Stay Out of that Room!

CLARE BILLS

MIDWESTERN BOOKS
POLK CITY, IOWA

Copyright © 2023 Clare Bills

All rights reserved. No part of this book may be reproduced in any form or by any electronic or mechanical means, including information storage and retrieval systems, without permission in writing from the publisher, except by reviewers, who may quote brief passages in a review.

ISBN 979-8-9880628-0-6 (Hardcover Edition)

LCCN: 1-12248613171

Cover design by: eBook Cover Designs

Published by Midwestern Books

801 W Washington Ave, Polk City, IA 50226

Contact: Info@midwesternbooks.com

To Aunt Polly
for providing us with unique adventures
and insights into her world.

Also to Ken, the cheerleader of my life.

PRAISE FOR STAY OUT OF THAT ROOM!

I SO ENJOYED THIS BOOK! In sharp detail (Pez dispensers! Hydrox!) Bills brings to life the bygone world in which many of us came of age. She writes with rich emotional imagination and a grinning way with similes ("earrings dangled like bait on a hook.") Cindy, her sweet-tart narrator, trembles (literally) on the brink of womanhood, trying to navigate Catholicism, cake, and curious cute boys. As Cindy might say, "Park your keester!" and enjoy an entertaining and evocative read!

    Irene O'Garden, Off-Broadway playwright, poet, author, and transplanted Midwesterner."

WHEN WEIRD GREAT-AUNT POLLY drags Cindy and Kitty to her crumbling lake house in the 1960s and orders them to stay out of the locked room on the first floor, the girls can't help themselves. They have to get inside it. Between embarrassing trips to the grocery store, fixing meals to satisfy their great-aunt's prodigious appetites, and trying to catch the attention of the boys next door, Cindy and Kitty snoop their way into trouble. Stay Out of That Room! is everything a mystery should be and more. Author Clare Bills keeps readers turning pages filled with renegade squirrels, glass eyes, swimsuit malfunctions, a pampered kitty cat, and summer romance. You'll laugh until you cry when Cindy and Kitty discover Aunt Polly's secret and see their eccentric, lonely relative with newfound compassion and respect.

Jolene Stratton Philo, author of See Jane Run! and the rest of the West River Mystery Series.

ACKNOWLEDGMENTS

I FIRST WANT TO THANK ANNE FLECK, who heard me speak about my Aunt Polly's secret room and encouraged me to write the story. She later guided me to shore it up and polish the rough edges.

I'm also thankful to Tom Walker of Midwestern Publishing, who took a chance on me and this book. He is not related to the Anthony Walker mentioned in the latter chapters of this book.

Brandi Doan McCann of eBook Cover Designs did an exceptional job blending humor and mystery in her incredible cover design.

Lisa Pelissier's eagle eye weeded out inconsistencies and kept close track of names and places—my eternal thanks to her.

Thanks to my seven sisters who added their Aunt Polly adventures to mine and pushed me to the finish line.

Finally, thanks to the readers of my first two books, Mountains of Trouble and Mending Helen's Heart, who left encouraging reviews and egged me on to write another book.

Stay Out
of that
Room!

Chapter 1

I CREPT DOWN TWO FLIGHTS OF STAIRS, avoiding the squeaky spots, and held my nose as the smell coming from the kitchen intensified. Mom was encouraging my younger sisters to "rise and shine" as I passed the four bedrooms on the second floor. Their school started later than mine.

If I was the first one down for breakfast, I could get the last piece of double chocolate cake which I had baked. But there was the little issue of the puppies. As I neared the bottom stair, my ten-year-old sister, Joanne, burst from her room and followed me, shouting, "Last day of school! Can't wait."

"Shhhh!" I hissed.

But it was too late. Our voices sent the puppies into a stampede. They charged the baby gate meant to keep them in the kitchen. It fell with a bang, and eleven wiggly, smelly puppies scrambled over it and rushed us. Joanne squealed in glee, plopped on the hallway floor, and opened her arms. They surrounded her with snuggles and wet kisses.

I peeked into the kitchen. "Oh yuck! What a mess!"

Joanne giggled. "Hey, you saw it first. You have to clean it up. Look, Cindy! This one with the black circle around his eye is my favorite. He's sooooo cute!"

"Don't get too attached. They're nearly old enough to give away."

Naturally, she wasn't listening. She shrieked and giggled from the puppy love. I would have joined her on the floor any other time, but today I wanted to make it to school without smelling like you-know-what. Today was the last day of school for the year, and we didn't have to wear our horrid brown wool blazers and gray plaid skirts. I sported a pale pink hip-hugger dress with a white Peter Pan collar. I had brushed my long, dark brown hair into a low ponytail held with a pink ribbon, and I felt good about myself. I knew I had to hurry because several puppies were clawing at my legs, begging to be held or fed. Their little whines tugged at my heart, and I knew I couldn't leave without getting them food and water, which meant entering the kitchen.

The newspapers mom scattered over the floor the night before were either shredded or full of puppy mess. I carefully stepped into the room and let Princess, the mama dog, outside for a break so I could clean up. Six hopeful, hungry pups followed me, while the other five continued to smother Joanne with kisses.

"OK, guys. Hang on," I said to six sets of brown eyes. Then I asked Joanne. "Help me find their bowls and wash the floor."

"I can't get up, Cindy. They won't let me. Call Mom."

I shook my head. "Mom's getting the younger kids dressed, and there's no shouting while Dad's still asleep." Dad never got up until we were all safely out of the house. Lucky guy. Besides, we had only one full bathroom, which he wouldn't have access to until we left.

I turned to my freckle-faced sister and sighed. What a sight! She didn't care that her jumper would be soiled, and she might be teased. Joanne was the first to burst out of bed every day, ready to embrace whatever trouble she could find. Her pixie-cut auburn hair was unbrushed, with a cowlick standing triumphantly. I envied her plucky confidence but couldn't imagine where it came from. It'd be easier to clean up the kitchen myself.

When I bent down to pick up the papers, I realized my dress was hugging a touch too much over my ample hips, and I had to yank it up to get the job done.

"What's happening?" Kitty startled me, holding her nose. She was so light on her feet I didn't hear her on the stairs.

"Thank goodness! I'm overloaded."

"Do you mean overwhelmed?"

"I guess. Whatever. Look at this mess! I'm trying to feed them before they maul me and ruin my new dress."

"I'll throw up if I have to pick up those papers." Kitty had a weak stomach, which got her out of many sticky messes. She was an inch taller than me, but her slight build made her look much taller. Her dark brown hair was softly curled and looked dramatic against her sunny yellow shift.

"OK, but Kitty, can you find their bowls and get 'em fed?"

Kitty nodded and kept one hand on her nose while she found three metal bowls and dug into a massive plastic container to scoop dry food. When they heard the hard kibble filling their dishes, they rushed at their food, some skidding on the slick kitchen floor as their bottoms swayed back and forth.

I filled several large bowls with fresh water, quickly cleared away the soiled newspapers, and shoved them into the large kitchen wastebasket. With a bucket and mop, I gave the floor a "lick and a promise" with vinegar water so the room smelled like pickled poo.

Despite the nature of my previous task, I was still hungry, so I reached on top of the fridge, took down the cake container, and turned to Kitty. "Want to split this with me?"

She fanned her face. "No. I still feel nauseous. And it's way too sweet for me."

Joanne hopped up off the floor. "I'll split it with you."

"Sure. You won't help me clean up, but you want cake for breakfast." I frowned but handed her a fork. Her reddish-brown eyes crinkled, and she grinned at her good fortune. We each took a bite of the chocolatey wonder just as Mom came down the stairs carrying two-year-old Ann Marie and trailed by seven-year-old Maureen and five-year-old Betty Jane.

Our parents churned out kids on the Catholic one-year plan as easily as shooting candy out of a Pez dispenser. Well, maybe not that easily. Mom probably would disagree with that. Critics said Catholics were trying to tip the population scales in their favor so we'd get a Catholic president, and for a few short years, we had one. But it's not polite to discuss politics and religion, so that's all I'll say about that.

Mom's eyes went wide. "Girls, girls. Honestly. Put that away."

Maureen bounced her strawberry-blond curls indignantly. "Cake! Why do they get cake?"

"Yeah! I want cake," Betty Jane demanded, squinting her deep purple eyes.

Mom took the platter from me and calmly put it back on top of the fridge. "No one's having cake. Let's get some cereal from the cupboard."

"Well, I think I deserved some. You should have seen the mess I just cleaned up. You agree, don't you?

"Cindy, cake for breakfast will not help you lose weight."

Eye roll. Why did every conversation revolve around the extra eight pounds that mysteriously landed on my middle over the winter?

My cheeks flushed. "No time for breakfast anyway. Let's go, Kitty."

Kitty headed toward the back door, and I followed. "We might as well not wait for Mary. She said she doesn't care if she's late. She'll still graduate."

Kitty, Mary, and I planned to walk together to our Catholic girls' school, Regina, as it was Mary's last day of high school. Kitty would be a junior and I'd be a sophomore in the fall. We usually walked at different times, depending on extracurricular stuff like the early debate team, but not anymore. Kitty and I were only thirteen months apart in age, what some call Irish twins, which has nothing to do with whether your ancestors came over on the boat during the potato famine. No one seems sure about our heritage, but we do love potatoes, so we're probably part Irish, and Dad says we're part Polish too.

Mom frowned. "Speaking of late, has Colleen come down yet?"

I shrugged. "Haven't seen her." Our newest teen was typically the last to get ready for anything. But it didn't matter to Kitty and me since she still went to school in the other direction. Next year she'd be in ninth grade, join us at Regina, and make us late every morning.

This whole puppy situation was Dad's fault. Six weeks ago, he came home from work with a female German Shepherd named Princess. When Dad walked in with her, our calico cat, Buttercup, jumped on her and dug her claws into the dog's fur. Princess sprinted several laps around the house howling in pain. To be fair, Buttercup had a litter of two-week-old kittens to protect. Mom finally cornered the dog, snatched the cat, and ordered Dad to bring the dog to the basement. Dad rarely took orders from anyone, so we watched in fascination as he sheepishly did as Mom asked. When he came upstairs, we circled him, waiting.

Dad's eyes danced. "A man came into my office today with this dog in tow. He said he was on the way to having the dog, Princess, put down because he couldn't keep her any longer.

He said she was purebred, and he even had papers for her. I hated to see her killed, so I took her."

Mom cocked an eyebrow. "Why would a man come into your insurance agency with a dog?"

Dad smiled dismissively. "Needed car insurance. The dog happened to be with him. Anyway, I said I'd try to find a home for her."

Mom's hands were on her hips. "You'd better find one soon. Notice her swollen belly?"

Dad shrugged his shoulders. "I thought she was malnourished"

Mom gave him a frosty look, which Dad ignored.

Dad clapped his hands together and changed the subject. "What's for dinner?"

At dinner that night, he sprang another surprise. "Cindy, I asked our priest to take you to visit the Poor Clare nuns and their cloistered convent."

I dropped my fork. "What? Why me?"

"I'm raising eight daughters, and one of you has to join a convent."

"But a cloistered convent where they never talk?" Was he kidding?

"Don't be dramatic, Cindy. I'm sure they'll let you speak at meals. Anyway, Father Ed will be here Saturday at 10."

I wasn't interested in any type of convent, much less one that had their members wear scratchy wool garments, sleep on horse hair mats, and garden, all of which gave me hives.

That weekend, I visited the convent, but after my eyes

puffed up and I couldn't stop sneezing, I was deemed unfit, much to my relief.

But back to the puppies. The day after Dad brought the dog home, Joanne went to the basement to let Princess out for a potty break. Eleven blind puppies were squealing and squirming around her. Joanne raced upstairs shouting, "Puppies! Puppies!" and continued to drum up excitement as sleepy girls in nightgowns awoke and ran downstairs to see for themselves. When she ran up to the third floor to tell Kitty and me, we headed to the basement. But Mary, who had a room all to herself, pulled the covers over her head and told her to "bugger off."

The rest of us were excited to see the newborns. In a flurry of activity, we found a large box and created a safe place in the basement laundry room where Princess and the pups could stay. But that only lasted for a few weeks. They quickly outgrew the box and then the basement.

Now that they were six weeks old, it was impossible to contain them. They were chewing, peeing, and pooing all over the first floor, and I worried they would learn to climb stairs and soil the rest of the house. But they were heartbreakers. Each one had different coloring and markings. Clearly, Princess had mated with a mutt. Their coloring was as varied as my sisters and I.

CHAPTER 2

THE DAY AFTER SCHOOL WAS OUT, I balanced Ann Marie on my wide left hip while complaining to Mom about the neighbor woman whose children I babysat. Mom was blackening a slab of beef and nodding to me. The smokey smell was tickling my nose. She looked up abruptly.

"Shhh! Listen! What's that noise?" She switched off the burner on the stove. We listened. There it was again. That dreaded honking—like a flock of disoriented geese.

Mom looked worried. "Cindy, go check." She turned the burner back on.

I dashed to the living room window, pushed the curtains aside, and peeked out, hoping it wasn't her. "Oh no!" I gasped. "It's too early, isn't it?"

Kitty crept to the window and glanced out quickly before hiding behind the curtain. "It's definitely her." She wrinkled her nose.

The honking continued as cries of, "Let me see, let me see," came from our younger sisters Betty Jane and Maureen.

Mom left the flaming meat to continue charring on its own and joined us at the window.

For most Minnesotans, summer arrived when snow tires vanished, puffy coats languished in closets, and kids ran screaming out of schools, but the blast from a 1952 Chevy meant the pandemonium of our family's summer was about to ramp up.

Like a migrating goose, our wackadoodle Great Aunt Polly found her way from New Mexico to our home in South Minneapolis every summer after first stopping at her decrepit mini mansion on the shores of Lake Minnetonka. She appeared without warning but always at dinner time.

Mom took Ann Marie from me. "Kitty, Cindy, go help her."

We dawdled off the front porch and down the steps into the blazing afternoon sunshine. The rusted, dented car encapsulated a woman with dyed red hair and a smear of matching lipstick that didn't stop at her lips. A turquoise patch covered one eye. Her earrings dangled like bait on a hook as she cranked down the window and gave a brief wave and halfhearted giggle. "Hello, girls!"

"Great Aunt" was her technical title because she was our grandmother's sister, but we would never consider her a great person. She did fit the other definition of great—enormous.

We tried to rustle up some enthusiasm as we tugged on her arms to release her from the car's grip, ignoring neighbor kids openly staring at the spectacle. She pulled down her turquoise muumuu to cover her massive, dimpled thighs. The bodice boasted orange and yellow embroidered flowers bursting from her bust. A longer dress would have been better, but at her height, most of her garments never reached her roly-poly knees. Black crew socks and tan orthopedic shoes with thick rubber soles completed her look. Does your family have an eccentric relative? If you don't think so, it might be you.

She snatched her oversized, black faux-leather bag and swung it onto her elbow to let us know she was ready for our attention. She put her arms out and demanded in her shrill voice. "Well? Don't I get a hug?"

"Sorry, Aunt Polly. I was waiting until we got inside." I leaned into her girth for a millisecond and quickly backed up lest I smash my face in her overblown bosom.

Kitty gingerly approached. "Hi. Nice. To. Have. You. Back," she staccatoed as Aunt Polly squeezed the breath out of her. She sucked in a lungful of air when Aunt Polly released her.

Aunt Polly clutched our arms to steady herself as we inched along the sidewalk and up the stairs. She was not only the tallest woman I'd ever seen, but the widest and slowest.

Our neighborhood flaunted solid homes built around 1900 and stuffed with children. Even the Protestants had at least four. One Catholic family had thirteen, another nine, and we had eight, so we never lacked players for a game of Murder at Midnight or Red Rover. But now we faced the snickers of neighborhood companions, watching as we were swallowed into our turn-of-the-century home.

Once inside, the ritual greetings and awkward hugs continued.

Aunt Polly sniffed the air. "Smells good in here. Dinner?"

Mom smiled. "Yes. Are you hungry?" Was she kidding? Aunt Polly was always hungry.

"Sounds delightful."

Mom whispered to me, "Put the captain's chair at the end of the dining table and set another place." Then she dashed into the smokey kitchen to rescue our dinner.

There was only one chair big enough to hold our great-aunt. It had sturdy armrests to help her get into and out of it, so she always sat at the dining room table for her entire visit. It was a good thing she did. Our purple silk sofa was so soft everyone sank into it and sounded like wounded bullfrogs when they tried to extricate themselves. Dad found it on clearance. He never let aesthetics get in the way of a good sale.

"My, it's warm in here," Aunt Polly said.

Colleen took the cue and went into the den to retrieve a small fan, which she plugged in and turned toward Aunt Polly to cool her.

Seven-year-old Maureen approached Aunt Polly holding a wiggly bundle. "We got a new puppy. Wanna hold him?" She shook her wavy blond hair out of her green eyes, but her bangs were sticking to her damp forehead. She was sweaty from playing on the swings outside and her faded green

T-shirt and frayed floral pedal pushers were streaked with mud—hand-me-downs from us older sisters.

Aunt Polly shook her head. "No. Oh my, where did that come from?"

Betty Jane pushed her way toward the captain's chair. "He came from the mama puppy." Betty Jane's milk chocolate bangs cut straight across her face, accentuating her huge purple eyes. She would be going to kindergarten in the fall, but loved to tell us that she already knew everything. Like Maureen, she wore faded and soiled hand-me-downs and carried the scent of sweat, wet grass, and muddy dog.

Maureen giggled at Betty Jane. "Our dad brought home a dog who had eleven puppies in our basement."

Aunt Polly's hand flew to her heart. "Eleven! Eleven?" She looked at me for confirmation and I nodded.

Joanne piped up. "Yup. Betty Jane petted the puppy. His name is Gunther. Dad said we could keep him. We have to give the rest away."

Aunt Polly wrinkled her nose. "Don't you have a cat?"

Joanne nodded. "Yup. Buttercup. She's getting used to Gunther. She didn't like the mama dog, so we have to find her a new home, but she's doin' better with Gunther."

Mom came into the dining room. "Maureen, why don't you put Gunther down? Dinner will be ready in about ten minutes. Aunt Polly, I'll bet the girls would enjoy hearing a song while you're waiting for dinner."

Kitty and I looked at each other and grinned. Here it

comes—the burglar song. Even Mary, who was reading in a corner chair in the living room, put down her book.

Aunt Polly had a song about a burglar and a spinster with a glass eye. We asked for it every summer. Truthfully, I wondered if she saw herself in the song, but she never seemed to make the connection.

Soon Mom called everyone to the table. No one was asked to wash their hands or change from dirty clothes. My parents felt germs would strengthen our immune systems and were meant to be shared.

Dad came home in time to cut the steak a little thinner that evening, giving us smaller portions of the tough, chewy meat so Aunt Polly could have her fill. I didn't consider this a sacrifice.

Typically, mealtime was as loud as a visit to the dog pound, with each of us barking over the other, vying for our parents' attention, but when Aunt Polly arrived, we shut down, hoping to avoid the request we knew was coming.

My saintly mother, wearing a faded house dress and sporting a come-as-you-are salt and pepper haircut, was always kind to her only aunt. Mom lobbed questions. "When did you arrive, Aunt Polly?"

Aunt Polly focused on the platters and bowls of food set in front of Dad so he could serve. "Uh, a few days ago." Her eyes roamed the table from platters to recipients as if measuring whether there would be enough for everyone, especially for her.

Still in his grey-striped business suit, Dad stood and

reverently led grace and then ceremoniously served Aunt Polly, Mother, and the rest of us as we passed large china plates from sister to sister down the ancient wood dining room table. The large slab of beef, known as family steak, was cut into thin slices, and served with roast potatoes, and peas.

Mother alone kept the conversation moving. "How was the drive?"

"Not too bad."

"Was there much traffic?"

"Only in the big cities."

Mom chewed, swallowed, and took a sip of water as we waited for the next tedious installation. "How's your car holding up?"

"It spent a few nights in mechanics' garages, but they got it running again."

I held my breath, not wanting to be the center of attention. My sisters did the same, except for Betty Jane, who was too young to remember much from last summer. Betty Jane kept staring at our great-aunt and finally blurted out, "What's wrong with your eye?"

Aunt Polly's face reddened. "How rude!"

But the curiosity of a five-year-old couldn't be contained. "But why do you have that patch on your face?"

Mom shook her head at Betty Jane to quiet her, but she continued to stare until Mary, the oldest of our crew, blurted out. "She has a glass eye, Betty Jane."

Betty Jane's mouth fell open. "Glass. Cool. I want to see it." She beamed with more curiosity and continued to stare.

A twinkle in thirteen-year-old Colleen's blue eyes appeared and she started to snicker, then Joanne joined her. Betty Jane, relishing her moment as the center of attention, blurted out, "Glass eye. Like a marble. I want one." She looked on both sides of the table from one of us to the other and proudly realized she had started a giggle fest.

In our house full of girls, an infectious giggle can turn into a rolling grass fire. A spark of a snicker catches the attention of one. The snicker turns into a snort across the table. A burst of pent-up cackling catches like dry timber, and soon the table is a roaring fire of chortling, stomach-holding howling and uncontained and uncontrollable hysteria. Even Ann Marie clapped her hand on her face, tossed her strawberry-blond curls, and giggled from her highchair. Mom held her napkin over her mouth and pretended to clear her throat, trying to hold back the spasms that shook her shoulders. While tears streamed down our faces, Dad remained stoic, chewing his tough, blackened meat. He had long ago realized no amount of disapproval on his part would squelch our merriment at times like this.

When the belly laughs turned into mere twitters, we wiped our eyes and turned our attention back to our burned beef. Aunt Polly looked from one to the other of us. "It's like you have your own language. Sometimes when I'm with you, I have no idea what's happening."

Dad swallowed. "I understand completely."

We turned quiet again and let Mom carry on, pretending it was over when in reality, we knew a spark from a smoldering snort could quickly turn into a full-blown fire again.

We reached for our water glasses, hoping to squelch the rumbles of silliness.

"Please pass the peas," I said to no one in particular, and when a bowl appeared, I spooned a heaping pile onto my plate as a decoy. While it looked like I was eating, in reality I was smuggling bites of beef under the table to Gunther, who never complained about overcooked food as long as it was meat.

The table grew quiet again as Mom carried the conversation ball alone. Don't ask about the house, I silently pleaded.

"How does the house look?"

Aunt Polly shook her head just enough to set her earrings swaying and gave a half grin as she looked up. "Well, uh, I could use help. I'm hoping a few of the older girls will come out for a few weeks."

There it was. Mom fell into Aunt Polly's trap, and now we'd be the victims. Again. We older sisters sneaked anxious glances at each other before pretending to eat our peas and hoping to be swallowed by the tablecloth. No one uttered a word. Not an "uff-dah" in sight.

Aunt Polly sweetened the pot. "I plan to ask the neighbor boys for a barbecue next week. Kitty, Cindy, you remember them. Jimmy and Charlie are about your ages."

Kitty glanced at me with questioning eyes. We knew those boys. She had tried to set us up with them the summer before, but they showed no interest in two girls from middle-class South Minneapolis.

Our mother, eager to help her aunt, was happy to martyr us for the task.

"Kitty, Cindy, that sounds fun. Why don't you two go?"

I knew this wasn't a suggestion, but I tried anyway. "I said I'd babysit for the judge's grandkids this week."

"How about you, Mary?"

My oldest sister's face scrunched up. "Me? Why do I have to go?"

"I mean, Mary, can you babysit instead of Cindy?"

"Oh, that. I s'pose," Mary nodded.

"Then it's settled. Go pack so you don't delay Aunt Polly."

Kitty and I shrugged our shoulders, scraped our chairs back from our massive dining room table, cleared our dishes, and climbed two flights of stairs to pack our small cloth suitcases. We shared a lilac bedroom shaped like a bowling alley on the third floor, affording us a view of the Minneapolis skyline from our windows.

Kitty tried to be upbeat. "It'll be fun to go swimming in the lake. And maybe Jimmy and Charlie will want to hang out."

A glimmer of hope arose in me. Now that I'd grown a bosom, maybe they wouldn't think I was too much of a baby. I packed my red two-piece high-waist swimsuit, wondering if this would be the summer Jimmy would notice me. Kitty already had set her hopes on Charlie. I threw in a tube of lip gloss, liquid eyeliner, and mascara, just in case. The packing was complete once my bell-bottoms, sundress, pedal pushers, shorts, and tie-dyed and plain T-shirts were smooshed next to my baby doll pj's. From my bookcase I selected a copy of The Mystery at the Moss-Covered Mansion, a Nancy Drew book that seemed appropriate. I brushed out my long hair and wrestled it into two ponytails.

Kitty brushed hers into a single ponytail. We both had dark brown hair and eyes, but that's as far as the similarities went. Kitty's hair had soft curls, and when she pulled it away from her face, her eyes looked huge. Her forehead was accented by wispy tendrils that models always had in teen magazines. And she was model thin.

My hair was stick straight except for the cowlick that sprung between my bangs. When I pulled my hair back, my eyes seemed to shrink and my nose looked like a mushroom on a plate of sauerkraut. Mom said I had my dad's Polish nose, but mine didn't look like his. I feared it would grow as big as my Polish grandfather's schnoz.

Mom took us aside before we left. "Be sure to wash all the dishes in her cupboards before using them. You know she puts them away without washing them."

I wrinkled my nose. "Gross. I will."

Kitty smiled sweetly. "We'll take care of things. Don't worry, Mom."

We piled our suitcases in the backseat of Aunt Polly's beater and then dashed back up the porch steps to help her shuffle to the car. We waved to our sisters and mother. No hugs. Physical affection stopped when we were very little. Our dad was already in his chair reading the newspaper when we left, and we knew we shouldn't bother him.

Kitty claimed the window seat, so I was squished in the middle. Rolls of peppermint candies flew at us from the dashboard when the car took off with a grind of the engine and a plume of black smoke.

I suppose I was ready to meet whatever the next few weeks held for us since I had no choice.

Chapter 3

I FIDGETED IN THE CAR like a puppy with fleas as we left South Minneapolis and headed to Minnetonka, where status-hungry residents bragged about life on the glamorous lake. It was less than an hour away but felt like an alternate universe. Kitty and I focused out the window of the Chevy as the comforts of home disappeared.

The day had been frying-pan hot with no breeze in sight, leaving us sticky in the crowded car. The smell of Aunt Polly's soiled body permeated the seats, leaving a stench that made it hard to breathe. I shifted closer to Kitty and tried to gasp fresh air from her open window.

Finally, we drove through an enormous arch and down a dark, private lane, past mini castles set far back from the road, with driveways that led to attached garages. What looked like a forest of pine and spruce trees provided fragrant relief along with year-round privacy from rubberneckers like me. After driving past lawns groomed with toenail clippers, we stopped at a single-car detached garage full of debris that left no room for even a unicycle, much less the Chevy. I looked out the window at knee-high weeds and knew mowing was in my future.

The scent of lilac bushes sent my nose twitching as I burst out of the car and inhaled the spring fragrance I loved, hoping to banish the car smells from my nose. I was aware the flowers didn't love me back, but I was desperate. I sneezed. Loudly. And again. And again.

"Quiet! You'll wake the dead," Aunt Polly commanded.

Kitty and I looked at each other, eyes wild. Behind Aunt Polly's back, I mouthed, "What dead?"

My heart raced as I wondered about the weeks ahead. Would I survive? Or would I sneeze my way to an early grave, leaving my dead body surrounded by a pile of used tissues? Kitty and I both toted our suitcases with one hand and helped Aunt Polly with the other. Slowly we crept along from the concrete slab behind her garage, down the path of broken stones, and into the back porch with the squeaky screen door. Our three-story home had plenty of character, but it was dwarfed by Aunt Polly's 1855 decrepit summer home. Stuffed into two levels were two living rooms, two dining rooms, an enormous, dark library, an eat-in kitchen, eight bedrooms, sitting rooms, bathrooms with marble sinks, and a room down the hall from the kitchen that was always locked. Massive screened porches faced the lake and wrapped the first floor in what Minnesotans call "natural air conditioning." This may sound like a magical home, but in truth, it was a place better suited for run-away raccoons.

We deposited our great-aunt on her favorite couch in the front living room, which was small compared to the massive formal living room down the hall. We crept up the creaking wooden stairs to see what hair-raising sights lay in wait for us. The dust from a hundred summers set my nose to twitching again as we walked from room to room, leading with our arms to fend off spider webs, and tried to decide where we were least likely to be attacked. Really, the choice was easy—the same room as last year, because our track record for survival there was solid. The front bedroom with two single beds that faced the lake caught the night breeze, so that's where we landed. We unlocked the stiff windows with the peeling paint and coaxed them open with our shoulders. Filthy screens on the outside of the windows slumped like drunken sailors. They were full of holes welcoming mosquitoes and moths at night and biting black flies by day.

I set my suitcase down on the bed closest to the wall, and a poof of dust blasted my way. "I'll take this bed after I shake it out and get rid of the dead bugs." Fearful of unknown attackers, I let Kitty take the bed nearest the hallway.

We carefully pulled up the cream-colored chenille bedspreads by their corners and held them like storks do when they deliver babies. At least like they do in cartoons. Kitty told me the true story about sex and birth at Aunt Polly's two summers ago. It took me months to get over the shock.

We crept down the long hallway seeking the bedroom

with a balcony, all the while watching for animals, dead or alive. We turned on the lights and checked for bats before we found the courage to open the creaky door to the balcony. We stepped out, hoping the rotting wood wouldn't deposit us into the weeds below, and gave our bedding a punishing shake. Back inside, we tiptoed past the stairway until we heard our great-aunt.

"Girls," she shrieked. "What are you doing up there?"

I nudged Kitty to answer since she was always the adults' favorite. "Just shaking out our bedspreads," she called down with a lilt in her voice.

"Don't go snooping around. Come downstairs."

We frowned silently, and Kitty responded, "Be right there."

I shook my head and whispered, "Now what? I hope she isn't mad."

Downstairs, we found her sitting on the lopsided couch in the first living room with a bag of Hydrox cookies on her chest, watching cowboys on her black and white television. The TV was in a small wooden cabinet that sat on the floor. A scratched oak coffee table, cluttered with paperbacks sporting ruby-lipped women in skimpy swimwear, sat between Aunt Polly and the TV. We stood near her, shifting from foot to foot, waiting for the next command.

As she spoke, her teeth covered in black cookie crumbs, she didn't take her eyes off the 10" screen. "Sit down. Gunsmoke's almost on." She reached into the package and grabbed three more cookies.

We glanced at the only other chairs in the small front

living room—platform rockers from the 1850s. The torn seat covers bore holes where something—mice perhaps?—had nested. I hoped I wasn't sitting on any animals, living or dead, as I nervously parked my keester and rocked back and forth on the rickety chair, unsure if the squeaks were from the ancient springs or suffocating mice. Kitty was rocking in tandem with me, creating an off-key symphony of screech-creak-whine-eek as we fidgeted, trying to get comfortable.

Aunt Polly scowled. "Shush! Can't you girls sit still?" She popped another whole cookie in her mouth without offering us one. "Now listen, girls. There are only a few rules I want you to follow while you're here. I'll let you do the cooking because I know you enjoy that." Sure we do!

"And I want you to pick up after yourselves and to be quiet when I'm watching my shows. And remember, don't go prying into the room off the kitchen."

She said this every year. I frowned the tiniest bit. "Can I ask why?"

"It's 'may I,' not 'can I' and the answer is no. It holds my private things, and you don't need to go in there."

Kitty tried to smooth things over before the vein in Aunt Polly's neck stood out. "We won't, Aunt Polly."

I rolled my eyes at Kitty for the umpteenth time, hoping my aunt wouldn't see me.

This was going to be a long evening, like most evenings with Aunt Polly. The days would be long as well. I feared we'd die of boredom, and no one would find our bodies until next summer, mummified on the platform rockers. One thing was sure—the girls on the covers of her paperbacks looked like they were having much more fun than we were. An old grandfather clock ticked away in a corner but marched to its own drumbeat, so the time was never accurate. Soon I timed my chair to creak in tandem with the clock's ticking.

Aunt Polly loved to entertain, although she didn't lift a finger to help. Our days would be filled with her requests for us to cook, bake, and clean, in addition to yard work, which always made me sick. I mentioned that I'm allergic to plants, remember? Instead of enjoying summer with our friends, sisters, or neighbor kids, we were holed up in a dilapidated, stuffy house with our unpredictable aunt. Again.

I must have sighed while deep in thought because Aunt Polly turned abruptly to me. "What's the matter with you, Cindy?"

What could I say? That I was secretly planning my funeral? Or sinking into a pit of despair? I reached for a simple, reasonable complaint, or so I thought. "I'm hot. Sorta stuffy in here, and I'm sweating."

She reared up, and her voice climbed an octave. "Nonsense! Horses sweat, men perspire, and women glow!"

"Then I'm glowing," I pouted and crossed my arms as I continued to totter back and forth on the creaky chair.

"Stop crossing your arms. It's disrespectful," Aunt Polly barked.

I couldn't sweat or cross my arms. Would pouting would be outlawed next? I tried to enjoy Gunsmoke, but my mind wandered to the mystery room. Telling me not to go in there was like telling me not to eat a chocolate cupcake that was sitting in plain sight. After what seemed like forever, I noticed Aunt Polly dozing off and decided to check the door, which was out of sight from the front living room.

I put a finger over my lips to tell Kitty to be quiet, crept to the door, and tried the handle. I jiggled it, but just like last year, it didn't give. I lodged my shoulder at it like I'd seen gangsters do in movies, but no dice. The thunk woke Aunt Polly.

"Cindy, what are you doing?" she called.

"Sorry. I just tripped and banged into the wall." That was believable, right?

Kitty came to my rescue. "Is it OK if we practice the piano?"

"Sure. I'd love to hear you girls play." Aunt Polly stayed on her couch as we crept down the dark hall and into the once-fancy living room at the front of the house. The musty smell was the first thing to hit our senses, probably from the threadbare, faded oriental rugs, peeling gold flocked wallpaper, and floor-to-ceiling olive-green velvet drapes faded in folds where the sun had scorched them.

Kitty sat down to play the old upright, and I strolled around the room examining portraits of distant ancestors with angled faces and necks tall enough to sport stiff collars and elaborate neckties. One woman had sausages of hair bursting across her forehead from a heart-shaped hat adorned with layers of lace and satin, forming a halo of absurdity. Another sour-faced woman stared at me, wearing miles of heavy wine-colored velvet for her skirt and just a few wisps of lace and ribbon on her low-cut bodice. A grim-faced, heavily mustached man looked at me disapprovingly from his perch on a settee, probably overheated because of layers of clothing—a ruffled shirt, brocade vest, and heavy wool waistcoat. Every portrait had one thing in common—the eyes followed my every move.

"How do the artists make that happen?" I said to no one at all.

"Make what happen?" So Kitty was listening.

"You know. Eyes and even heads seem to follow us around the room."

Kitty got up and we strolled a few laps around the cavernous room, pretending we carried parasols and dainty lace handbags. "They seem to turn their entire bodies as we walk," Kitty said.

I felt we should whisper in case these creatures were listening. "Yes. If these are our ancestors, maybe some still haunt this house."

Kitty shook her head. "Don't be ridiculous."

"What do you think she's hiding in that room?"

"Probably just junk like in the garage."

"How do we know there isn't a corpse in the forbidden room?"

"Cindy, just forget about it."

I nodded, but I didn't really agree.

This sad living room boasted hardwood floors under the rugs, and chairs, slouching couches, and settees that seemed to shout, "Don't sit here." Not only were they covered in dust, but several tipped to one side because of broken or missing legs. At the far end of the room was a rolltop desk with a straight-back chair in front of it.

I walked over to the desk and yanked on it to open the top, but it didn't budge. "This house is full of locks."

Kitty whispered. "We shouldn't snoop. She'll get mad and tell Mom and Dad."

Kitty rarely got in trouble. Me? I was used to it.

I kept my voice low, but my hands scavenged the exterior of the desk. "You can sit there if you like, but I'm going to look around."

Kitty sat to play the out-of-tune upright but was quickly frustrated. She stage-whispered to me. "Middle C is missing. So is G. Nothing sounds right."

"Figures," I said. Why would we expect the hundred-year-old piano to have all its parts when the rest of the house didn't?

Despite her frustration, she continued to coax music out of the defective keyboard.

When the rolltop wouldn't yield, I searched for secret drawers. Come on, desk! I know you want to spill your guts. In frustration, I sat on the floor and looked up at the underside of the desk. A key covered with brittle tape clung to the wood like an inchworm clinging to a branch. With a bit of persuasion, it fell into my hands. It was a large skeleton key, too large for the keyhole on the desk.

I hopped up and dashed over to the piano. "Kitty, look! Maybe this is the key to the locked room."

Kitty stopped playing and looked at the metal key. "We can't get into trouble. She has a wicked temper."

"We'll be careful."

"Not WE. I don't want any part of this."

I slid the key into the pocket of my pedal pushers. Perhaps this summer wouldn't be so dull after all.

Chapter 4

Each night Kitty and I opened the windows to let in the refreshing breeze off Lake Minnetonka and with the cool air came the swarm of mosquitoes, black flies, and moths through torn screens. But without fans we felt we'd suffocate in the heat. We pulled sheets right over our heads as we slept, but we could still hear the whine of mosquitoes as they tried to bite us through the fabric. At times I could also hear the soft flapping from the moths' wings. They were less offensive, but all of it meant waking several times a night to shoo away whatever pest was bothering me.

During the day, Kitty and I were in exile. We cleaned, dusted, fetched, and carried for Aunt Polly while hoping to see the O'Reilly brothers, who seemed to have vanished. We relished our time alone when we first awoke, before Aunt Polly's call to action, usually to make and serve her breakfast. We didn't vary much from the routine of eggs, oatmeal, or cold cereal.

"Let's do something different today," I said, bouncing up and down on the brass bed, causing the springs to croak like bullfrogs at night. "I'm going batty here." We were still in our baby doll pajamas.

"Like what? It's not like we could take her car into town, and there's no one to hang out with."

"Let's find a way into that room off the kitchen. What's she hiding in there? Dead bodies? I still have that key I found under the rolltop desk."

Kitty crinkled her nose and whispered, "I don't know. She'd be furious if she found out we snooped around."

"Think of something else, then." I jumped up to look out the filmy window toward the O'Reillys'. I squinted through the grime and saw closed windows and drawn curtains on the house next door. "They must be gone still."

"Where have they been all week?" Kitty asked. "I was hoping to see Charlie again."

I put my hands on my hips. "You're sure it's Charlie now?" It didn't matter. Both brothers were crazy about Kitty last summer. I had a crush on Jimmy. Neither of us was fond of their older brother, Wayne, but I had a hunch that Mary had a thing for him.

Aunt Polly called in her high, screechy, bird-like voice, sounding upbeat, "Girls, GIRLS, do you want to go out for breakfast?" I'm not sure if she didn't know our names or if it was easier to call us both "girls."

We bounced off our beds, flew to the top of the stairs, and looked down at her. She was dressed in a blood-red muumuu.

"Breakfast. Great. Yep, that sounds fun." My eyes popped from the scarlet hue of her dress, but I didn't want to say anything that would keep me from getting breakfast.

She half-smiled up at us. "Pancakes sound good?"

"Can I get chocolate chip?" My favorite was anything with chocolate.

One eyebrow shot up. "Oh, that sounds delicious. How 'bout you, Kitty?"

"I'd love a strawberry waffle."

"Perfect. Get dressed and fix your hair, girls, and we can leave in a few minutes." Aunt Polly thought hair should be contained in some fashion—braids, ponytails, pigtails, whatever. But long, untamed hair was a faux pas in her book.

I grabbed my hairbrush and comb and then wrangled my thick hair into two lopsided braids tied with light blue ribbons.

Kitty made pouty faces in the mirror as she pulled one side of her hair behind her ear, fastened it with a large barrette, and repeated the process on the other side.

We slipped into pedal pushers and light-colored T-shirts perfect for a warm June day.

We bounced downstairs just as Aunt Polly stepped out of her bedroom sporting an American flag patch over her glass eye, red dangly earrings, and matching lipstick. "Just to be a bit festive on Flag Day," she said. Kitty and I stifled snickers, relieved we wouldn't see anyone we knew at the pancake house.

We helped her shuffle to her car. She was slower than a

barge coming into Duluth harbor. We watched the car tilt under her weight as she finally settled behind the wheel. Kitty sat next to her in the front seat, and I rode beside the window this time. I cranked it down and stuck my nose out, gulping the fresh air. The day was promising to be steamy, with hardly a cloud in the sky. Aunt Polly's hands shook as she stiffly shifted the car into reverse. She didn't look in the rearview mirror as we jerked back to clear the short driveway. With a hard brake, we lurched forward, and then she shakily shifted again, pinning us to the back of our seats as rolls of peppermint candies torpedoed toward us.

Going out to eat was a big deal for us. As a family of ten, we rarely set foot in a restaurant. The last time we tried going out for breakfast on a Sunday after church, we had to wait over an hour for them to find enough empty tables near each other to push together to accommodate us. While we worked to entertain little Ann Marie and our younger sisters, Dad grumbled, "We could have made eggs and pancakes in half the time this is taking." We never again went out for breakfast.

Aunt Polly snapped the radio on in the car. Now and then she reached over to pat Kitty's knees in rhythm to the radio. Cases of peppermint candy rolls continued to bounce on the dash as we chugged along. I was glad she was happy, but time spent with her was a delicate dance. My sisters and I were terrified of her temper, which sprang up in unexpected places. When our fiesty ten-year-old sister Joanne visited, she was sent home early for standing with her hands on her hips.

We pulled up to a parking spot at the neighborhood restaurant, and Aunt Polly turned the key to cut her engine, but her car had other plans. It kept revving and lurching forward like a bull about to charge. I sank lower in my seat, hoping no one would see me. Even though I was miles away from my friends and neighbors, I was still embarrassed. Finally there was a loud clank as the car shuddered and stopped, expelling black smoke from a pipe in the back. A few hungry restaurant-goers had stopped to watch the spectacle but scattered like cockroaches in the light when we stopped, no doubt hoping to get a table far from us inside.

After pulling on Aunt Polly to extract her from the car, I gingerly took her elbow to help her into the restaurant, and we waited as they searched for a table with a queen-size chair. On the march to our table, we spotted the O'Reillys. My stomach did flip flops. Like everyone else, they were staring at our little parade as if we were naked lepers with open wounds.

Kitty smiled sweetly and rolled her shoulder slightly. What was that? Some sort of flirting signal? "Hello, Mr. and Mrs. O'Reilly. Hi, boys!"

Aunt Polly stopped too. In her best screech owl imitation, she swooped down on the opportunity to embarrass us. "Well, hello there. The girls have been hoping to see you. They've walked by your house every afternoon," she twittered in a voice that made my ears burn and my cheeks flame. "Haven't you, girls?"

I tugged on her arm. "I think our table is ready." I avoided looking at the boys. "We should sit down."

"We've just gotten back in town," Mrs. O'Reilly said.

"Well, let's get these kids together soon. Perhaps a barbecue."

Was it my imagination, or had the whole restaurant gone quiet to witness our shame and embarrassment? I glanced at tables near us and noticed no one was eating. Patrons sat wide-eyed, with forks and knives held midair, staring at the spectacle that was our aunt, hiding smiles under cupped hands. Her presence and voice were enough to cause stares, but with the addition of a patterned patch over her eye, smeared lipstick, and crimson dress, even the most well-mannered couldn't help a sideways glance and eyebrow raise. If people hadn't noticed us before, after Aunt Polly's high-pitched announcement, everyone knew crazy-town had arrived, and many waffle-eaters stared openly.

"Yes, certainly," Mrs. O'Reilly nodded as she dabbed the sides of her mouth with her white linen napkin. "I'm sure you boys would enjoy that, wouldn't you?" She shot a glance at the tables nearest to her.

Jimmy and Charlie shrugged and took stabs at their food. "Yeah, sure." The O'Reillys seemed eager for our parade to move on lest we incriminate them as allies.

Kitty glanced back and flashed a quick smile at the boys, but I pressed forward.

I hoped our table would be in a dark corner in the back so I could melt into the floor, but it was in the middle of all the action. Humiliation was my punishment for a plate of pancakes.

When the peppy young waitress brought us water, Aunt Polly ordered a four-egg omelet with extra cheese and bacon, a stack of pancakes, and a slab of ham. "Oh! And, uh, heavy cream and sugar in my coffee. It's Flag Day, so I'm treating myself," she told the waitress. To her, every day was Flag Day, National Donut Day, or National Scream for Ice Cream Day.

We made small talk while we waited for our breakfast and avoided the subject of the O'Reillys. Kitty stole glances at their table and then shot tiny shrugs and hopeful looks my way. Once the food arrived, Aunt Polly was a study in concentration, approaching her plate as if it were her job to clear it before a falcon swooped in and gobbled it. She inhaled every bite with sounds of scraping, chopping, and chewing. I had happily worked my way through part of a stack of pancakes when her shaky, beefy hand reached over. She nabbed my last pancake and ate it in two bites. I wanted to protest but feared she'd snarl at me, causing further public humiliation. Kitty picked up the pace on her waffle, but Aunt Polly reached across and forked the last of it into her mouth. Then she twittered a sort of giggle at us. Was that her apology?

After we helped her out of the restaurant and squeezed her into the car, I held my breath until the old saddle-brown beater chugged to life. Aunt Polly cranked into reverse without looking and backed up until she hit another vehicle. Then she yanked the gear into drive, heaving us against the front seat. As we tootled back to the wrinkled old house, I peeked out the window, hoping an angry driver with a dented bumper wasn't following us.

Within minutes, sirens blared behind us, and lights flashed.

"Aunt Polly, the police are following you. I think you should pull over," I said.

"Yes, yes, I know what to do," she snapped as she stopped the car and rolled down her window.

A no-nonsense officer stepped up to her window. "License and registration, Ma'am."

Aunt Polly dug in her vast black purse until she retrieved the documents. "What seems to be the problem?"

"Your driving. You've been weaving back and forth, in and out of lanes. I need to be sure you aren't impaired." Then he looked at us and asked, "Is she your grandmother?"

"No, our great-aunt," Kitty said. "We just had breakfast."

"Uh-huh, well, please step out of the car." He opened her car door and watched as Aunt Polly struggled to get to her feet. His eyes widened as he took in the sight of her in her red muumuu and flag-patched eye.

"Have you been drinking, Ma'am?"

"Orange juice and coffee."

"Can you balance on one foot?"

"Listen here, young man. I haven't been drinking, and if I try to balance on one foot, I'll fall, and if I hurt myself, I'll sue the city."

The officer stared ahead as she glared back with her good eye.

"Are you licensed to drive with only one eye?"

She shook her license in front of him. "I passed the eye exam."

He marched to his squad car for a few minutes and then returned with a piece of paper.

"I'm giving you a warning. Watch your driving and stay in your lane."

Aunt Polly harrumphed and plunked back into the car with a thud. She reached for a roll of peppermint candies, popped three in her mouth, and we were off again.

Chapter 5

ONCE HOME, EYES GLAZED from the massive breakfast, Aunt Polly headed to her first-floor bedroom near the kitchen. "I need a nap, girls. Entertain yourselves."

"Sure. We will, Aunt Polly. We brought books," Kitty said, her voice all sweetness and sunshine. Then she turned to me, eyes wide and mouthed, "Finally!"

Time to ourselves. We quickly dashed upstairs to rehash breakfast and develop a plan while we still had some freedom.

I flopped on my bed. "How embarrassing seeing the O'Reillys."

Kitty tossed her hair. "So what? At least we know they're here. I hope they ask us to go sailing."

"You can hope, but they didn't look very excited when Aunt Polly mentioned a barbecue."

Kitty took out her barrettes and brushed her hair while admiring herself in the cracked mirror on top of the dresser.

"Probably because adults would be there. I'm sure they want to see us. Charlie threw me a little smile."

"I wanted to melt into the floor. Everyone in the restaurant was staring at us."

Kitty turned back and hissed. "Not at us. At her."

"Well, she's asleep now, so let's do something."

"Like what?"

"Let's see if that key fits the room."

Kitty set down her hairbrush and turned to me. "I guess it wouldn't hurt to see if it fits and take a peek. But we can't go in there."

I got the key and we hurried down the wooden stairs barefoot, trying to avoid the squeaky spots, and headed past both living rooms and into the kitchen. The locked room was between the kitchen and the back porch.

Kitty took the skeleton key. I hung back, watching for signs of our aunt. In a moment, Kitty found me, shook her head, and whispered, "Not even close. Wrong kind of key. Now what?"

"So you're on board?"

"I wouldn't mind a little adventure. Where do we start?"

I thought for a moment. "Let's keep looking for the right key."

"We'll have to be very quiet."

I nodded. "Come on." We crept back upstairs and started searching in the tiny upstairs bedroom in front of the house, farthest from Aunt Polly's room. We searched the small dresser, single bed, and night table. No key. We moved into the sprawling bedroom across the hall from ours that boasted a dressing room with two marble-topped vanities and twin beds in a connected space.

Kitty stealthily yanked on the drawers. "Why don't we ever sleep in this room? It's so much nicer."

"The mouse. Remember? We found that dead mouse in my bed a few years ago. I can't stay in here again."

Kitty shivered. "Oh. I forgot about that. Anything in those drawers, Cindy?"

"Mouse poop and bugs. I wish I had gloves. Yuck!"

The drawers squeaked as we carefully shoved them closed. We stopped and listened to make sure Aunt Polly wasn't calling us.

I whispered. "Coast is clear. Let's move down the hall."

We tiptoed up to the crack in the floor over the porch below. "I can see daylight from the porch. Look. It's much worse than it was last year."

"This is too much for Dad to fix. Is this house splitting apart?"

"Probably," I shrugged. "Let's hope it doesn't split while we're here. Let's keep going." We inched our way down the hall to the bedroom with the balcony where we shook out our bedspreads when we arrived. A beautiful velvet fainting couch sat near the door of the sitting room, along with two antique dressers.

Kitty dramatically threw herself onto the couch and pretended she was fainting. As soon as she did, a plume of dust burst into the air, triggering a sneezing fit from me.

"Shhhhh. She'll hear us," Kitty shushed.

"I can't help it. I'm allergic to dust." My eyes started to water. "You look in here. I'm going to the bathroom to find a tissue."

I passed another three bedrooms before I came to the bathroom. It was large enough to practice dance steps, with a tiled floor, two marble sinks, and an oversized claw-footed tub. Because there was little dust, I breathed easier for a few moments.

Kitty soon found me and excitedly held out a small silver key. "I found this in one of the dressers. Not a skeleton key. I don't know if it'll fit, but let's try it when she's not looking."

"Like now. Why wait?"

"OK, but we need a signal. I'll try the key, and you stay on the lookout. Sneeze if you hear or see her."

"What if I have to sneeze for real? That won't work."

Kitty let out an exasperated breath. "What then?"

"How 'bout if I say 'donut'?"

"Donut! Are you crazy? She'll think we have secret donuts, and it'll send her into a frenzy. Something else."

"OK. I'll snap my fingers."

We crept back downstairs, and once again, Kitty took the key, and I posted myself near Aunt Polly's bedroom to keep watch. Moments later, Kitty found me and shook her head.

Back upstairs, we hid both keys and decided to take a break from our sleuthing to read. An hour or so later, we heard Aunt Polly screeching our names.

"Kitty! Cindy! Where are you?" So she did know our names!

We ran to the top of the stairs. "Just up here reading."

"Let's go swimming. It's such a warm day. Get your suits on, girls."

We shimmied into our swimsuits and pulled our hair back into ponytails. Aunt Polly's house overlooked Lake Minnetonka, but the sandy swimming beach was a short car ride away. To our surprise, Aunt Polly was already waiting for us at the bottom of the stairs. She looked flustered.

"Can you girls help me?"

We ran down the stairs and asked what was wrong.

"I couldn't zip my suit," she said and turned around to show us a gap of at least four inches where her suit wouldn't come together over rolls of back fat that looked like Crisco shortening.

"You want us to zip your swimsuit?" I sighed, dumbfounded. This was a new one.

I nudged Kitty to give it a try. She stepped behind Aunt Polly, eyes wide with disbelief. She bit her bottom lip as she tugged both sides of the suit. "Help me," she said, and I inched in to work the zipper while she struggled to make the fabric stretch, but it wouldn't budge. The knit material was strained as far as it was willing to go.

After several minutes of pulling and groaning, I timidly spoke. "I think this is the wrong size, Aunt Polly. Do you have another one?"

"Nonsense! You girls aren't strong enough. Never mind. I'll find someone at the beach. Let's go."

I was aghast. "The beach? But what if no one can get it zipped?"

"Don't be silly. I always find someone. Get in the car," she said and moved toward the door.

Kitty and I shook our heads behind her, grabbed our towels, and headed to the car like a funeral parade with our aunt's swimsuit gaping open in the back, exposing rolls of fat and the crack at the top of her butt. We glanced around the backyard, relieved that the O'Reillys weren't outside. I hoped they weren't ogling us from a window.

As Kitty and I walked to the car's passenger side, I whispered, "She always finds someone? This is a regular thing?"

Kitty shrugged and looked appalled. You'd be horrified too, wouldn't you?

We hoped there would be few other swimmers at the beach, but Minnesotans rarely miss an opportunity to swim on the few days when the weather is good. Once Aunt Polly's car stopped coughing at the parking lot, we waited to see her plan for the gaping swimsuit. Within minutes she spotted an athletic-looking young man and rolled down her window as far as it would go.

"Excuse me," she chimed. "Can you help me?"

Kitty and I froze. This was the plan? I secretly prayed God would scoop me up and plant me on the moon. NASA was working on that, right? Not in time to help me in my moment of mortification.

"Help me out of the car, girls."

As the handsome—did I mention he was

gorgeous?—young man approached, we realized to our horror it was Jimmy O'Reilly, the boy I secretly adored. My first heartthrob. Jimmy. He was about to witness a sight he'd never be able to unsee.

We dashed around the car to Aunt Polly and pulled her out just as Jimmy reached us.

"Hey," Kitty said weakly.

I looked away, not wanting to let him see our shame.

"Can you zip my swimsuit?" Aunt Polly asked him with no trace of embarrassment.

Jimmy raked his hand through his blond hair, cocked his head to one side, and swallowed a smirk. "Say what? You want me to do what?" He was surely cataloging this outrageous moment to relive with his buddies.

Aunt Polly giggled. "Just, uh, zip me up. The zipper's stuck, and the girls aren't strong enough." She turned and showed him the gap caused not by a faulty zipper but by a bathing suit several sizes too small.

"Oh wow. I see the problem." I thought I saw him gag a bit, but he budged the pudge little by little in a show of strength.

Jimmy had sweat on his forehead when he finished. "There you go. All done." His blue eyes crinkled slightly at the edges as if he was trying not to laugh.

"Thanks. Now you and the girls can go for a swim," Aunt Polly said. Like a penguin, she tottered to the water's edge, and without any hesitation to adjust to the cold water, she dove in and floated away.

We three stood watching in awe and awkwardness. Finally, Jimmy broke away. "I'm going to swim. See you around." He pranced off, shoulders swaying in rhythm to his steps.

Kitty and I spoke in tandem. "Yes, see you. Thanks for helping." What can you say after the most mortifying experience of your life? Would I ever be able to look him in the eye?

He dashed toward a different part of the beach. I sighed as I watched him go, wondering if we'd ever see him again. I dreamed of kissing him, but I knew he was too good for me… so sophisticated and dreamy.

Kitty broke the silence. "Wow. That's one episode I'll never forget."

"Why couldn't it have been a stranger we'd never have to see again?"

"Our sisters will never believe it when we tell them."

"Mary will. I think she had some weird experiences here last year."

"We might as well swim… or sunbathe."

We grabbed the faded, fraying bath towels we brought from Aunt Polly's linen closet and timidly made our way down the vast beach. The scalding sand made us regret our decision to go barefoot.

Sunbathers on that swanky beach looked like they were born to lay in the sun. Many had proper beach towels long enough to lie upon without getting sand in their hair. Others reclined on chairs fitted with umbrellas to keep their delicate European skin from burning. It was a scene from a travel magazine with flat-stomached women sporting the latest two-piece swimsuits, sandals, and hats, lying next to tanned men with bulging muscles.

Self-conscious about her gangly figure, Kitty wore a modest navy two-piece suit trimmed in white. I must have been highly optimistic when I shopped for my swimsuit because I now sported a red, high-waist suit adorned with tropical fruit, which was probably a touch gaudy for this crowd.

We bravely looked for an empty spot on the beach to lay our towels. As we walked by one family, a young boy shouted, "Hey! She's got a pineapple on her butt." And everyone started to laugh.

I whispered to my sister. "Is it true?"

"Yes, there's a large pineapple on your right butt cheek."

Why hadn't I noticed that before? Now the only way out was to plunge into the water and stay there until the beach was empty. We dropped our towels in a heap near some rocks and headed to the icy shore. In Minnesota, even when the air temperature is warm, it takes months to warm the massive lakes, and usually by the time they've warmed up, Mother Nature blows a fuse, the birds leave town, leaves fall, and we reach for our puffy coats and wool sweaters. There was no point waiting for the water to warm. I prepared to embrace it. I headed to the diving platform as Kitty inched her way into the chilly water, adjusting as the water swarmed her feet and legs. Before I had a chance to change my mind, I dove in and then burst back up into the sunshine. Kitty gasped and put one hand over her mouth, and I thought it was because of the water temperature.

Kitty gestured frantically at me when I popped up from my dive into Lake Minnetonka, waving her hands at my top. I heard a wolf whistle and realized my swimsuit top was pushed around my neck, not covering my boobies. It all happened in seconds, but my embarrassment would be with me for years. I dove back underwater and adjusted my suit, relieved I didn't know the boy who whistled. I hoped I never saw him again. There was a growing list of folks I never wanted to see again. Mostly guys.

I swam over to Kitty. "I wish we could go home. This day has gone from bad to worse."

Kitty was dog paddling. "Hardly anyone saw you, and we don't know anyone here."

"Other than Jimmy."

"He went to another part of the beach. Try to forget it."

"Which part? Jimmy having to zip her suit? Or me exposing myself to the world?"

Kitty stifled a laugh. "It'll be funnier next year when you think about it."

"Or when I'm an old lady. It'll be funny then. Maybe."

"We're here now, so let's enjoy the water," Kitty said.

"We'd better keep an eye out for Aunt Polly, though."

"She's hard to miss, Cindy."

"Yes, but we don't want her wandering around the beach calling for us."

"I see your point. Let's swim closer to where she floated off."

That turned out to be a smart move. After about twenty

minutes, Aunt Polly swam close to us and announced it was time to leave. We swam to the shore, retrieved our towels, and wrapped them around us for modesty and warmth. But like a confident puppy, Aunt Polly simply shook herself off and plowed her way through the sandy beach to her Chevy without bothering to dry off. When she landed inside the car, her wet suit made a sucking noise on the synthetic fabric, and water oozed onto the floorboard. Undeterred and not a bit cold, she started the car, and we were off in a plume of smoke once again.

CHAPTER 6

AFTER A WEEK AT AUNT POLLY'S, Kitty and I sneaked into the front living room, and I dialed the heavy black rotary phone that sat on a side table near Aunt Polly's usual couch. Aunt Polly had fallen asleep in a recliner on the large porch that wrapped the lake side of the house.

Our eldest sister, Mary, answered the phone. "Hanson's hen house. Which chick do you want?"

"Hilarious, Mary. It's me, Cindy. Is Mom there?"

"Are you still at Aunt Polly's?"

"Yes."

"I wondered why it was so peaceful here."

"Very funny. We've been cleaning, fetching, cooking, and doing dishes, and we're sick of it. Is Mom there?"

"So, no boys then? Not even Wayne?"

"No!"

"Too bad."

"Could you please just get Mom?"

"Mom!" Mary hollered loudly, near enough to hurt my ears right through the phone. "It's Cindy."

After a pause, Mom answered.

"Hi, Cindy. What's up?"

"Hi, Mom. We want to come home. Can you come and get us?"

"Come home? Why?"

"We're bored. And we'd like to see our friends."

"Aunt Polly said she'd arrange a barbecue with the O'Reilly boys. That should be fun."

"Well, she hasn't done it. All we've been doing is cooking and cleaning for her."

"Where is she now?"

"On the front porch snoozing."

Mom sighed. "I'm glad you're being helpful, but sorry, dear, I can't come to get you. She needs your help. And we'll all be there for the July 4th party. Why don't you stick it out and come home after the party? Now, is Kitty there?"

"Yes." I handed the phone to Mom's favorite.

Kitty made the same plea with the same result. No dice. We had to stay for another two weeks. She hung up the phone dejectedly. "Mom says we need to take all the dishes out of the cupboards and wash them."

"Did you tell her we've done most of them?"

"She says with company coming, we need to ensure the pots and pans are clean."

"Fine, but let's try the window to that mystery room. See if she left it unlocked. Maybe we can pry it open."

"She might hear us."

"You stay here and keep watch. If you hear her, whistle."

"Whistle? What song should I whistle?"

"It doesn't matter, Kitty. How 'bout 'Yankee Doodle'?"

"'Yankee Doodle'? How'd you come up with that one?"

I shook my head. "Kitty, just stay here. I'll check the window." I crept onto the back porch, pushed on the window, and felt it give—just a bit. I was about to put my fingers in the crack when I heard Kitty whistling 'Three Blind Mice.' It wasn't the code, but I stopped anyway and crept into the hall.

Aunt Polly was moseying down the hallway, her eyebrows pinched close together. They created such a deep crevice in her forehead I was afraid her glass eye would pop out, and I didn't want to see what was behind it. "What are you two doing?"

Kitty was quick with an answer. "We were just about to do some spring cleaning. We thought we should wash the dishes in the cupboards before the big party."

"Good. When you girls finish, let's go into town to get the food for the big event."

"It's not for two weeks," I protested.

"We have to get ready." Our great-aunt sank into her favorite couch and turned on I Love Lucy. "Could one of you please get me the Lorna Doones?"

Kitty found the cookies in the snack cupboard, opened them, and we each sneaked a buttery cookie before we brought the crinkly package to her. We slugged into the kitchen and emptied the first cupboard of soiled dishes while Aunt Polly reclined in leisure.

Elbows deep in sudsy water, I hissed at Kitty, "This isn't fair. We didn't make this mess. Why do we have to clean it up?" I wanted to be sitting on the couch eating Lorna Doones like Aunt Polly. You can't blame me, can you?

Kitty shook her head and whispered back, "Mom asked us, so we have to. It won't take long."

"Not long? Are you kidding? Our childhood will be over by the time we finish."

"Quit complaining. Let's just hurry up and get it done."

As I reached into a second lower cupboard, I screamed.

Kitty jumped back. "What? What is it?"

"The cupboard's alive with squiggling, wiggling creatures. Mice! A nest of mice. Yuck! The big one just jumped out, and there must be a dozen little ones in that cupboard."

"Gross! Like three blind mice?"

"Not funny, Kitty. Maybe your song brought them here."

"I think I'm going to throw up."

Aunt Polly called from her couch, "What's going on in there?"

We rushed into the living room. "I found a nest of mice. The mother got away. Now Kitty's going to throw up." Kitty stood by me, ready to bolt from the room if she was about to hurl.

Aunt Polly wasn't surprised, disgusted, or nauseous, which I thought were appropriate responses. Instead, she said nothing until we became afraid she'd fallen asleep with her eyes open. Well, with one eye open. Kitty and I exchanged glances as Kitty kept up her deep breathing to hold in her breakfast.

Finally Aunt Polly said, "Let's call Mr. O'Reilly. He'll know what to do." She picked up her phone and dialed.

This was good news and bad news. On the plus side, maybe he'd get rid of those mice. But what if he brought his sons? We hadn't brushed our hair or applied lip gloss or a swipe of mascara. What would they think if they saw us? I could see Kitty chewing on her bottom lip, and I suspected she was pondering the same thing. But this was an emergency, and we didn't have much control of the situation.

Aunt Polly put down the phone, and we hovered over her to learn our fate. I blurted out, "What did he say?"

"He's coming over."

I was in a panic. I felt my hands involuntarily start flapping at my side. "Just, just… just him? Or, or is he bringing… anyone?"

Was Aunt Polly hiding a wee little smile? "He didn't say. And stop stuttering."

Kitty and I bolted upstairs to primp, just in case the O'Reilly boys came to our rescue along with their dad. Kitty's nausea disappeared faster than a packet of Lorna Doones on Aunt Polly's lap. We were on a mission as we dashed to the bathroom with hairbrushes, makeup, and toothbrushes in hand. We didn't want to look like we were trying to impress them, but our pride wouldn't let them see us looking and smelling like mangy raccoons.

As I peered into the mirror, I said, "The last time we saw Jimmy was at the beach, so let's hope things seem more normal this time."

"Cindy, there is nothing normal about this. Cleaning up someone else's nest of mice will be just another notch in his belt of stories."

"Well, we don't want to make it any weirder." We swapped soiled T-shirts for fresh ones, took 3.4 minutes to glam up, and then headed downstairs, trying not to sound breathless as they arrived at the door. Mr. O'Reilly, Jimmy-the-heartthrob, and Charlie, Kitty's crush, approached wide-eyed, all dressed in tennis whites.

Kitty opened the back door, flipped her hair back, and nervously greeted them. "Hi! Thanks so much for helping us. Come on in."

"No problem. We're happy to help," said Mr. O'Reilly in his best Minnesota-nice voice.

They walked through the back porch and into the living room where Aunt Polly was on full display, lounging on her couch with crumbs on her face and chest. She threw back her head and giggled in a flirtatious manner. "Hello there! The girls are afraid of the mice, so I thought you could help. Cindy, show them."

I wasn't about to open that cupboard again, so I gestured, pointed, and wrung my hands. "Well, um, it's mice. A lot of them. One got away, but you'll see them if you look in the cupboard, uh, there, uh, under the sink."

Mr. O'Reilly took the lead as his sons gawked at Aunt Polly and avoided our eyes. He marched to the kitchen like a man of action, and Jimmy and Charlie followed, ready to do battle.

"I see you have a nest of little ones. I'll remove them, but you'll need traps to find the mama." He didn't scream or squirm, which I found abnormal.

Kitty and I moved to the formal dining room, unable to witness the removal. We heard some rumbling. The porch door opened and closed several times. Finally, Mr. O'Reilly found us cowering. "You'll need to wash everything that was in that cupboard. Do you have any traps?"

Traps? Did we look like trappers? I shook my head.

"I'll send the boys over with traps tomorrow." Jimmy and Charlie looked at us, nodded, and then looked at the floor, hiding smirks. None of us could think of a thing to say.

After a brief exchange with Aunt Polly about the weather, always a safe subject, Mr. O'Reilly said they needed to leave for a game of tennis doubles.

We nodded mutely as they marched out in single file, leaving Kitty and me alone on the porch.

Kitty whispered. "Traps? Now we have to start trapping mice?"

"Like frontier pioneers, I guess, but without bonnets. Could this get any worse?"

"At least we got to see Jimmy and Charlie. And they'll be back tomorrow."

"Yes, but they didn't say a word."

"How could they with Aunt Polly sitting there?"

I sighed. "Let's get the cupboard cleaned out." Was this how other girls spent their summers? I felt like a charwoman in an Eastern European novel. Old before my time, without hope or rubber gloves.

"Girls! Girls! Wake up!" I was having a nightmare where mice were crawling all over me, and I was supposed to tame them to do circus tricks while Aunt Polly shouted orders with a Dilly Bar in her hand.

Then I awoke and realized parts of the dream were accurate. Aunt Polly was calling for us from the bottom of the stairs.

"Kitty, get up," I mumbled as my feet hit the hardwood floor. I stumbled to the top of the stairs and looked down. "What is it, Aunt Polly?" No Dilly Bar.

"We need to have an early breakfast because I have a hair appointment. Get dressed and come downstairs."

I nodded and relayed the message to Kitty as she sat dazed on the edge of her bed.

She whispered. "Why? Why do we have to get up so early? I was enjoying a dream about Charlie."

"She's got a hair appointment. I don't know why we have to go with her." I snatched the skeleton key from the dresser drawer and pocketed it so I could continue to look for something it would unlock.

Aunt Polly was chipper as she directed us to put moldy strawberries, milk, and stale cereal on the wobbly table on the front porch. The porch was enclosed entirely in floor-to-ceiling screens so the mosquitoes wouldn't feed on us while we picked through our breakfast. We obediently brought out bowls and spoons and started to pour milk over our cereal when Kitty sniffed. "Stop! That milk is sour."

I sniffed the carton and pulled back. "Ewwww. She's right. It's curdled."

Aunt Polly took a sniff. "Nonsense! Don't be ridiculous. It's fine. It must be something outside." And she snatched the carton and poured sour milk all over our cornflakes.

We sat stunned for a few minutes, watching our great-aunt dive into her bowl.

"What's the matter with you girls? Start eating!"

Kitty and I took tiny bites, but when our aunt wasn't looking, we spit them into paper napkins we held in our laps. Aunt Polly kept telling us we were imagining things and plowed ahead, eating all her cereal. I'm pretty sure I know when milk has soured, don't you?

"Pass the cornflakes, please. I have milk left in my bowl."

I passed my aunt the cereal box and tried to figure out how to make it look like I was eating.

"Finish your breakfast. I need to get to the beauty parlor."

I took another tentative bite and pretended to cough into my napkin as I spit out the disgusting mushy mess.

Aunt Polly eyed me suspiciously but reached for the curdled milk. "Now I have too much cereal."

She seesawed between adding cereal and milk and kept munching away, eating four bowls of sour flakes.

Meanwhile, Kitty and I continued to push the sour mess around in our bowls. Finally, the telephone ringing in the front living room saved us. I put my napkin down and raced to answer it.

"It's for you, Aunt Polly," I called as I returned to the porch.

Aunt Polly got up and we saw our chance.

By now, my cereal had disintegrated into a pile of sour mushiness.

"Quick, grab your bowl," I said as I heaved my bowl toward a hole in the screen. Kitty followed in quick order, but instead of going through it, the mush hit the screen and stuck.

Kitty turned to me and whispered. "Great. Now we're in trouble. Why did you make me do that?"

I snapped back at her. "I didn't make you. I thought it would go right through."

Just as gravity got hold of the clotted mess and it began to slide to the floor, Aunt Polly reappeared and scowled. I held my breath.

"What happened here?"

"Uh, would you believe a big wind came along, and our cereal blew into the screen?" I lied.

"A big wind, huh? No, I would not believe that."

"How about flying squirrels swooped in and thrust the bowls at the screen?" Would humor help?

"Nice try, but I don't believe that either." Aunt Polly stood looking from one of us to the other, and then, to our surprise, she burst out laughing and told us to clean up the slop. She behaved like a marionette puppet cut off from the puppeteer, unpredictable in her movements and speech. When she stopped laughing, she sighed and shook her head.

"You girls are spoiled. In my day, we had to eat what was in front of us."

I shot back. "But the milk was curdled."

"Rubbish. Clean that up. Now I'll have to go to my appointment without you."

Kitty nodded. "We're sorry. We'll clean it up. But we should stay here anyway because Jimmy and Charlie are supposed to come over with mousetraps."

Aunt Polly hesitated. "Jimmy and Charlie, huh? I don't want you entertaining while I'm gone."

I crossed my arms. "We're not entertaining. They're bringing traps, remember?"

"Don't get snippy with me. And uncross your arms! Honestly, you'd think you girls were being raised by ruffians. And don't get into trouble while I'm gone." With that, she propelled herself to her car and left.

I waited until I heard her engine backfire like a rocket blasting into space. I exhaled.

"She's gone." I felt like I could turn cartwheels if I was coordinated enough. I wanted to run from room to room bellowing like the scruffy hobos in downtown Minneapolis who stand on corners and warn about incoming aliens, the end of the world, or a coming shortage of shortbread cookies. For the first time in days, we had the house to ourselves. "Let's look for another key after we clean this up."

Kitty shrugged. "OK."

She was nauseous again, conveniently, so I cleaned the curdled cereal mess. I didn't mind, though, because we finally had a little freedom. Freedom! I dumped out the rest of the sour milk and sang as I cleaned the screen. But first, we raided the snack cupboard and snatched Twinkies to fuel us for the hunt.

Riding a sugar high, we dashed upstairs and down the long hall to a dreary bedroom that hadn't been visited since 1875. Plum wallpaper covered the sitting room's walls with an elaborate floral design that nearly camouflaged the plum fainting couch, tall cherry dressers, desks, and, most importantly, the door to a closet stuffed with vintage garments. A filmy crystal chandelier with strands of spiderwebs dangling from it cast yellow patterns on the items below. Beyond the sitting room was another cavernous bedroom with two beds, side tables, lamps, velvet chairs, and filthy windows with torn screens on the outside. Even my eyes felt dusty as we disturbed the decomposing critters and bugs that covered every surface.

I fastened a scarf around my nose and mouth as we rummaged through the dressers and desks and searched in the back of the closet looking for hiding places. We found none. I was sure we'd find dinosaur skeletons hoping to come back to life.

Kitty pulled out a scarlet ball gown embellished with rows of tiny jewels and beads. She shook it out and then plastered it against her small frame. "Do you think it would fit me?"

"It's beautiful. Try it on."

She quickly slipped into the dress and twirled around, a cloud of dust rising as she did so. "It fits. I wonder if this is silk. Imagine wearing this to a ball."

"Imagine what would happen if she came home and found you wearing it."

"Spoilsport!"

"Sorry. You look beautiful, but I live in fear of that woman's temper."

Kitty slipped the dress off and continued to search with me. We pulled a dresser away from the wall a few inches, and I ran my hands behind it and was thrilled to find a blue key taped to the back. "Kitty, look! Another one. Come on. Let's see if this fits." We bolted downstairs and tried it, but again were disappointed. It looked like it would take an act of Congress to get into that room, and even then, Congress moved like a sloth in a coma.

Kitty's eyebrows furled and she put her pointer finger to her lips. "What about the window? Do you think it's locked?"

"No. It's just stuck. Probably dried paint."

"Let's try it together." We went onto the porch. Just as we put our shoulders to it, we heard a knock. We looked up. Jimmy and Charlie were standing outside the back porch door watching us through the screen. Busted.

Jimmy's blue eyes twinkled. "Locked out?"

Kitty brushed her hair out of her eyes. "No, um, we just wanted to be sure the window was locked." She opened the door and the guys walked onto the porch.

Charlie nodded. "Yeah, sure. We brought a couple of mousetraps."

"Thanks. But, um, what do we do with them?" Kitty asked.

Charlie looked amused. "Put 'em under the sink." He thrust them into Kitty's hands.

I doubted it was that simple. "Just like that?"

"Do you have any peanut butter for bait?" Jimmy asked.

Kitty held the traps out as if they had already held dead animals. "Bait? Um, I think so. But where do we put it?"

Charlie took the traps back and smirked. "You've never set a mousetrap?"

I didn't want him to think we were simpletons. "No. We don't have mice at home." We probably did, but I wasn't going to admit it.

Charlie stepped up, his brown eyes sympathetic. "Let's go into the kitchen, get the bait, and I'll show you how to set the trap."

Kitty grinned her most flirtatious grin, shook her hair, and made her voice sound like the woman on the radio selling Brylcreem for men. "Thanks, Charlie. I knew you'd know what to do."

Now I was the nauseous one. Was this how flirting was done?

The four of us traipsed into the kitchen. Charlie showed us how to put a dab of peanut butter on the trap and pull back the lever. "When the mouse eats the peanut butter, this lever will snap back."

I was horrified. "To kill it?"

Jimmy laughed at me. "Yes, to kill it. What did you think? We were going to take it to the zoo?"

My cheeks burned. "Well, no. Will it suffer?"

Jimmy looked into my eyes, and I nearly fainted. "No. It'll happen very quickly."

Charlie put two traps in the lower cupboard. "They usually come out at night, so check them in the morning."

"Will you come back if we catch one?" Kitty asked Charlie as she batted her eyelashes. I couldn't help wondering if she was having a stroke or something.

Charlie shook his head in disbelief but smiled. "Just give us a call."

We stood in silence, not sure what should happen next. I didn't want them to go, but I had no experience speaking to boys.

Kitty brightened. "Would you like a cup of tea?"

Jimmy laughed. "Tea? What is this? Nineteenth-century England?"

She smiled weakly. "I guess I've been reading too many Jane Austen novels."

How were we supposed to know what boys liked? "Orange juice, then?" I asked.

Jimmy shook his head. "Nah. Thanks. We'd better go."

No one moved. We glanced nervously from one to the other and then at our feet. Kitty was chewing on her lip, no doubt thinking of how to trap them to stay. "So, um, the weather's going to warm up."

Jimmy brightened and thrust a hand through his golden hair. "Right! We could go sailing tomorrow if you like."

"Yes!" we said in tandem before remembering that girls weren't supposed to act eager.

Charlie was not-so-secretly eyeing Kitty. He smiled. "Sounds good. See you tomorrow."

They left through the back porch, and we watched them stroll next door, laughing and punching each other in the arms in some unknown brotherly code.

Kitty whispered in awe, "Sailing tomorrow! I can't wait."

"Right, but what do we know about sailing?"

"I think we just have to sit in the boat. Or is it on the boat?"

I didn't know. "What should we wear?"

"Swimsuits. If we're in the water, we have to expect to get wet. So glad I got a new navy suit."

Swimsuit! I pondered my pineapple-butt suit with the top that didn't stay in place. Would they make fun of me?

Chapter 7

I TUGGED ON ONE OF MY BRAIDS. "I'm not so sure I want to go sailing."

"Don't be crazy, Cindy. We've waited all year to see them again."

"But my swimsuit! They'll make fun of me."

"Wear shorts over your suit or bring a big towel and keep it around your waist."

I bit my lip. Maybe that would work. At least I'd get to see Jimmy again.

The following day, we told Aunt Polly about our plans to go sailing.

"Wonderful. It'll be nice for you to spend time around kids your age."

"Yes, we're looking forward to it," Kitty said politely.

Aunt Polly looked to a far corner of the room. "We spent a great deal of time on the lake when I was your age."

"With boys?" Oops! I hadn't meant to say that out loud. But it was out there now.

She smiled slightly. "Sometimes with fellas our age, yes."

I was glad she seemed happy for us but wondered if Aunt Polly was sick of having us around all the time. Either way, we were going and could hardly eat lunch with our nerves raw in anticipation. Waiting until early afternoon when the temperature was at least 70 degrees was torture. Luckily there was no rain in the forecast, just a perfect June afternoon.

We grew up swimming in several South Minneapolis lakes, but Lake Minnetonka was the queen of them all, vast and deep, with many islands, inlets, bays, twists, and turns. Not a lake you could run around, like, say, Lake Harriet. No, Lake Minnetonka was home to celebrities, mini castles, and the hoity-toity Lafayette Club, where wealthy residents rubbed elbows and exchanged tips on becoming more affluent and staying rail thin. At least, that was my idea of what they were doing. In truth, I never set foot in the place because Aunt Polly couldn't afford to join. We did attend the fireworks each year on the 4th of July. I'll tell you about that later.

Our mother was a water safety instructor who taught us how to swim in the murky lakes, so we weren't spooked by the fish and seaweed that skimmed our legs and wrapped itself around our ankles. We grew up like mermaids, preferring water to land in the short summer months. Life jackets had been invented, but my parents didn't subscribe to safety items, so we learned to dive and swim, even in the deepest waters, without any protective gear. Sunscreen had also been invented, but we didn't bother with that either, so we suffered many sleepless nights with raw, red skin after lying on the sandy shores in the blazing afternoon sun. Sometimes after a particularly painful burn set in, we poured apple cider vinegar on our skin. It didn't help the burn, but it kept the mosquitoes at bay and caused strange cravings for pickles.

After lunch, I tried on my swimsuit and stretched around to see my rump in the bathroom mirror. Kitty was watching me. "Don't worry about it. No one will notice the pineapple."

I shook my head and reached for a pair of shorts, a large towel, and my sense of humor, just in case.

We walked next door in our flip-flops with towels slung over our shoulders. Kitty was wearing her navy-blue swimsuit, which looked tame next to my fruity red one. The O'Reilly's rose bushes were in full bloom, and we stopped for a moment to enjoy them. Before we had a chance to knock, their door opened, and Jimmy and Charlie filled the threshold. Their older brother, Wayne, darkened the doorway when they stepped out into the afternoon sun. All three were wearing swimming trunks and T-shirts, so at least we passed the correct dress-code test.

As Jimmy passed me, my pulse quickened to be so near him again. What was happening to me?

"Mother wanted me to go to make sure there's no hanky-panky," Wayne said.

Kitty and I tried to hide our smirks. We avoided looking at each other lest we explode into a fit of giggles. With a house full of sisters, we were never sure how to behave around boys.

Our father insisted we attend an all-girl high school to ensure we wouldn't become loose women, so we had to ride on the memories of boys we knew from middle grades before most hit puberty. We were navigating unfamiliar waters with boys sprouting facial hair and cello-like voices.

Wayne looked disapprovingly at my bare midriff. I sucked in my stomach. Was he scowling at my swimsuit top or my fluffy middle?

"Let's go," Wayne commanded, and we stepped in line.

We walked to the inlet across the railroad tracks behind our homes, boys in front and Kitty and I trying to keep up with their long strides. When we reached the dock, Jimmy set a small cooler of drinks inside the boat. They removed the tarp and set the sails in place as we stood awkwardly on the dock, unsure what to do or how to help.

Charlie turned to us as he shook his dark brown bangs out of his eyes. "Hop in." He gestured broadly, so we gingerly navigated the side of the boat and sat huddled together in the middle of it like football players who've been benched. Charlie turned away and went back to his sail. After he stripped off his T-shirt, Kitty followed his every move. His bare torso was an object of fascination for us. We didn't dare look any further south or wonder what was inside his trunks. That might be a mortal sin.

Jimmy was taller than Charlie and even more muscular. I tried to keep my mouth shut and not drool as I watched them get the sails ready, tying and untying heavy ropes.

Wayne turned to us and scowled. "You can't sit there. Go to the starboard side."

I shrugged. "The what?"

He rolled his eyes. "Oh, great. Over there, you two." Wayne pointed as the others moved the sails into place. Wayne was utterly different from his brothers—short and stodgy, with a crew cut and perpetual sneer.

Kitty and I quickly shifted spots, flicked the bugs off a bench, and waited as they hollered words like "jibs," "sail ties," and maneuvering the boat "into the wind." It was a choreographed dance with only the wind and seagull squawks for music. And then, suddenly, we were off, and for a few glorious moments, I felt the same exhilaration I experienced as a child riding my bicycle down a hill. So this was sailing! I understood the appeal.

Kitty and I threw our heads back and relaxed into the sensation, pretending we were models on a luxurious yacht. It was as if the sky had been brushed free of clouds, making the dazzling sun sparkle across the lake like jewels. Jimmy and Charlie smiled and offered us cans of pop. I watched as Charlie handed Kitty a cola, smiling as his hand grazed hers. "What do you think?" he asked her.

She grinned back. "It's far out! I feel so free."

"Groovy," Charlie replied, nodding. That said it all.

As we sipped, they pointed out the summer homes of the rich and famous. Most we'd never heard of, but we pretended to be impressed. Everything was going well, and I couldn't believe how easy sailing was. Until the wind switched.

"Ready to tack?" Wayne yelled to no one in particular. And then, "Come about!"

I thought he said, "Come on out!" An invitation to move to the center of the boat. I stood up and stepped forward just as a giant sail swung at my back. I flew through the air and landed on my belly in the water with a loud slap.

The blow knocked the wind out of my sails and sent my sense of humor out to sea. For a moment, I thought I'd drown but you already know I didn't, or I wouldn't be here to tell you about it.

With my hands, I pushed my way to the surface and took a deep breath. I quickly checked my bikini top to ensure I wasn't flashing anyone. Jimmy, Charlie, and Kitty looked down at me, concerned. Bossy Wayne seemed only irritated.

Jimmy shouted so I could hear him over the wind, "Do you need help?"

I wasn't sure what kind of help he meant. Help identifying fish? Or getting seaweed off my legs? Or help with my hearing? "Yes," I said feebly.

They slowed the sailboat, and I swam close to it. Jimmy reached over the side. I took his hand, but the wind picked up, and the boat jerked away. I swam closer again and reached up to grasp the boat's side, but it was too high. I bounced up and down, trying to get enough momentum, but I wasn't strong enough to propel myself up and over the edge. Each time I attempted to get back in the boat, I feared my bikini top would slide up, a fate worse than death. Finally, I got both hands on the boat's side. Jimmy grabbed my forearms and hauled me gracelessly over the edge and into the sailboat. I landed with a thud on the bottom of the boat. Cold. Embarrassed. Tired.

Kitty handed me my towel.

Jimmy leaned over me. "Are you OK?"

"Just wet. I'm fine."

He nodded and smiled. "'Come about' means the large sail is swinging from one side to the other. So next time, stay low."

"I thought he said, 'come on out,' so I stood up."

"First time sailing?"

"Is it that obvious?" I smiled and knew it was.

A brief flash of sympathy shone in his blue eyes, sending a wave of jitters up my spine. "Sit over here and don't move. When you hear commands like 'come about' or 'ready to tack,' stay low in your seat."

I whispered in Kitty's ear, "I'm so embarrassed." She nodded, but her eyes continued to follow Charlie's every move.

In spite of my plunge into the lake, we spent a luxurious hour sailing. After, the boys worked their magic and put the sailboat back in its original position. They were animated on the way home, but I felt subdued after my spill in the lake.

Kitty walked alongside Charlie. "Thank you so much! That was fantastic!"

Charlie bounced along. "Glad you liked it. We sail as often as possible, so if you want to go again, just let me know."

She brightened, eyes wide. "OK, we will. Thank you."

"How long are you staying with your aunt?" Jimmy asked us.

"Great-aunt," I corrected.

Kitty continued, "She's my grandmother's sister. Only until the 4th. Our family's coming for a party and for the fireworks."

Charlie's puppy-dog-brown eyes lit up. "Cool! You'll be at the fireworks. I mean, you'll love them."

Kitty beamed at him. "Hope so. Will you be there?"

His enthusiasm bubbled over like a can of pop after vigorous shaking. "Of course." But was he excited about the fireworks or that Kitty would be there? I wasn't sure.

I didn't want them to think we were strangers to the festivities. "We go every year. Our whole family comes over for the day, and then after dinner we walk over to the Lafayette Club."

Wayne piped up. "We thought you wouldn't go to the fireworks because your aunt isn't, you know, a club member. And we assume you aren't either."

Kitty and I exchanged glances and shrugged. "Didn't know you had to be a member to sit outside and watch," I said.

Jimmy inserted, "I'm sure anyone is welcome."

Wayne snorted. "Even the unwashed masses."

"Stop it, dude," Jimmy said.

But Wayne couldn't let the moment pass. "How many are in your family?"

Kitty responded politely. "Ten, including our parents."

Wayne smirked. "Wow! They must mate like rabbits."

Jimmy shushed him. "Wayne, honestly."

"No wonder you can't afford to join a country club with so many kids," Wayne said.

I raised my chin and huffed. "Our father works very hard.

Just because we don't join a club doesn't mean we're poor." As if being poor was a crime.

Wayne's sharp words burst the bubble of fun we'd been floating in. We walked the rest of the way in silence. I was seething and wanted to say something to put him in his place but couldn't think of anything that would sting without causing a problem with Jimmy and Charlie. I imagined him swimming in a pool of dog waste instead. It's not a sin if you only think it, right?

CHAPTER 8

THE NEXT DAY, Aunt Polly went to the dermatologist to have her warts treated. We'd have the house to ourselves for a few blessed hours.

Today, nothing was going to stop us from getting into that room. Once we heard her car backfire, we knew the coast was clear.

"Let's start with the window. I felt it give last time I tried to open it. I don't think it's locked."

Kitty nodded. "OK. I'm in."

We walked onto the back porch with all the determination of NASA astronauts preparing for launch, put our shoulders to the window, and shoved. Something loosened.

"Don't break it!" Kitty hissed.

"It was just the frame creaking." I shoved again, and it opened a few inches as peeling, once-white paint chipped around it. With renewed excitement, we both put our fingers in the opening and pushed, pulled, heaved, and yanked until it was open about a foot. And then it wouldn't budge.

"It's stuck! Let's see if you can squeeze in there."

Kitty pushed back. "Me? Why don't we push you through the window?"

"Because you're the skinny one. Come on. We're so close. Just get inside and unlock the door."

"Yuck. There are cobwebs on the window frame and probably dead creatures inside."

I dashed back into the kitchen, grabbed a rag, and put it on Kitty's head.

"Why is this on my head?"

"To protect you from cobwebs. You'll need to go in headfirst."

"No way. I'll limbo my way in feet first. All those dance lessons will pay off."

"OK. Take the rag with you."

The window was about four feet off the ground, so Kitty backed up a bit and then swung one leg up and propelled it through the window. She bounced up and down on her other leg. "How am I supposed to get my other foot in?"

"I'll get a chair." I ran into the kitchen and brought out a straight-backed chair.

"How's that supposed to help?" Kitty asked, still hopping on one leg.

"I thought you could sit on the chair and hoist your other leg in."

"How can I sit on that chair with one leg stuck in the air?"

I sighed. "I think it'd be simpler if you went in headfirst."

"Fine!" She drew her leg out, put the rag on her head, and stuck her head through the opening. "Give me a little push."

I did, and she wiggled her shoulders and arms through, but there was nothing to land on except the floor. With another push, she was in. She landed with a thud. Two pushes. Just like childbirth, or the little I knew about it, without all the mess.

"You all right?"

"This floor is filthy!" She jumped up and crossed the room to unlock the door. It opened, and we were in. Finally.

I found a light switch for the single overhead light and surveyed the room as my eyes adjusted to the dimness. I saw a rack of clothes on one wall, an old metal bed frame, dresser, and desk on the opposite wall, and what looked like a blanket-covered bench in the corner. Don't ask me which wall was north or south. Directions were never my strong suit.

We started with the clothes, searched through pockets, and found little of interest. But when we opened the dresser's top drawer, we pulled out an ancient photo album with a raised design on the cover. The pages were yellowed and felt as if they'd crumble in our hands. We sat on the bench and began to carefully turn pages. There were black and white pictures of Aunt Polly, our grandmother, their parents, and a slew of folks we didn't recognize.

Kitty pointed to a picture. "Aunt Polly's almost pretty in these."

"She was nearly as tall as her father though, and much heavier than he was."

"But not so blubbery. She looks sturdy."

"Nice way to put it. Let's hide this up in our room so we can take a closer look later," I said.

"Good plan. I'll finish looking through the dresser."

I hightailed it upstairs, and when I came back after stashing the album in our dresser, Kitty was holding baby clothes.

"Look what I found in the dresser."

"Weird. I wonder if those were hers from when Aunt Polly was a baby? Or she was planning to kidnap someone's baby and bought the clothes just in case?"

"Don't be silly, Cindy. These look vintage. Not like any baby clothes I've seen."

"She never brings infant clothes when our new sisters arrive, so I doubt they were meant for a gift. Why did she hold on to them?"

Kitty scratched her head. "Let's keep looking."

I moved to the dresser and found a few newspaper clippings about institutions for patients with mental disabilities. I showed them to my sister.

"Maybe they were going to admit her?" Kitty's eyes were dark as she chewed on her bottom lip. She moved to the bench in the corner, and I sat next to her as we silently scanned the articles. Nothing unusual stood out. As we stood up, the blanket slipped off the bench.

"Cindy, this isn't a bench. Look. There's a lock on the front with a large metal clasp over it and two side clasps."

"And handles on both ends. This must be where she stores the skeletons."

"I have goosebumps."

I knelt and took a closer look at the side. "It's a shipping label."

"Can you read it?" Kitty asked.

"Hard to see in the dark. Help me move it under the window."

"Good plan. It'll make it easier to get through the window if I have something to land on next time."

"I thought you were worried about getting caught."

"My curiosity has taken over."

Now I was the cautious one. "As long as Aunt Polly doesn't notice we moved something."

"I doubt she ever comes into this room. Let's do it," Kitty said.

We struggled to move the heavy metal trunk but finally shoved it under the window, the only good light source. I squinted to read the label but couldn't.

Kitty tapped my shoulder. "Let me try. I have better eyes." She knelt and read, "Polly Schultz—1917 Paris, France. She went to France! Was that during World War I?"

"I'm not sure. I wish I'd paid better attention in history class. The only war date I remember is the War of 1812."

"Who fought in that one?"

"I can't remember. But I can tell you what year it was fought."

Kitty grinned. "Nice."

"Let's see if any of those keys will fit this trunk."

The excitement in Kitty's voice was palpable. "Yes. Go get 'em. I'll keep watch for Aunt Polly."

I hurried upstairs and retrieved the three keys from inside the bottom drawer of our room's dresser. When I brought the keys into the secret room, Kitty showed me a small leather box she found on the floor in the corner. It had a lock on the front and an elaborate design on the cream-colored top. I ran my finger over the top, and it came away black from years of dirt.

"Looks like a jewelry box. But like everything else, it's locked," Kitty said.

"OK. Let's try these keys on the bench first, and then I'll see if the smaller one unlocks the jewelry chest." The skeleton key was too big, the blue key didn't fit, and the smaller silver key went into the trunk's lock but wouldn't turn anything. I sighed. "What's with all these locks?"

Kitty was thoughtful. "I assumed her life was pretty simple. No husband, no kids. She went to college and works as a teacher down south. What's she got to hide?"

I shook my head. "She doesn't act like she's had many adventures. Never mentions past trips, experiences, or even people. Just works through the school year and then comes here in the summers and expects us to entertain her and wait on her." My limited imagination was running out of ideas.

"I've often wondered how she could afford this house on Lake Minnetonka on a teacher's salary."

"I never thought about it. But we can chat later. Let's try the small key on the jewelry box." Kitty held the box, and I worked the tarnished key into the lock. "Look, Kitty! It fits!"

We were finally about to uncover something. At least, that was our hope. Of course, nothing as exciting as the secret to my dad's fried chicken recipe or how magicians sawed people in half and put them back together or Stonehenge. But something!

I held my breath as we opened it. We peered into the faded red velvet lining and exhaled. What? To our disappointment, the only things in the box were a few beaded necklaces and another key, a tiny one with a brass finish. I held it up. "This is the fourth key. I'm going crazy!" I turned and quickly tried it on the luggage trunk and then the door to the room, but neither was a fit.

Kitty was feeling antsy. "Let's take the keys and get out of here. I'll lock the door from the inside and climb back out the window."

As I left the room, I heard Aunt Polly's car coughing. I pocketed the keys to save for another adventure. "She's here. Hurry, Kitty!" I dashed through the door and around to the porch to help Kitty climb through the window. We had it nearly closed as Aunt Polly approached. We stood in front of the window like soldiers guarding the Vatican, with Kitty holding the rag I had given her earlier. Not at all suspicious.

"What are you girls doing?"

"We thought we'd clean the porch to prepare for the barbecue," Kitty said.

She looked at us for a long moment and finally moved toward the door. "Yes, we'd better finish planning that party. Bring me some cookies before you sweep the porch."

I was going to Hell for all this lying.

Chapter 9

I DREAMED JIMMY AND I were sailing to Hawaii in a small boat, eating pineapples and drinking Dr Pepper, with seagulls sitting on our shoulders, when Aunt Polly's shrill voice pierced my dreams. "Girls! Girls! Wake up." I reluctantly left Jimmy behind and floated to the surface of consciousness.

Kitty poked my shoulder. "She's calling. Wake up."

Slowly we got out of bed and went to the top of the stairs. "What is it, Aunt Polly?"

"Get dressed. We need to go out."

Kitty asked hopefully, "Are we going out for breakfast?"

"No. We're going to get the groceries for the July 4th party."

I put my hand on my hip. "But that's ten days away," I said.

"Take your hand off your hip. It's disrespectful. Now get dressed and hop in the car."

There was no "hopping". The three of us slogged to her car and dodged flying candy rolls when Aunt Polly backed up and lurched forward. I'm not sure why they were called "Life Savers" since they were a danger to us as they shot toward our faces every time Aunt Polly accelerated. The peppermint candies had been replaced by butter rum, which I secretly wanted to taste, but I assumed I'd get into trouble if there was booze in the sweets. Besides, I never liked sharing food with our aunt. I rolled down the window to find a bit of fresh air as we rambled along, but between the stale smell of the car and the smoke coming from the exhaust, it was hard to breathe. When we finally reached the grocery store, I quickly opened my door, but she stopped me.

"No, no. Just stay in the car." She honked her horn repeatedly until a middle-aged woman with short, no-nonsense hair, wearing a Red Owl uniform came outside to see about the racket. I scrunched down in my seat as Aunt Polly handed the woman a piece of paper and some money through her rolled-down window.

The woman put one hand on her hip. "Say what? You want ME to pick out your groceries?"

I wanted to say, "Hey lady, at least you don't have to zip her swimsuit," but I kept my trap shut.

Aunt Polly was indignant. "Yes. Just bring me the change."

The woman looked at Kitty and me. "Can't they come in and do it?"

"I can," I offered, but Aunt Polly stuck her hand out to stop me.

"You'll do a better job," she said, and grinned at the woman.

The woman in the uniform shook her head after she snatched the list and money. She mumbled something unintelligible on her way back into the grocery store.

What were we? Chopped liver? I sighed and again sank lower in my seat. Just as sure as there were mosquitoes every summer, Aunt Polly would continue to find ways to embarrass us.

"Was that a list you gave her?" I said hopefully.

"Yes."

"Is milk on the list?"

"Yes, it is." She offered no other hints about what the list contained.

Kitty's voice was just out of the polite range. "Why didn't you want us to get the groceries?"

"I'll be here all summer without help, so I want them to get used to watching for me," Aunt Polly snapped.

"But we're here now," I said.

"You won't be for long. It's too difficult for me to walk through the store, so I need the grocery folks to do it for me."

As we waited, I looked at our aunt's face with the sunlight shining on it through the windshield. Her skin looked like rawhide, which I assumed was from years of living in New Mexico's desert and our family's tendency to shun sunscreen. Our Minnesota grandmother, who was ten years older than Aunt Polly, had baby-soft skin with few wrinkles since she stayed indoors most of the year. She feared both the cold and the heat, which was any temperature over 75 degrees. It left her with about thirteen days suitable for a stroll in the elements—and perfect skin. After we sat in the baking car for what felt like a month of Sundays, the same woman opened the back door to the vehicle and unceremoniously dumped two bags onto the seat. She handed Aunt Polly her pocket change, slammed the car door, and disappeared into the Red Owl grocery store.

Kitty and I straightened up in our seats as Aunt Polly jerked the car into reverse, hit a bumper, and then lurched ahead so we could hightail it out of the parking lot. However, just as her stick shift jerked forward, the owner of the car she hit came running and yelled for her to stop. She sped away as Kitty's eyes bugged out, whispering to me, "Did you see that?" I nodded. I watched in the rearview mirror to see if the police would find us, but it was a clean getaway.

We were relieved to finally have fresh milk, ripe strawberries, and bread without mold. We hurried through breakfast, hoping we might see the O'Reilly boys again, but no one came by. As we washed dishes, I noticed an unpleasant smell. I sniffed several times in the direction of the lower cupboards. "What is that smell?"

Kitty sniffed the air. "Gross! You need to check the traps for corpses."

"Why do I have to look?"

"Because I might vomit. I'll go into the living room so you can take a quick peek. If you find dead mice, we'll call Jimmy or Charlie."

"What if they're not home? Or they're busy? Or they don't want to get rid of dead mice? What's plan B?"

"You'll think of something. They said they'd help, and you know I'm not good with bad smells and dead critters."

"Fine. I'll look, but you have to call Charlie if I find anything. Not me."

Kitty smirked. "I guess that's fair." She went into the front living room and found Aunt Polly in a cookie coma on her couch. She had devoured the Fig Newtons we picked up at the store.

I sucked in as much air as possible and held it as I quickly opened the lower cupboard. Then I slammed it shut and dashed into the other room.

I flapped my hands up and down, hyperventilating. "Yuck, yuck, yuck! Yes. Dead. Two dead. Call Charlie!"

Kitty shivered and then picked up the heavy black phone and dialed the number she had memorized.

In minutes, Jimmy and Charlie were at the back door. We stood back as they swaggered into the kitchen like two bulls ready to do battle and emerged with traps holding the remains of dead mice. "We'll just set these out in the bushes. Do you want to see how it's done?"

Kitty and I covered our noses and mouths, shaking our heads. "No, no. No, thanks," I said.

When they returned with empty traps, they set them again and put them under the sink.

Aunt Polly finally awoke and brightened at the sight of two strapping young males. "What are you two up to today?"

Jimmy spoke first. "Kitty asked us to empty the traps. Two dead mice under your sink today."

She seemed unruffled. "Oh, yes. Just part of summer."

Charlie frowned. "We don't have mice. Until you get that hole in the roof fixed, animals will keep getting in."

Aunt Polly nodded. "Yes, well, thanks, boys." They took that as a cue and walked to the back door.

Kitty and I followed them like lost puppies, hoping to think of a reason for them to stay. The very air we breathed seemed to change when we were with them. As they opened the porch door to leave, Charlie turned, pointed toward the window to the secret room, and whispered, "Say, have you gotten in there yet?"

"How did you know?" I whispered.

Jimmy responded. "We saw you trying to break in, remember?"

Kitty's eyes grew wide. She put a finger to her lips and shook her head as she whispered back, "We can't talk about it."

Jimmy turned to me. "Any idea what's in there?"

My heart raced being so close to him. I shrugged my shoulders nervously but didn't want to reveal anything. "Probably dead people."

"Groovy!"

A nervous giggle was bubbling up in my chest. "No, I mean, I don't know. Probably not dead people, really. But it's always locked, you know, so there might be something interesting. Right?"

Charlie whispered, "Right. No point locking the door if it's just rubbish."

"Let me know if I can help you," Jimmy said to my adoring face. He walked quietly to the window and put his shoulder to it. It inched up.

I dashed over to the window and shook my head. "We can't let her see it's open."

The boys nodded and left.

I went into the formal living room to practice the piano and rid myself of the anxiety I felt. The honking for help, the angry car owner, finding dead mice, and seeing Jimmy again… It was all too much for my fifteen-year-old nerves. I pounded on the ivory keys, even those that made no sound, and tried to take myself mentally to a safe place. Wherever that was.

How did Aunt Polly manage the rest of the year while teaching in New Mexico? Had she trained an army of people to attend to her? I also wondered what a bizarre teacher she must be. I tried to imagine her in front of a classroom of first graders. Did she sing them the song about the burglar who crept into the old maid's room at night? Did she eat cases of candies and bushels of cookies in front of the children?

All my life, I had accepted her eccentricities, but this summer, they were on full display as I saw with mature eyes this was not normal behavior. I also worried that her weight issue was somehow genetic, and I would blow up to sumo-wrestler proportions. I banged on the piano to chase away fears clogging my brain like cobwebs.

Chapter 10

The next few days were a flurry of activity in preparation for a neighborhood barbecue. Although Kitty and I were about as excited as we would have been to have a cavity filled without Novocain, we pressed on with our duties. Aunt Polly came up with a guest list of neighbors, including the O'Reillys and two elderly couples who lived on the other side of her house, the Ericksons and the Petersons. The Ericksons' home was magnificent from the outside. Of course, we'd never been invited into it, but Kitty and I loved to walk along the sidewalk nearest the lake where we could access their wishing well and throw pennies into it, hoping for boyfriends, bigger boobs, and a cave where we could escape for hours each day. But this time, we walked up to the oak door in front and used the large brass lion door knocker. A young woman dressed in jeans and a T-shirt answered, along with an exotic long-haired cat.

"I'm the cleaning help," she explained with a light laugh

when we thought she might be the lady of the house. "Step inside quickly so the cat doesn't escape."

While we waited for Mrs. Erickson to come to the door, we peeked into the expansive entry. A marble floor sparkled under an enormous crystal chandelier. The cat watched us for a moment, but when we tried to pet her, she skittered away, leaving us to strain our necks to view the living room through the large, arched opening. As we scanned the room with mouths open, a towering woman with brown hair and broad shoulders and hips peeked into the entry. She had a pleasant smile.

"Well, hello, girls. Are you selling Girl Scout Cookies?"

Before we could answer, a diminutive woman with closely coiffed white hair came down the curved staircase holding onto the polished wood banister. She was wearing a long caftan and fluffy slippers. At the sight of her, the blue-eyed white cat swished around her feet until she scooped it into her arms.

"I don't want any cookies. We don't eat sweets," she snapped.

Kitty put on her sweetest smile. "No, we're not selling anything. Our great-aunt, Polly, asked us to invite you and your husband, or, well, all of you, to dinner on Thursday." She nodded toward the tall woman.

Mrs. Erickson gestured. "This is my niece, Marjorie."

Marjorie smiled at us. "Thanks for the invitation, but I'm afraid I have other plans on Thursday."

Mrs. Erickson turned toward Marjorie. "You and your friends. Always planning something."

Marjorie shook her short curls and her green eyes lit up. "I'm only in town for a few weeks, so I want to see as many old friends as I can."

Mrs. Erickson turned back to us, but seemed confused. "Now who is inviting us?"

Kitty nodded her head up and down as though that would help the older woman remember. "Your neighbor from down the lane, Polly Schultz."

Her sunken eyes widened behind rhinestone cat-eye glasses. "Oh, yes. That… woman." She peered at us over the glasses and took a long look at our figures as I sucked in my stomach. "She's your aunt?"

"Great-aunt. We're helping her for a few weeks this summer," I said and reached out to pet the cat.

Mrs. Erickson's eyes were fixed on the soft dome of my middle. "That's nice of you girls."

"Thank you. What's the cat's name? She's so soft."

Marjorie answered. "Anastasia. She's a Balinese cat."

I leaned in to examine her features. "I love her blue eyes."

Mrs. Erickson seemed pleased at our admiration. "Yes. She's a show cat. She's won several awards for her beauty and poise."

I continued to pet her. "Hi, Anastasia. She's very calm."

"This breed is known to be calm. She's my precious." Mrs. Erickson then addressed her cat. "You're Mama's baby, aren't you?"

"She's purring," I said as I continued to pet her.

Kitty cleared her throat. "So, Mrs. Erickson, do you think you're available Thursday?"

"Oh yes, yes. Nothing much goes on here. No family nearby. Our dear Marjorie is visiting, but she's busy. Our friends are all dead or dying, so we're always available."

Our next invitation was to the Petersons, who lived further down the lane. Stone columns led to their front door and defined the edge of their estate. When I peeked around the side of the house, I could see a private tennis court and beautifully kept gardens. Kitty and I strolled up and again were greeted by a maid after ringing the bell and hearing the chimes inside. Mrs. Peterson quickly came to the door in a white tennis dress which showed off her petite figure and sagging thigh skin. Her blond wig was fixed in a bouffant style, making her head look out of proportion to her tiny body.

She waved her hand like she was swatting flies. "We're not buying anything." Nice greeting. Our conversation ran along the same tracks as our chat with Mrs. Erickson, but without a cat. They were available Thursday evening for dinner, even though they barely knew Aunt Polly.

When we were out of earshot, Kitty said, "These are our aunt's friends? I hope she doesn't have any enemies."

It was to be a casual event with twelve of us. We'd have drinks on Aunt Polly's expansive front porch and dinner in the dining room she rarely used. But of course, Aunt Polly didn't cook, clean, or bake, as I've mentioned before, so Kitty and I helped her devise a menu that included all precooked foods from the grocer in town. When Kitty noted that the menu didn't include any vegetables, Aunt Polly said she'd look for a green salad, which meant lime Jell-O, which could be used as a salad or dessert.

The morning of the party, we accompanied Aunt Polly into downtown Minnetonka to collect foods that would be transformed into a "homemade" barbecue. We were astonished when she got out of her car, and we followed to watch her select food for the feast. This was no ordinary grocery run. I wielded a grocery cart, and she tossed in Velveeta cheese, sliced beef and turkey, barbecue sauce in a jar, Wonder Bread, cold macaroni salad, green Jell-O with shaved carrots and celery topped with mayonnaise, ginger ale, a can of pineapple tidbits in heavy syrup, and lemonade. Once we left the store, we swung by the Dairy Queen and bought a case of Dilly Bars, which she considered a staple food like milk and eggs. Aunt Polly knew no one would think she made those, but it seemed like the perfect ending for a warm summer night by the lake.

Once home, Aunt Polly reclined on her couch and barked orders. Her walk around the store had tired her as if she'd just swum across Lake Minnetonka. "I need to save my energy to entertain tonight," she told us.

After we schlepped in the groceries and put away the cold food, we put the sliced meats in small pans with prepared barbecue sauce. After all, it couldn't be called a barbecue unless some tasty red sauce was present.

Aunt Polly directed us to pour the entire can of pineapple and syrup into a bowl and to put it in the freezer with the Dilly Bars.

Next, we checked Aunt Polly's fondue pot for mouse poop, and, finding none, set the squishy "cheese" into it to melt. We toasted bread and cut it into cubes for the fondue. Then we searched cupboards for serving bowls so the purchased food could be transferred into presentable bowls. While we looked through the cupboards, Aunt Polly told us to get out a huge, round punch bowl. Later, before the guests arrived, she told us to fill the bowl with ginger ale, lemonade, a bottle of rum, and the frozen pineapple tidbits. We carefully put the punch bowl on a low table on the porch, and Aunt Polly took out a packet of straws and added them to the punch.

Aunt Polly emerged from her room ready for the party, wearing a teal floral eye patch, large dangly earrings, and a teal-colored dress that clung to her form like a baby monkey clings to its mother. Thick, rubber-soled black shoes completed her look.

Kitty and I dressed in knee-length cotton pastel dresses and sandals, hoping to stay cool on this warm and humid day. Not sundresses. We had to have our shoulders covered according to the guidebook "Rules to Live by for Puritan Girls." Or in other words, Aunt Polly's antiquated rules. We took extra care with our hair and added a splash of makeup. I was as nervous as a baby bunny in a forest full of owls with all we had to do. I was also nervous about spending time with people I barely knew. And, of course, Jimmy would be there. I didn't want to make a fool of myself around him, but I had no idea how to act. Kitty seemed edgy as well. Her hand shook as she added another coat of mascara.

The guests arrived in small groups, acting as if they were surprised Aunt Polly was already back for the summer. Of course, she'd been back for weeks, but I guess it's always better to pretend you're happy to see someone you don't really care about. At least that's what it seemed like to me. The two older couples, the Ericksons and Petersons, had gone to some trouble getting ready, dressing as if they were going to dinner at a fancy restaurant instead of their neighbor's decrepit summer home. Mrs. Erickson wore an elegant blue silk dress and must have bathed in rose water, which clashed with Mrs. Peterson's Tigress perfume. Mrs. Peterson wore a crisp linen shift dress in lemony yellow. Their husbands wore plaid trousers and white button-down shirts, looking like a game of golf might break out at any moment. The women nodded at each other as if scrutinizing each the other's figure, dress, jewelry, and wrinkles.

Mrs. Erickson turned to Mrs. Peterson and sniffed. "I see you're looking well. Arizona must be helping to keep you fit."

Mrs. Peterson looked Mrs. Erickson up and down. "Yes, we had a good winter. We're still playing tennis, you know. And you must be doing something right. As slim as ever."

Mrs. Erickson replied, "Yes, I'm quite careful with my diet and I take daily constitutionals in the neighborhood to stay fit. Unlike…" With that, she not-so-subtly nodded her head toward Aunt Polly. Eyebrows were raised and smiles subverted as Aunt Polly turned to greet them.

The O'Reillys arrived as a unit and were kind enough not to ask if we had any mousetraps they needed to empty. They looked like they were ready for a photo shoot for Fashionable Family magazine, if there were such a thing, wearing coordinating slacks in navy blue with white polo shirts. Mrs. O'Reilly was the spark in the middle with a white linen blouse and red plaid skirt.

Aunt Polly seemed excited to have so much company in her home. I wondered if her family entertained hordes of people when she was a kid.

We set out sticks for the fondue, and people indulged, careful not to spill the hot cheese on their clothes. We teens were offered cans of pop to drink, and the adults were directed to the large punch bowl where they could choose a straw to suck on.

Mrs. O'Reilly seemed hesitant about the communal punch bowl, but the men dove in as if they hadn't had anything to drink for a month. I saw Mrs. O'Reilly shaking her head at her husband when she thought no one was looking. "Not very sanitary," she whispered to him loud enough that I picked it up.

"The rum will kill the germs," he whispered back. My first lesson in killing germs with rum. A handy bit of information to take with me into adulthood.

Kitty and I played hostesses, fetching, carrying, and serving food, but in between we mainly paid attention to the three brothers from next door—at least the younger two. Wayne seemed more comfortable with the adults and was delighted to claim a straw and partake in the communal punch. Talking to Jimmy and Charlie with their parents hanging around wasn't easy. At one point, Wayne looked me over with squinty eyes and said, "Still bruised from the boat?" I could smell the rum on his breath.

I turned red and shook my head, but it was too late. Suddenly the adults went quiet as Mrs. O'Reilly said loudly, "What's that about the boat?"

Wayne was happy to explain. "Cindy here had never been on a sailboat. So when I said 'come about,' she stood up and got thrown into the water. It was a hoot!" He burst out laughing. I sneered at him.

Mrs. O'Reilly frowned at her oldest son. "Wayne! That's not funny. Were you hurt, Cindy?"

I wished there was a trap door I could disappear into. "No, just a little bruised. Jimmy helped me back into the boat." I glanced at Jimmy gratefully. He nodded and seemed to stand a little taller.

"She was only in the water for a few minutes. Right, Cindy?" Jimmy's eyes told me I needed to agree.

"Yes. No big deal. I'm fine."

Mr. O'Reilly took center stage in his best stern-parent manner. "Sons, if you take a guest out sailing again, you must give them instructions on how to stay safe. Is that clear?"

If things weren't awkward before, they certainly were now.

I felt responsible and thought I could score points with Jimmy by taking the blame. "They did. They gave us instructions, but I didn't listen very well. It was my own fault."

Aunt Polly decided it was time to move the party along. "Cindy and Kitty, why don't you get dinner on the table."

That was our cue to serve, which was a relief after all the unwanted attention.

In the kitchen, Kitty whispered, "That Wayne's a jerk. You could have been really hurt."

"Thank goodness Jimmy was there to help me." Sigh.

Dinner stuttered along with talk of the weather, outdoor activities, and the stock market, and long pauses in the conversation. Aunt Polly brushed off questions about her full schedule of activities. Finally their plates were empty, and I thought we'd survived this uncomfortable evening. Aunt Polly called for dessert and suggested we all "go through into the living room," the way they do in English manors, so I headed to the freezer and brought out the bag of ice cream treats, not coffee and mini cakes as the English might. I was surprised when even the women who said they never touched sweets wanted one. But then Aunt Polly suggested I play the piano for our guests.

"Oh, no. I'm not very good. And the piano is missing some keys. Maybe Kitty could play?" Kitty gave me the stink eye, so I took a quick bite of my dessert and put it back into the freezer as the dinner guests moved into the formal living room, Dilly Bars in hand. They carefullly examined the portraits of our ancestors and looked around at the platform rockers, love seats, and antique settees to see which were strong enough to hold them and which tilted to one side because of broken legs. After examining their options, the men said they were more than happy to stand.

Good thing I brought my piano music. I sat down to play. After a few painful moments of listening to the tinny sound and missing notes, I doubted they wanted me to continue and again wished for an escape route. I was just about to launch into the "Minuet in G" when I was saved by a loud scream.

CHAPTER 11

I JUMPED UP TO SEE MRS. ERICKSON throw her Dilly Bar on the worn carpet and shriek. "A squirrel! A squirrel just darted across my lap."

Jimmy and Charlie sprang into action and tried to trap the squirrel. The Petersons and Ericksons ran for the door and quickly said their goodbyes, all clutching their dessert except for Mrs. Erickson. Aunt Polly nodded to them calmly from her chair as they escaped, not a bit surprised or embarrassed.

Jimmy came back into the living room, breathless from the excitement. "We couldn't catch it, but Charlie held the door, and I managed to shoo it outside."

Mr. O'Reilly moved toward the door and gestured with the remaining ice cream on a stick. "Thank you, boys. Polly, you need to fix that large hole in your lower roof. All manner of rodents may be living in this house."

Wayne chirped in with a smirk, "Any more mice?" His father grabbed his arm, and the family left in a hurry.

Party over. Kitty and I cleaned up the Dilly bar mess and the dishes and collapsed on lounge chairs on the front porch where Aunt Polly was finishing the rum punch.

"That was fun," Aunt Polly said. We looked at her, aghast. "It was nice to see the neighbors again."

How could we respond to that? She lived in her own reality. Perhaps in her world, having a squirrel create a commotion was the exit strategy to get rid of guests who'd outstayed their welcome. She no doubt had been craving the last of the punch and finally saw her opportunity.

Upstairs, Kitty and I rehashed the evening after checking our room for rodents and stuffing a blanket under the door.

She sat on the bed with her legs drawn up and her arms holding them close. "Charlie looked cool!" she said.

"Kitty, how can you think about that now when we have squirrels living with us?"

"That was so embarrassing."

"And creepy. And those neighbors aren't her friends. Why did she invite them?"

Kitty wrinkled her nose. "Did you notice how they looked around at all the old furniture, dingy lamps, and fading drapes? And at her?"

"It's like she's a freak show. Mom's always kind to her because she's her mother's sister, but I wonder if she has any true friends."

We pondered this for a few minutes, and then I spoke the words ping-ponging around my brain. "Do you think we'll see Jimmy and Charlie again?"

Kitty shook her head. "Charlie barely said anything to me all night. And they left in such a hurry."

"Everyone left in a hurry after that dang squirrel. And we were pretty busy serving and stuff. Maybe they didn't want to say much because their parents were watching."

Kitty was philosophical. "I suppose their parents think we're not good enough for them."

"True. We don't play tennis, speak French, or know how to sail a boat. We need to forget them."

On that solemn note, we pulled the sheets over our heads to keep the bugs at bay. I tried to sleep, but with every scratchy noise, my nerves kept thinking a wild animal was about to burst in and chew on my nose. Or toes. Or worse.

We were quieter than usual as we cut the mold off strawberries, checked for spoiled milk, and set out a box of puffed wheat cereal. Now that we thought we'd never see the O'Reilly boys again, we felt adrift. If we couldn't conspire to spend time with them, how would we survive the long, tedious hours and days?

When she finished wolfing down her breakfast, Aunt Polly looked from me to Kitty. "You girls tired from the party?"

"Kinda. I mean, it was a lot of work," I said.

She raised her eyebrows. "Work? Didn't you enjoy seeing the O'Reilly boys?"

"Yes, but I meant the cleaning and dishes were work."

I expected her to chastise me for an unknown infraction, but instead, she shook her head a bit. "Hmmm. Well, uh, maybe we can play games later. I have to go to the podiatrist this morning to get my corns shaved off, but we can play board games this afternoon."

Kitty brightened and said a bit too enthusiastically, "Sure. That sounds fun."

She stole a quick glance at me, and I knew the fun part would happen while Aunt Polly was away. Long walks along the lane on previous days gave us the luxury to plot and scheme without worrying about being heard, but today we'd have the chance to continue our search for clues to the secrets of this house.

Once she left, we recounted what we knew so far. I started. "Let's see. I found the skeleton key under the rolltop desk in the living room, and so far, that hasn't fit anything. And I found the blue key behind the dresser upstairs. It hasn't fit anything either."

Kitty continued. "I found the small silver key in the fourth bedroom upstairs, which fit the jewelry box we found in the secret room. But the brass key that was inside the jewelry box hasn't fit anything. Why would they lock a key in a jewelry box?"

"None of it makes sense. But maybe it will if we keep searching. We still need to find a key to the travel trunk in the secret room and the rolltop desk in the formal living room. We know we can get into the secret room through the window so that key isn't urgent. Where does this leave us?"

Kitty was thoughtful. "We still have three more bedrooms and the larger bathroom upstairs, so let's start in the fifth bedroom."

"Right. And we have to finish going through the picture album to see if we recognize anyone in the old photos, but we can do that tonight. Let's start on the bedrooms while Aunt Polly's gone."

Upstairs, we moved down the hallway to rooms we had never slept in. The fifth bedroom was dark, with little light from a lamp on a side table. The room held two single beds, covered like the others with cotton chenille bedspreads, two dressers, side tables, and a small armoire for clothes.

"I'll start with the dresser drawers," I said and began to yank and pull drawers that had been shut for decades.

Kitty went to the armoire and opened it. She ran her hands over dresses and coats, checking pockets, but came up empty. Finally, she snatched a mink coat off the hanger and tried it on. "Take a look at this! A full-length mink."

"That's a lot of dead animals," I said. We stroked it and couldn't help purring over the velvety texture of the fur.

Kitty put her hands deep in the pockets and frowned. "I can feel something hard, but it's not inside the pocket."

"What? Like a secret pocket? Or a skeleton bone?"

"You're obsessed with skeletons." She whipped off the coat and threw it on a bed so we could take a closer look. "Can you see the outline here?"

"I'll get scissors." I ran to the kitchen and retrieved small scissors which we used to remove some of the stitching from the coat's lining. Inside, we found a small pocket and cut it open. A long gold key fell into my hands. "Woo hoo! Key number five!"

Kitty hung the mink coat back in the armoire, and we both bounced down the stairs like Lewis and Clark looking for the Missouri River.

The key was too long to work on the lock in the rolltop dresser. We headed to the secret room, where we found it was too small for the door, but, like Goldilocks, we found it was just right for the travel trunk. We heard a click, pulled the brass lock up, and opened it. Inside was an empty, shallow tray covered in fabric, which we removed.

"Check for mice. We don't want to find any more dead animals," Kitty said.

I cautiously looked into the deep trunk and pulled out a white scrapbook with a floral design on the cover. We closed the lid and sat on it, searching for answers in the clippings inside the scrapbook.

"This one's about Aunt Polly going to college."

"They put that in the newspaper? Why was that newsworthy?" I asked.

"Mom said Aunt Polly's dad, our great-grandfather, was some bigwig in the grain industry, so they were always in the paper on the society pages. And besides, it was unusual for women to attend college in 1911."

"Wow, that was some pressure. What if she flunked out? Would they print that?"

"Probably, but here's an article about her graduation from the University of Minnesota."

I tried to read over Kitty's shoulder while pinching my nose to keep from sneezing at the dusty newspaper. "Does it list her major?"

"Yes, teaching. Makes sense since that's what she does. But it says she was going to go on a cruise around the world before looking for a teaching position."

"How long would that take?"

Kitty looked at me, aghast. "And who could afford that? They clearly didn't have eight kids like Mom and Dad."

"Look! This one says she went to France for months and ran out of funds, so she asked her father to send money. How embarrassing to have it included in a newspaper article."

My nose twitched, and I sneezed over and over in a full-blown allergy fit.

Kitty was eager to learn more. "Let's keep reading. This one is from 1917. She joined the Red Cross to help with the war effort. That explains the date on the shipping container. I've never heard about this. I wonder if Mom knows."

I was getting nervous that our aunt would come home and find us. "It's too much dust for me. Let's hide this upstairs before she gets home. Maybe we can pump Mom for information."

I took the scrapbook upstairs as Kitty locked the room and crawled back out the window. When I came back downstairs, I said, "Let's call Mom."

"Call Mom now?" Kitty asked. "What if Aunt Polly comes home while we're on the phone?"

"Then we'll change the subject. We're allowed to call our mother, for Pete's sake."

I went to the heavy black phone and dialed. This time Mom picked up. "Hi, Mom," I said. "We miss you."

"I miss you too. Sounds like you're all stuffed up."

I could hear our youngest sister crying in the background. "Allergies. What's wrong with Ann Marie?"

"Time for her nap. I'll put her down in a minute, but first, tell me what you need. Are you sick?"

"No. Just sneezing. So dusty here. We were thinking about the party on Sunday."

"Uh-huh, what about it? We'll bring the food. Have you washed all the dishes?"

"Yes. And Aunt Polly bought a ham a week ago."

"Ugh! I hope it's still good. Is that why you called?"

"No. We, ah, we found some clippings about Aunt Polly from when she was younger."

The crying in the background seemed to get louder. "What kind of clippings?"

"Newspaper clippings about college and trips to Europe. We have questions."

"I hope you aren't snooping around where you shouldn't be. Listen, I need to get this one to bed. Let's talk Sunday when I see you."

"OK. We'll talk Sunday."

Kitty leaned into the phone, and we both closed out the conversation. "Bye, Mom!" We hung up.

"Ann Marie cried in the background the whole time, so she had to go."

"Was she mad we found the clippings?"

"Not really, but she warned me not to snoop around."

Kitty was nervous. She wasn't used to breaking rules, especially if it threatened her status as Mom's favorite. "Then how will we explain where we found all this stuff?"

"We'll think of something."

Chapter 12

On Sunday, the Fourth of July, Aunt Polly took Kitty and me to her local Presbyterian church so no one could accuse us of being heathens. She wore a flag eye patch that coordinated with her crimson muumuu. We'd never gone to anything but a Catholic church, but there were rumors that we'd soon be allowed to visit other denominations, so we kept our traps shut and went along, not that we had a choice. We agreed we wouldn't tell Mom or Dad, just in case.

Later that afternoon, Kitty and I changed from our Sunday dresses into red pedal pushers and navy tops with white embroidery around the neckline. And then, suddenly, a station wagon with wood siding pulled into the driveway and our family surged out like a tidal wave, most wearing the colors of the American flag. Kitty and I raced outside to greet them as they poured out of the car. Mom opened the front passenger door, took Ann Marie off her lap, and deposited her onto the grass. The two-year-old jumped into my arms, and I hugged and squeezed her. "I've missed you so much! Did you miss me?"

Ann Marie wriggled her nose. "Miss you." She gave me an Eskimo kiss, rubbing her nose to mine. She smelled like baby lotion, and I held onto her wriggling form until she spotted Kitty. I put her down and let her run to Kitty, who twirled her around and smothered her in kisses.

Next, I snatched Gunther who was barking and running in circles.

"Come here, boy!" I knelt on the grass and he barreled toward me. I scooped him up. "I've missed you too!"

I stood as Maureen and Betty Jane wrapped their arms around my waist in a group hug. It had only been a few weeks, but it felt like an eternity. The younger three, Maureen, Betty Jane, and Ann Marie, wore matching dresses with red and white striped full skirts beneath blue bodices. "New dresses? You look so pretty," I said, and they began spinning like tops to show how full their skirts were.

"I have a loose tooth," Betty Jane said. She opened her mouth and wiggled her bottom tooth like it was an attraction at Ripley's Believe it or Not.

Next, we hugged Joanne and Colleen, who were less enthusiastic, but still happy to see us. Both wore navy pedal pushers and red blouses with white Peter Pan collars. Our oldest sister, Mary, rebelled and dressed all in black. She gave me a nod and marched into Aunt Polly's house carrying a large bowl of food as she barked orders to Joanne and Colleen. "Hurry up and help with the food! Stop messing around!"

Younger sisters reached in the back of the station wagon and carried bowls of Jell-O salad, potato salad, and coleslaw.

Mom greeted us with a smile, carrying a platter of meat and cheeses. "Hello, girls!"

"You got into the spirit," I said, looking at her navy-blue dress with a print of red and white apples on the skirt.

"Hi, Dad," I shouted to him as he wrestled with a ladder attached to the roof of the car.

Once we all pressed into the kitchen, I asked Mom about the ladder.

"He's going to see about patching that hole in the roof by the sleeping porch."

"I hope he can. It's creepy to go down that hall to the porch. You have to jump over the crack. We keep finding mice in the kitchen, and last week a squirrel ran through the living room while Aunt Polly had guests."

"Never a dull moment," Mom said. Nothing fazed her. "Stay away from that side of the house."

Aunt Polly came out of her bedroom carrying a piñata and wearing a form-fitting navy-blue dress with sturdy shoes. Instead of her flag patch, she sported one with red, white, and blue stripes. Her red earrings dangled to match her lipstick, and a string of white faux pearls completed the flag color scheme. "Look what I brought from New Mexico." She said it was already full of candy, and we could take swings at it after dinner to release the treats.

I turned to Kitty and whispered, "Graveling on the floor for candy again?"

She giggled. "Shh. I think you mean 'grovel.' The little ones'll love it."

I nodded. "Do you think we'll see Jimmy and Charlie at the fireworks tonight?"

"Hope so. But it'll be a huge crowd."

Mom turned to us. "What are you two whispering about?"

Kitty smiled. "Nothing, Mom. Just excited about the fireworks."

Aunt Polly sniffed. "Bad manners to whisper in front of others."

Mom nudged us, so Kitty and I tried to look contrite. "Sorry, Aunt Polly."

Our younger sisters loved exploring the house as much as we did. They ran up and down the dark stairs and explored the hallways leading to the many bedrooms. Kitty and I were nervous they'd find the scrapbook and photo albums we had stashed, so we stayed upstairs while they searched. In the late afternoon, Mom came upstairs.

"I need Ann Marie to rest awhile since she'll be up late tonight." She shooed the others downstairs, but before Kitty and I left, we asked her to sit with us for a few minutes. She held Ann Marie and gently swayed while we peppered her with questions about our great aunt.

"Her parents were wealthy, so each of their daughters went to college, which was unusual, especially in the early 1900s. And yes, girls were encouraged to major in nursing or teaching."

"Is she wealthy?" I asked.

"No, just the opposite. I'm afraid she's gone through any inheritance."

Kitty patted Ann Marie, who was getting restless. "Then how can she afford this house?"

Mom put Ann Marie's head on her shoulder and swayed back and forth. "It was a gift from her parents. But she doesn't have the money to keep it up. That's why your father helps her with repairs."

"But what was she doing in France?" I asked.

"That's a long story, girls, and we don't have time for it now. Why are you suddenly so interested?"

I blew out a breath. "What else do we have to do here? We're bored."

"I thought you were spending time with the neighbor boys?"

Kitty shook her head. "We wish. We had fun sailing one time, but they were really distant at Aunt Polly's barbecue."

I flicked a dead bug off the bedspread. "We figure we need to forget about them."

"You can come home with us tonight. I have plenty of chores to keep you busy. But right now, I need to put this little one in a quiet room for her nap."

We left and quietly walked into a bedroom down the hall.

Kitty shut the door. "I'm excited to go home and all that, but I wish we could see the guys again. I feel like they're mad at us."

"That barbecue was awkward, with the adults watching us. Maybe we'll see them tonight."

Dad came inside in time to eat dinner. While we sat in the formal dining room eating big juicy slices of watermelon for dessert, I questioned him about his repairs. "Is the hole in the roof fixed?"

He scratched the back of his neck as if he could still feel roof debris clinging to him. "Yes and no. I got the hole patched, but I need more shingles to finish the job. I'll come back next week, but no more animals should get in for now."

Aunt Polly sat at the head of the table and nodded to Dad at the other end. "That's why you're my favorite nephew-in-law."

Dad let out a deep breath. "Let's hope this keeps that crack from getting worse. No guarantees."

After dinner, our younger sisters took turns swinging a bat at the piñata. Mary refused to watch and sat on a recliner on the front porch reading a grim murder mystery. Kitty and I hung back, letting the little ones try until they became frustrated. Then I stepped forward.

"Look out, everyone." I swung hard. Candy poured out, causing a frenzy of squeals as sisters dove to the floor in search of chewy toffees, chocolate creams, squares of coconut, and other wrapped delights. I snagged a few favorites and pocketed them quickly.

Mom quickly collected candy from the three youngest sisters, causing groans and complaints. "Let's save some of this for the fireworks. Just one piece now."

Finally, it was time to gather blankets, mosquito spray, Aunt Polly's folding chair, and snacks and walk to the grounds of the Lafayette Club, just a half-mile away. The evening was still warm and humid, causing bugs to feast on our moist skin. We found a perfect spot on the grassy hill and laid down our blankets, but before we sat down, Mom sprayed us each with bug spray. It left a disgusting film on our skin and clothes and smelled so bad even the mosquitoes avoided us. I guess that was the plan.

Next, Mom reached into her large canvas purse and produced two boxes of sparklers. Before we could enjoy them, Mary plunked herself down on a blanket and leaned back on her elbows. "These are way too dangerous for little kids."

Mom raised her eyebrows at Mary. "Yes, but the older girls can keep track of them, even if you don't want to. You can watch Ann Marie."

She handed the toddler to Mary, who mumbled under her breath. "She's your kid, not mine." Mom ignored her.

Kitty, Colleen, and I supervised Betty Jane, Maureen, and Joanne and showed them how to light the fire sticks and make letters in the dusky air. After their turns, we each took one and were whirling around giggling when Jimmy and Charlie walked up wearing Burmuda shorts and plain T-shirts.

"Hey there. Having fun?" Charlie asked.

"Yup. Just showing our little sisters how to write their names."

Jimmy looked at the gaggle of little girls. They stared silently at Jimmy as if he were an other-worldly creature. He waved hesitantly. "Hi. Wow. Sure are a lot of you."

I laughed nervously. Was he making fun of us?

Kitty jumped in. "Mom and Dad, this is Jimmy and Charlie from next door."

She pointed at our sisters and named each one.

Mary perked up. "Where's Wayne? Didn't he want to see the fireworks?"

Charlie gestured to a spot further down the hill. "He's over there with our parents. Go and see him if you like."

Mary sniffed. "No, thanks. I was just wondering, that's all."

Kitty smiled brightly at Charlie, no doubt trying to find a way to start a conversation. Finally she sputtered, "Did you have, I mean, are you having a nice 4th?"

Charlie shrugged one shoulder. "Ok, I guess. How 'bout you?"

"Yes. We had a piñata. Have you ever seen one of those?"

"Something you ate?"

Kitty giggled way more than was necessary. "No, it's a papier-mâché bird stuffed with candy. The little ones took turns swinging at it to break it open."

Looking at our small sisters, Charlie seemed impressed. "Which one was strong enough?"

Kitty put one hand on a hip. "Well, none of them, so Cindy stepped in."

Jimmy was listening in. "Good one, Cindy!"

"Thanks—I think. It's just a fun tradition. Aunt Polly brings us one every year."

Kitty and I exchanged glances hoping to keep the boys

near us a little longer. "So, not watching from your boat?" she asked.

"Not this year," Charlie said.

Jimmy looked at our parents. "Nice meeting you. I think the show's about to start." They left to rejoin their family.

A single rocket shot in the air, and its boom caused little screams of surprise. We all sat on our blankets and leaned back on our elbows for maximum viewing. Although we attended every year, the show was never dull, with new displays of colors and shapes to ensure we'd ooh and ah as we watched. I named each blast—velvet, wedding dress, circling dancers, flowers, and so on.

The night started with showy pyrotechnics shot across the lake from the bottom of the hill. I wondered if the partiers in sailboats and yachts got burned as flaming particles drifted lazily toward the lake. I heard sizzles as some ashes hit the water, but others certainly must fall close to the boats. There were only honks of appreciation, so I decided not to worry.

The fireworks had our full attention with the rhythmic blast, the vivid colors, followed by quiet as the workers reset another round.

But as we watched, a live spark from the sky fell into the pile of waiting fireworks. One after the other, they caught fire and blew up, sounding like gunfire as flames shot into the air in multicolored horror.

Was this a new technique? The crowd around us gasped. I sat up and gawked. The sight was mesmerizing until we all realized it was an accident. Almost instantly, we jumped to our feet and grabbed our blankets and snacks amid the smoke and the hullabaloo.

"Girls, take your sisters' hands." Mom carried Ann Marie who clung to her like a baby koala. The rest of us created a chain of hands as quickly as we could, but the crowd made it difficult to move, as people began to panic and push each other to leave the grounds.

Dad pulled Aunt Polly to her feet, collapsed her folding chair, and held her arm to hurry her along. But racing up the hill proved more difficult than walking down it, and Aunt Polly yelped. I let go of Joanne's hand and went back to help.

"What's wrong?" Dad asked.

"I hurt my ankle," Aunt Polly said.

Dad shouted to my mother, "Go on ahead." He sat Aunt Polly back down in her chair and checked her ankle to see if it was broken. "I think you just turned it." He helped her to her feet again, and slowly we took a few steps amid the impatient crowd, with Dad helping Aunt Polly and me carrying her chair and my blanket.

Within minutes, the fireworks were spent, and an eerie quiet descended. I glanced back at the smoking mess on the shores of the lake. Several men raced down the hill to check on the two men in charge of setting off the pyrotechnics to ensure they weren't injured.

As we made slow progress, Charlie appeared at Dad's side. "Need any help?"

"Thanks, Charlie. Yes, Polly hurt her ankle. Would you take her other arm?" We hobbled along as people streamed by in a rush to get to safety, unsure whether another explosion was possible.

When we reached Aunt Polly's house, she collapsed on her sofa. Dad turned to Charlie and shook his hand. "Thanks very much, young man."

Charlie looked around shyly and caught Kitty's eye. "It was nothing."

Kitty's eyes were wide. "I'll bet you're glad you weren't in your boat with all those explosions."

"I thought of that as they started blowing up. Hope the boaters were able to get out of the way quickly," Charlie said.

"It certainly was an evening to remember," Dad said.

Charlie turned toward the door and gave a little wave in Kitty's direction. "I'd better get home."

Kitty discreetly waved back.

Mom got an ice pack and put it on our great-aunt's ankle. Then she took Kitty and me into the kitchen. "We can't leave her like this. You girls will have to stay at least another week."

"Why us?" I whined.

"Because no one else has a change of clothes. Sorry, girls."

Kitty didn't look upset. I realized she must be hoping for more time with Charlie.

We brought our suitcases back upstairs.

"At least we don't have to worry about squirrels," Kitty said.

"But now we have to play nursemight along with everything else."

"Nursemight? You mean nursemaid. Maybe it won't be so bad." Why was she always so optimistic? It was exasperating.

Back downstairs, we enjoyed the last of the Dilly Bars as we all replayed the evening.

"I hope no one was injured," Mom said.

Dad's eyebrows looked like moving caterpillars as he analyzed what might have caused the problem. "I suppose a dud fell back into the pile and ignited them all."

"I thought it was a new type of show at first," Colleen said.

"I thought we were all going to die," said Maureen.

Betty Jane's eyes lit up. "It was cool!" And we all laughed.

Mary frowned. "Well, someone'll get sued over it, for certain."

Kitty was licking the chocolate coating on her ice cream. "Too bad it was all over so fast. We look forward to it all year, and then poof! Done."

I nodded. "Yes, but I'll bet we never forget these particular fireworks. It's always when things go wrong that we remember."

Aunt Polly sat up on her sofa. "Despite my hurt ankle, it was so much fun having you all here today."

After everyone left and Aunt Polly hobbled to bed, Kitty and I retreated to our room.

"Aunt Polly must be lonely," I said.

"She seemed relaxed and even happy today."

"Of course. She had people waiting on her and Dad fixing her roof. But I think she must actually like our family."

"She must. But it would be nice if she'd show it more often."

Chapter 13

Kitty and I awoke on our own and remembered all that had happened the day before. My mind was still picturing the blast of fireworks. "I can't stop thinking about all those fireworks going off in three minutes instead of thirty."

"It was amazing. And wasn't that sweet of Charlie to help Aunt Polly home last night? We always think these rich boys are too good for us, but he was helpful."

We didn't get long to chat before we heard Aunt Polly calling us, so we quickly dressed and scooted down the stairs.

"I have a doctor's appointment this morning," she said. "Let's have a quick breakfast."

"Do you need us to go with you?" Kitty asked.

"No, just help me get into the car. The doctor's office said they'll have a wheelchair ready when I get there."

Once she was safely on her way, we knew we'd have time to explore.

"I can't remember which keys haven't opened anything yet," Kitty said.

"OK, let's review. The skeleton key so far hasn't fit anything. But the small silver key opened the jewelry box, where we found the tiny brass key."

"Right. And the long gold key opened the trunk. But what about the other key? The blue one?"

"That was the one we found taped to the back of the dresser upstairs. But so far, it doesn't open anything."

"Let's separate the keys into piles and put the ones we know will work into in a separate drawer."

"OK. Then the ones that are still a mystery we can keep out so we can try them in different places. Great idea, Kitty. The skeleton key, blue key, and tiny brass key so far don't fit anything."

"I guess this is where we start. Have we tried that tiny brass key on the rolltop desk?"

"No. I forgot about the desk. Let's try it now."

We ran downstairs but slowed our pace as we entered the large formal living room and walked past the portraits of our ancestors.

"I feel like we're not alone whenever I'm in this room," Kitty said.

"We're on a mission. Don't think about them." The desk's lock was easy to spot on the dark oak finish, a small brassy opening below the curved top. My hands shook as I inserted the tiny brass key, which clicked when I turned it. I could feel Kitty breathing near me.

"Well? Did it turn?" she asked.

"Yes. Maybe we don't want to know what's in here."

Kitty looked at me seriously. "Do you think we'll find out something horrible and never be able to forget it?"

"Kinda. I mean, if Aunt Polly's life was so great, why is everything locked away?"

"True. And why won't Mom tell us about it?"

We paused and looked at each other, waiting for an answer, a reason to stop. But our curiosity was stronger than our worries. Together we raised the stiff oak slats.

I gasped. "Bingo! Look. Old letters."

"Well, duh! What did you think would be in an old desk? A dead squirrel?"

"Don't laugh. I was worried about that. But I'm excited to find letters."

At first, we were afraid to touch them. Yellowed with age, they were decorated with faint lettering that might disappear if exposed to the light. Some were addressed to Polly Schultz, while others had been sent to her parents. A small number were addressed to Anthony Walker.

"Who's this dude?" I asked the room of dead portraits.

Kitty shrugged.

I gingerly rifled through the pile and chose a few for closer inspection. Kitty did the same.

We sat carefully on the settee as if the delicate papers would dissolve into dust if we made any sudden movements.

Kitty looked at the pile and suggested we sort them. "Let's put the ones addressed to Mr. and Mrs. Alexander Schultz in one pile and those to Polly Schultz in another. We can make a third pile if there are others, like the ones to Anthony Walker, whoever he was."

"Perfect. Then let's put them in chronological order."

We felt like true detectives looking for patterns to emerge. We made three piles in our laps, sorted them by date, and opened a few of them one at a time.

The earliest letters addressed to our great-grandparents were from 1911, so we started there.

"Of course, that was the year Aunt Polly went away to college," Kitty said.

"But I thought she went to the University of Minnesota?"

"She did, but remember, her parents lived in Colorado, so she was far away. How amazing that her mother saved them all."

We flipped through the dates and glimpsed letters telling of her college days and, later, her cruise around the world.

"These stamps are amazing. They're from all different countries—Italy, Switzerland, England, Ireland, even India. What an incredible trip. Look how many there are from France."

Kitty examined letters with French stamps and held them up to her eyes to see the dates. "Looks like she stayed there for months in 1917."

"We saw those newspaper clippings that said she was in France then."

Kitty's eyes were a study of concentration. "But why was she there?"

I put the letters back in fragile envelopes. "I feel like we're eavesdropping on a private conversation. I wish we could just come out and ask her."

Kitty nodded. "But then she'd know we were snooping. Let's take a peek at the letters addressed to Aunt Polly."

I picked up the pile on my lap. "Here are a few with scrolly handwriting. These should be interesting." I opened the letters and looked for the signature. "From Margaret," I read.

"Who was that? A friend?"

Kitty read over my shoulder as I skimmed the lilac-colored paper.

"She mentions Mom and Dad as if she's a sister."

Kitty pulled back and frowned. "But Aunt Polly had only one sister, our grandmother, Catherine."

We searched for more letters with the same handwriting and got lost in the world we entered while reading them. They were time capsules that held clues but no answers. The familiar sound of Aunt Polly's car coughing up black smoke jarred us back to reality.

Kitty jumped up. "It's her. I'll take these letters upstairs." I made a mad dash to relock the desk and deposit the key in my jeans. I flew into the living room, turned on the TV, and pretended I was watching The Dating Game. Kitty made it back downstairs and flopped onto the couch just as we heard the back porch door close.

We tried not to sound breathless as we greeted our great aunt, but our cheeks were flaming, and we were still breathing more quickly than usual, which wasn't lost on her.

"Watching the Dating Game, eh? You girls thinking about dating? You're still quite young."

Kitty sat up taller and giggled. "No, not really. This is just a funny show. How's your ankle?"

"Just a sprain. They gave me a walking cast to wear for a week or so, but I'll be better soon."

I nodded, hoping to keep the conversation going so she wouldn't ask us what we'd been doing. "That's great. Looks like you can walk better with the cast."

Aunt Polly looked suspiciously at us. "Yes, it's better. What have you two been doing while I was gone?"

"Reading," I said just as Kitty said, "Watching TV." We looked at each other and nodded.

Aunt Polly frowned. "So, reading and watching TV at the same time?"

Kitty smiled. "Well, no. We were reading before, and then we got bored and thought we'd see what was on TV."

I nodded. "Right." Then I squirmed in my seat, wondering how we were getting so good at lying. Aunt Polly surprised us. "If you're bored, let's play a game of Parcheesi. We can set it up in the library."

Kitty hopped up and turned off the television. "Great. We love board games."

The library was a dark room on the other side of the hall from the formal living room. There weren't any windows, and one entire wall was lined with shelves packed with books. The furniture was heavy, and the lighting wasn't great, but this room held a game table we adored. It was made of different colors of inlaid wood and seemed to jump into a three-dimensional pattern if you looked at it long enough. It wasn't a huge table, only about four feet across, but it was perfect for board games. We pulled up three chairs and set out the pieces. Aunt Polly easily won the first two rounds and was in a great mood, but we decided to take a break for lunch.

"Cindy, would you make a cake after lunch? It's such a rainy, chilly day, and it'd be fun to have a warm treat. I have a cake mix in the cupboard."

"Um, sure. That sounds fun. What should I do for frosting?" I loved to cook and bake, but I usually used a cookbook, something that was foreign to our aunt.

"Whatever you can drum up is fine with me."

Kitty made sandwiches for lunch while I put the cake in the oven. When it was baked and cooled, I rummaged around for ingredients to make frosting and found brown sugar and butter. I knew I'd made a caramel frosting before but couldn't remember all the ingredients, so I called home, and Colleen answered the phone.

"Hi, Colleen. Hey, go get my Betty Crocker's Cook Book for Boys and Girls because I need a frosting recipe. It's in the bookshelf in the kitchen nook."

I could hear the ridicule in her voice. "You mean 'please.' "

"OK, yes. Please."

"You're still using that little kid cookbook?"

"Will you please just get it."

She let the phone dangle from the wall in the kitchen, and I could hear the dog breathing nearby.

"Gunther! Is that you, boy?"

More heavy breathing.

"Come here, Gunther." I was sure I could hear a small whimper. Finally, Maureen returned.

"Who were you talking to?"

"Just the dog. I miss him. Did you find the cookbook? I'm looking for caramel frosting. I think it's called penuche."

"Ah yeah, must be your favorite section 'cuz the pages are dirty and torn. What do you do to the cookbook while you're baking?"

"Colleen, just read the ingredients."

"One stick butter, one cup packed brown sugar, one-fourth cup milk, and two cups confectioner's sugar. Should I read the directions?"

"No, I remember them. Thanks."

"When are you and Kitty coming home?"

"Not sure. Aunt Polly's in a walking cast, so we're still helping her."

"Well, I'm taking all your babysitting clients."

Great. My only source of income. After seeing Colleen in action, I just hoped they'd still want me to babysit. She was the baby whisperer and could charm any toddler. With her sparkling blue eyes and curly blond hair she looked like an angel and kids adored her. I didn't enjoy changing disgusting diapers and wiping snotty noses, and I was quickly bored spending long afternoons with other people's kids. But I put up with it for the money.

"I'll be able to get a real job soon, so maybe I won't need

all those babysitting jobs. Anyway, thanks for the help." We hung up.

"Um, Aunt Polly, I need powdered sugar."

"Just go next door and ask for some."

I hesitated. "Next door? You mean the O'Reilly's?"

"Yes. I'll bet they have some."

The chubby girl asking for more sugar. "Kitty, why don't you ask them?" I said.

She brightened. "I'll go with you."

We combed our hair, applied lip gloss, and headed next door. We were sorely disappointed when Wayne answered, but he quickly retrieved a bag of powdered sugar and sent us on our way with a request. "If you don't eat it all, bring some back here."

I stopped. Pressure. This had better be delicious. Girls were expected to know how to magically take a few ingredients and transform them into edible delights. Sometimes my attempts worked. But not always.

CHAPTER 14

I WAS DETERMINED TO SUCCEED with the frosting now that I'd promised to share some of the cake. I melted butter, brown sugar, and milk into caramel and brought it to a boil, then set the hot pan in a bowl of ice water to thicken. When it was ready, I found a small hand mixer and beat in the powdered sugar, hoping it wouldn't clump, and whipped it into a thick caramel frosting, which I spread on the cooled cake.

We were all salivating by the time I served the confection. Cakes were my specialty. Well, that and cookies. Each of us had special duties, and I was the family baker, making cakes whenever there was a birthday, feast day, or when we were out of cake, which was often. With so many in our family, I often tripled cookie recipes and whipped up a massive batch after school if my mother was out with one of her many volunteer jobs. My sisters and I could work our way through several pans of cookies before our parents came home. But I digress.

Aunt Polly finished her cake in four bites and asked for another piece, which I brought her.

Kitty took a few small bites, then set the rest on the table. "It's too sweet."

I nodded. "Yes, but I still love it. I think it's the caramel that makes it irresistible."

Aunt Polly agreed. "Hand me your slice, Kitty." She finished that piece in seconds.

At this point, I was afraid Aunt Polly would try to finish the cake and faint from all the sugar. We didn't know if she had diabetes because she refused to have her blood tested, but my mother assumed she had it.

I hopped up. "Why don't I share some cake with the neighbors since they provided the powdered sugar?"

"Save a few pieces for later," Aunt Polly instructed, which I did.

I carefully lifted the rest of the slices, put them on a large paper plate left from our Fourth of July dinner, and snatched the bag with the remainder of the powdered sugar.

"Kitty, want to come with me?"

She giggled. "Sure, but look in the mirror. You'd better change your blouse and brush out your hair first."

They don't call it powdered sugar for nothing. When I first turned it on, the mixer exploded with a cloud of sugar, and I was too focused to notice. White powder covered my dark blue blouse and bangs, so I went upstairs to make myself presentable.

Kitty smiled when I came into the living room. "Much better. Let's go."

We walked next door and I carried the paper plate as if it held treasure from a sunken ship or a king's crown. I shuffled reverently, slowly, lest I trip and fall, planting the whole works into my face.

We knocked and waited. And waited for several moments more. Finally, we tried the doorbell. We could hear a commotion, so we knew they were home. Finally, Jimmy threw open the door and beamed at us, sending my pulse racing.

"Hi Kitty, Cindy. Whatcha got there?"

Kitty blurted out. "Cake. Cindy made it. It's really sweet, but we thought you might like it."

"And I brought back the rest of your powdered sugar," I said, swinging the half-empty bag.

At this point, Charlie pushed in next to Jimmy at the open door. "Did I hear you say cake?"

We were grinning back at them as if they were Greek Gods holding molten chocolate.

I giggled nervously for no reason. "I made this cake and thought you might like some." I thrust it and the sugar into Jimmy's hands, which he happily accepted.

"Thanks, Cindy. Far out."

Charlie nodded. "Yeah, groovy! Say, would you two like to go sailing again? It's perfect today with just the right amount of wind. We were just about to head out."

Jimmy's eyes lit up. "Great idea. And Cindy, I promise to watch out for you so you won't go in the drink."

I wrinkled my nose. "In the drink?"

"Into the water," Jimmy explained.

"Oh, right. No. Um, no more in the drink for me."

Jimmy cocked his head, probably wondering if I was having a stroke. "Why don't we meet back here in, say, thirty minutes?"

We were already backing up, ready to sprint. "OK. Fine. Yes. Thirty Minutes. Be back," we echoed each other and took off for Aunt Polly's.

Aunt Polly was reclining on her couch, tired from the cake's sugar load, and seemed relieved to have us out of the house for a few hours so she could nap in peace.

Upstairs, Kitty and I excitedly changed into swimsuits and found beach towels in the bathroom cupboards, which we had recently washed to rid them of animal droppings. We were ready to go in ten minutes. We didn't want to appear too eager, so we sat on our creaky beds chatting like chipmunks in anticipation of the annual sunflower seed celebration.

"You need to pay attention when you hear commands and don't stand up unless you know where to go."

"Yes, yes. I remember, Kitty. Don't be so bossy."

"I just don't want to see you hurt."

"Fine. I hope Wayne doesn't come this time. He's such a killjoy."

"Agreed."

Our wish came true when Jimmy and Charlie stepped outside to greet us without Wayne. The four of us laughed and talked on the way to the bay where the sailboat was tied up. There was less tension without Wayne, and for the first time, I started to feel more relaxed in the presence of the two handsome, athletic brothers.

The sun was beating down when we were ready to sail, and Charlie pulled out sunscreen, which we rarely used. But I told you that already.

"Might want to put some of this on," he said as he tossed it to Kitty.

She applied some to her face and arms and then turned to Charlie coquettishly. "Would you put some on my back?"

He was at her side faster than a seagull to a trout. "Sure." He rubbed her shoulders and the parts of her back not covered by her swimsuit top. Then he tossed the cream to me, and I smeared it over myself as quickly as possible.

Jimmy was watching me, and he cocked his head and asked, "Would you like some help with your back?"

"Oh! Um. OK. Sure," I sputtered.

He gently rubbed cream into my shoulders and back, and I felt myself leaning into his touch like our cats tilt toward us while we pet them. I kept myself from purring. I think I surprised him when I offered to apply sunscreen to his back.

"Sure! Great. That's nice of you."

Nice nothing. It was a thrill to feel the muscles in his shoulders and back. I found myself in a hypnotic state as my hands moved in circles over his back.

After a few minutes, Jimmy broke in. "That's probably enough, Cindy. Thanks," he said and broke the spell.

The brothers finished preparing the sails, and we pushed off into the water. The sun danced across the water as we cruised along. I turned my face toward the wind and let it cool me and wondered how I had lived this long without ever feeling so free and so happy. The camaraderie was getting easier. Maybe they didn't see us as the poor kids from the city after all.

After a few hours, we helped them tie up the boat and headed back. Charlie nudged Kitty, grabbed her hand, and swung it back and forth as we walked. I felt silly until Jimmy quietly put his hand in mine, and we strolled home, slower than we needed to, not wanting the afternoon to end. When we reached their house, they let go of our hands and turned to go inside. Charlie turned back, smiling casually. "That was fun. Want to see a movie tomorrow night?"

Jimmy nodded. "Some great movies playing."

Kitty and I nodded like bobbleheads. "Yes. Great. Sounds. Fun. See. You. Tomorrow."

Our feet hardly touched the grass as we walked next door, greeted Aunt Polly, and headed upstairs. We flopped on our beds and sighed.

"Wasn't that wonderful, Cindy? We finally got to see them again without all the adults around."

"This summer is turning out to be a lot more fun than I ever thought it would be."

That evening, Aunt Polly headed to her bathroom on the first floor. We heard water running, so we assumed she was drawing her bath. We could watch whatever we wanted on her small TV, so we turned the knobs until we found Bewitched, a favorite among my sisters and me. The program was almost finished when we heard our great-aunt calling for us. We hurried down the hall and stood outside her bathroom door.

"What's the matter?" Kitty asked.

We could hear frantic splashing. She finally answered. "I can't seem to get out of the tub!"

Kitty and I looked at each other in horror. Certainly, we weren't strong enough to pull her out. Not only that, whatever we saw, we couldn't unsee. We'd be scarred for life.

"Should we call the neighbors?" Kitty asked.

Apparently, even Aunt Polly had her limits. Her high, shrill voice answered, "No, better call the fire department."

I stood immobile, chewing on the inside of my lips, and prayed for a different solution. I couldn't think of any.

"Just call!" Aunt Polly commanded.

Kitty moved into the living room and dialed "0" for the operator. "Yes, Hello! My great-aunt is stuck in her bathtub. Can you please send someone to help her get out?"

I waited in silence as she listened for the response. Then she continued. "No, I don't think she fell. Let me ask her." Kitty ran back down the hall.

"Aunt Polly, did you fall in the bathtub?"

"No, I got in fine. I just can't get out. Are they coming?"

"Just a minute, Aunt Polly." Kitty ran back to the phone.

"No, she didn't fall in the tub, but somehow she's stuck." She listened again.

Indignantly Kitty responded, "No, this isn't a teen prank. Uh-huh. OK, just a minute."

Kitty and I ran back to the bathroom door. "Aunt Polly, is there something you can grab onto? Like a towel bar?"

We heard a great deal of splashing and then a plop. "I just ripped the towel bar out of the wall. Tell them to get over here!"

We ran back to the living room and Kitty picked up the phone. "I think she ripped the towel bar out of the wall. We need help."

I put my ear next to hers so I could listen but heard only mumbles.

Kitty was getting frustrated. "No. I'm not strong enough to help her. She's, um, rather large."

Silence again.

"You know, large. Tall and big in every direction." More mumbling from the operator.

"No, our father isn't here, and she doesn't have a husband."

I could hear the operator saying, "OK, no need to shout."

"Look. Our great-aunt is really, really large, she's hurt her ankle, and no one here is strong enough to get her out."

"Why didn't you say she was hurt?" the operator shouted loud enough for me to hear. "Someone will be right there."

Kitty gave them the address and hung up.

We hesitated as we walked down the hall and called through the door to tell her help was on the way. I feared she'd ask us to help her, and there was no way I was going to open that door. Next, we hurried to the back door to wait, praying they wouldn't use sirens, lights, and whistles to announce themselves.

But they did. Of course, they did.

We heard sirens in the distance and soon saw the flashing lights in the driveway. Three strong men emerged from the truck ready to do battle, wearing black helmets, heavy coats, and knee-high rubber boots.

"Hi!" we said weakly, leading the way. "She's in here." Duh, I thought. Of course, she's in there. That's why we need help.

We were nearly speechless, partly from embarrassment, but mainly because these men were a vision to behold. Strong, handsome, and swoon worthy. We were sheltered teens who rarely were near strong, handsome, swoon-worthy men. Except for the O'Reilly brothers, naturally. But they were a new phenomenon. We led the way and stood back so we didn't have to witness the extrication.

Moments later, they came out stifling grins and announced that she was getting dressed. "You girls OK?" one asked. We nodded. "Have someone install a shower for her," another handsome face suggested. "And you might have to mop the floor." They marched out the door and climbed into their firetruck. As they drove away, I gave a thumbs-up to the small crowd of onlookers. Then I quickly shut and locked the door. We needed time to think.

"Could this day get any weirder?" I giggled quietly and knew that it could.

Aunt Polly soon came out of the bathroom in her nightgown and didn't mention the drama with the firemen. She plunked herself on the couch and ordered me to make popcorn with plenty of butter. So I did. Kitty mopped the water on the bathroom floor. Then, as if nothing unusual had happened, we watched television for a bit. Aunt Polly didn't say a word about the humiliation she must have suffered.

Later, as Kitty and I sat and bounced on our beds, we wondered how Aunt Polly managed when no one was there to help.

"Did you see all those people gathered outside?"

Kitty nodded. "Yup. Kinda creepy. I hope they don't ask us a bunch of questions."

"You know they will. People are always snoopy. What should we tell them?"

"Clearly there was no fire, so we can't say that."

"And they didn't carry her out on a stretcher, so what should we tell people?"

Kitty started snickering. "No one will believe us if we say she was stuck in the bathtub."

"I still can't believe it myself."

"So let's go with that. The truth. Who cares what people think?"

I nodded. "OK, but let's ask her about it tomorrow."

The following morning, Kitty approached the subject over a bowl of cornflakes. "We, eh, we saw some of the neighbors outside last night."

Aunt Polly focused on her food. "That's nice."

Kitty tried again. "I mean when the fire truck was here."

"Nosy neighbors!"

"Yes, but if they ask why the firemen were here, what should we say?"

"First of all, firemen work on trains. Those were firefighters."

I sighed. "OK, but if people ask why we had firefighters in your house, what should we tell them?"

Aunt Polly shrugged. "Just say I had a little trouble in the bath."

We weren't sure if that was code for something else, but that became our official answer.

Chapter 15

WE WERE AS NERVOUS AS WALLEYES on fishing-opener weekend in Minnesota. The night before our date, we took baths, washed our hair, and rolled it in pink sponge rollers, which we slept on. We left the rollers in while eating breakfast, which we discovered was against another etiquette rule, known only to those born before 1900.

Aunt Polly shook her head. "It's impolite to wear rollers while you're eating."

Kitty's eyebrows rose. "Oh, we're sorry. It's humid today, and we want our hair to look nice tonight."

"Tonight?"

"You remember, we're going to a movie with Jimmy and Charlie tonight. We told you last night," I said.

Aunt Polly shook her head slightly. "I thought you were going to ask your mother for permission."

Kitty's eyes brightened confidently. "She's fine with it.

We're leaving about 6:30, and we can have dinner before we leave."

"Don't let those boys get too friendly with you, if you know what I mean," she warned.

We weren't exactly sure what she meant, but we had an inkling, and we hoped they would get friendlier tonight. Before we left, we brushed out our hair, swiped black mascara over our eyelashes, and blotted pink lipstick to make our lips more kissable. Our skin was still red from sailing, so we didn't need any blush. Besides, I found the more time I spent with Jimmy, the pinker my cheeks became.

We were happy we had packed light summery dresses weeks ago. Now we had a reason to wear them. Kitty's was apricot with a white collar, while mine was sky blue with a square neckline. Both were tunic styles and ended just below our knees. Kitty was twirling in front of the mirror. "I need to find a way to hitch up this hem. All the girls wear miniskirts, and here we are with these long dresses."

"We could pin them if we find a bunch of safety pins."

"We've been all over this house and in every drawer. Have you seen any safety pins?"

"Only the one I use for my mascara. How 'bout staples? We could staple the hems up a few inches."

"Cindy, wouldn't that be scratchy? And the staples would show. No good. We'll just hem them when we get home. For another time."

I shrugged nervously. "Hopefully this won't be the last date of our lives."

Kitty frowned. "What's the matter with you? This is the beginning. Think happy thoughts."

"I was just kidding. Really." Now I had to convince myself.

When we couldn't wait any longer, we walked next door. Jimmy and Charlie eagerly opened the door and greeted us. In the entryway, Mrs. O'Reilly looked us up and down in our out-of-date dresses, making me want to escape into Middle-earth. But we smiled.

"How's your great-aunt doing?" Mrs. O'Reilly asked.

"Much better. She has a walking cast and gets around fine," Kitty answered.

Wayne appeared at the door, and for a minute, I was afraid he was coming with us to the movies. "Well, that's good. She wouldn't want to be any slower than she already is," he said.

"That isn't very nice, Wayne," Mrs. O'Reilly corrected.

But Wayne the pitbull rarely took a hint. "Why was the firetruck here last night?"

Kitty took a breath and gestured with one hand. "Our great-aunt had a little trouble in the bath."

Wayne threw his head back and howled. "Little trouble? LITTLE TROUBLE? You mean like she got stuck?"

In a small voice I answered, "Yes, something like that. She was very embarrassed."

Mrs. O'Reilly's hand flew to her chest. "That must have been awful. It's not funny, Wayne." She glared at him and he piped down and moved away from the door.

Jimmy stepped out and took charge, keys in hand. "We need to be off so we're not late to the movies." He and Charlie ushered us to their parents' three-car garage. Jimmy held the front passenger door for me, and I slid into a navy Plymouth Barracuda, while Charlie opened the back door for Kitty and then crawled in next to her. I was excited not only to be with Jimmy but to sit in the front seat.

When we were a short distance away, Jimmy turned on the radio and cranked up the volume. We sang along to "Wooly Bully," "Help," and an eclectic mix of music from the Beatles, Beach Boys, the Temptations, and even Elvis Presley. Movie choices in 1965 included a range of sweet movies like The Sound of Music to great dramas like Dr. Zhivago and The Greatest Story Ever Told. But this night, our choice was Beach Blanket Bingo," a romping, lively tale with music, dancing, and lots of gyrating teens on beaches in swimsuits.

At first, I was embarrassed to see all the busty actresses and burly men clad so skimpily. I wondered what exactly was beneath those swimming trunks. The nuns in school had given us some idea, but I doubted they knew what they were talking about because, you know, they were nuns.

I tried to tell myself to enjoy the sights and concentrate on the music, dancing, and the thin plot line. Still, after we devoured a shared bucket of popcorn, Jimmy put an arm around my shoulder, and I could hardly focus on the movie. My parents rarely hugged us, and this older boy was sitting close and touching me. What did it mean? Was I his girl now? Was he planning to kiss me? I knew I didn't want to become a cloistered nun, but sheesh! Boys were uncharted territory.

Jimmy drove us to a drive-in restaurant when the picture finished, and we all ordered root beer floats. It's basically light ice milk, not ice cream, sunk into a glass full of root beer, which doesn't contain alcohol, so not really a beer. You'll just have to trust me on this. They're delicious.

While I was sipping away, Jimmy turned to me. "What do you two do all day in your great-aunt's house? I mean, you must be going stir crazy."

I giggled nervously. "We do get bored. But sometimes we like to explore the house."

He frowned. "What do you mean, 'explore'?"

Kitty sat up in her seat to face Jimmy. "There are lots of bedrooms full of old furniture and clothes and stuff."

Charlie perked up. "What kind of stuff?"

Kitty and I looked at each other uncertainly. How much should we tell them?

"Well," I started, "we found an old travel trunk from 1917. We think Aunt Polly may have been doing something in France during World War I."

"That's cool. Yes, 1917. The date is right. Any idea what she was doing?" Jimmy asked.

Kitty cautiously replied. "We found some old letters but haven't read them all."

"I think she'd be furious if she knew we were nosing around," I said.

Jimmy nodded thoughtfully. "We won't say anything."

"Do you think your parents know anything about her past?"

"We can ask. I'll think of a way to bring it up without telling them about your detective work," Jimmy said.

"Please don't get us into trouble," Kitty said. "We've probably said too much."

Jimmy reassured us. "If there are newspaper articles, that's out in the open, and this is a small neighborhood."

We drove back to their house, and Jimmy got out and opened my door. Charlie said, "I'll be there in a minute." He and Kitty cuddled up in the backseat, and I tried not to see what they were doing.

Jimmy walked me to Aunt Polly's and leaned in for a quick kiss. I blushed but didn't back away. We chatted for a few minutes waiting for Kitty, knowing we'd better go in together. Her face was flushed when she and Charlie walked up to the door.

She threw her arms around Charlie and hugged him. "Thanks again, Charlie."

Was I supposed to do the same? I wasn't sure, so I just smiled and thanked Jimmy. Kitty and I floated inside.

Aunt Polly was nodding off on her couch with the television blaring. She seemed irked. "What time is it? Where have you two been?"

Kitty was quick with an answer. "Not late. We went for root beer floats after the movie."

Aunt Polly frowned and looked from one of us to the other. "Your cheeks are sure red. You're spending too much time in the sun."

"You're right. Well, good night, Aunt Polly," I said, and we made a clean exit.

Kitty flopped down on the bed and sighed. "Wow, that was amazing."

"The root beer floats? Yes, they were delicious."

"No, silly, the whole night. And wow, can Charlie kiss."

"Is that what you were doing in the car when we got out?"

Kitty giggled. "Yes. It was dreamy. Did Jimmy kiss you?"

"Yes, just a quick peck." I blushed. "It was a fun night. But do you think they'll tell their parents we've been searching through her stuff?"

"Don't be silly. I thought I was the worrier, but you're getting worse."

"I just don't want to get into trouble with her. She has such a wild temper. I thought she would get mad when we came home, but I think she was too sleepy."

"Even if she did blow her stack, nothing could erase my great mood after this evening."

I nodded. "It was wonderful. And to think, we thought they didn't like us."

"And that we weren't good enough for them. Not cool enough. But I guess I was wrong."

We got ready for bed, changed into our baby doll pj's, and prepared for a warm, buggy night with the sheets over our heads. Jimmy's face was all I saw as I drifted into the fuzzy state of dreams. My first kiss. It wasn't much, but he must have liked me at least a little. He wasn't repulsed by me. I sighed and passed out.

CHAPTER 16

A THWACK OF LIGHTNING, followed by a snare drum rumble of thunder bolted me out of bed the morning after our movie date.

It was a rude awakening after a night of cotton candy dreams. Thunderstorms take on a different tone when they have an enormous lake to bully. They whip the waves and punish the giant trees along the shore, all the while sending patio furniture on adventures. The storm left the air damp and chilly.

Kitty and I reluctantly left the warmth of our beds and pulled on jeans and sweatshirts. July was usually a month that kept its promise to be hot, hot, hot. But on this day, the contract was broken. I took it personally, thinking somehow I was being punished for having fun with a guy I barely knew. Silly, I realized. But guilt is like that. It arrives at strange times, takes your heart, rolls it around in gritty dirt, and then spins your head around, so you aren't sure if you've done something wrong or experienced unexpected joy. Catholic parents specialize in guilt, sprinkling it liberally on their children to ensure they learn valuable lessons, such as there's no such thing as a free lunch. Expect nothing and you won't be disappointed. What comes around goes around. If you're sad, you need to find something to clean. They also told us not to cross our eyes, or they'd get stuck that way, but I'm rarely tempted to cross my eyes, so I ignore this advice.

Aunt Polly loved watching storms as if they were major motion pictures. Was this the only excitement in her life? Her phone rarely rang, and no visitors popped by for a cup of coffee or to share her stash of cookies. She never seemed to have friends to meet for lunch or to attend a play with even though the Minneapolis theater scene was legendary. Even our high school had a link to the famous Guthrie Theater and their student program. This morning, she sat on her front porch, mesmerized by the raging storm, eating donuts, and drinking coffee with cream and sugar while we stayed upstairs after a quick breakfast.

"It's so humid! I'm smothering."

Kitty looked up from her book. "You mean suffocating."

"Whatever. You know what I mean. It's so stuffy in here. I know it's chilly, but the rain's stopped, so let's go outside for a walk."

She smirked. "Hoping to see anyone in particular?"

"That would be fun, but I really need to get out of this room."

Kitty shut her book. "It's almost time for lunch. Let's

make grilled cheese and then when Aunt Polly's watching her 'stories,' we can escape."

Mom said television soaps were too racy for us, so we usually went upstairs to read, but since we'd spent most of this morning reading and staring into space, I was going crazy.

On our walk we talked about our next strategies in searching for clues.

"We've searched all the bedrooms and most of the formal living room, but we haven't spent any time in the library."

Kitty chewed her bottom lip. "True, but what reason do we have for going in there? I don't want to make her suspicious."

"We could say we're going to play a game on that cool table with the unlaid wood."

"You mean inlaid. It makes my eyes jump the way it goes from two dimensional to three."

Aunt Polly was still watching TV without her eye patch when we strolled in from our walk. I noticed her good eye was looking hazy.

Kitty waited until a commercial break. "Aunt Polly, is it OK if Cindy and I play checkers in the library or find something new to read?"

Aunt Polly looked up. "Sure. But bring me a package of cookies first."

We found a new package of chocolate-covered graham crackers and brought it to her.

Next, we set up checkers on the game table to look like we were playing, but then started searching the room. Almost every room had so far yielded a key, so we tipped heavy leather chairs over and ran our hands along the bottoms but found nothing. We did the same with the end tables and heavy brass lamps sitting on them.

Kitty kept her voice low. "This seems like the perfect place to hide something. Let's not give up. What about the books?"

"Yes! In one of the Nancy Drew mysteries, they found items hidden inside hollowed-out books. But where should we start?" An entire wall of old tomes lay before us, with shelf after shelf bursting with titles.

"You start at that end, and I'll work over here. Let's begin with shelves we can reach and then get a chair for the taller shelves."

This seemed like an endless task, but since we had nothing better to do, I started pulling books out one at a time, examining the spaces behind them and then opening them to see if they were hollow. The dust from the old tomes was getting to me, and a sneezing fit rocked me like an internal earthquake.

"One, two, three, four…" Kitty counted to see if I'd break my record of seventeen sneezes in a row, but luckily for me, the fit stopped at eleven.

My head was swimming from the violent sneezes. "I think I need to sit down," I said, but before I could get to a chair, I lost my balance and fell into the wall of books.

"I think I felt something move," I groaned.

"I think you hit your head too hard," Kitty replied.

"Push on the bookshelf," I suggested. "I'm not sure if it happened or if my brain is getting soft from sneezing."

Kitty squealed. "It moves! Get up. There's something weird behind the bookshelves."

My head was still fuzzy and the room seemed to spin around me. "Did it really move?"

"Look! The wall moved." Kitty gave me a hand, and I stood. She put an arm around me to steady me for a moment. Together we gently pushed one side of the wall of books. The entire thing creaked and croaked as it rotated enough to let us peer into what looked like an empty space. "Far out!" we said in unison.

We didn't hear our great-aunt dragging her casted foot down the hallway until she appeared in the doorway. She looked at the bookshelf wall and gasped, "What are you girls doing?"

"A sneezing fit made me dizzy, and I fell. The wall moved!"

She walked over to the exposed wall and peered in. I held my breath and waited. She was too large to walk into the space but stood at the entrance, seemingly lost in thought, until she stepped back and looked around. "I heard about this when I was a child, but I didn't think it was real."

Kitty carefully prodded her for information. "What did you hear? What is this space?"

Aunt Polly slumped into one of the leather chairs. "The house was built by my grandparents just before the Civil War, and my mother told us she hid silver spoons and other treasures to keep soldiers from finding them."

Kitty's face screwed up. "Soldiers? Looking for silver?"

The teacher in Aunt Polly was on full display. "Yes,

sometimes they would ransack homes looking for food or valuables to sell. And they might be on the lookout for runaway slaves. My grandparents were part of a network that helped slaves escape the South. Kitty, can you slip in and see if anything's still in there?"

"Sure." My slender sister slid sideways into a long, narrow, windowless room that looked like it might lead to outer space. "It echoes. Imagine hiding in here. There's not much space, and it's dark."

I peeked in. "Is there anything left in here?"

"It's so dark I can't tell."

Aunt Polly chirped, "Cindy, get the flashlight I keep in the kitchen drawer to the right of the sink."

I was happy to have a job, as long as I didn't have to slither into that dark space. Within minutes I retrieved the flashlight as if I were carrying the torch to the Olympic games and handed it to Kitty, who was still hovering at the opening of the dark room. "Watch out for dead animals," I whispered.

She frowned at me and whispered back, "Thanks a lot. You're obsessed."

I watched as Kitty shone the light around the room and then walked to the back of it. She came out holding a small box. "I found something," she said excitedly as she slid back into the library and handed the box to Aunt Polly. It was about a foot square, made of dark wood, and only a few inches high.

Aunt Polly held it in her lap for a moment before she tried

to lift the lid. We edged near and peeked over her shoulder. "It's locked."

Kitty and I looked at each and gave a small shake of our heads. Another mystery.

Trying to be helpful, I suggested she look under the box, but it was smooth. No hidden key. I wondered if the blue key we found on the back of the dresser would fit, but I didn't dare say it out loud. But since Aunt Polly seemed to be in a good mood, I decided to see what we could find out. "So, um, Aunt Polly, if this house was your grandparents, how did you come to own it?"

She seemed pleased to have us take an interest in our ancestors. "My grandparents built this house in their later years. They had only one child, my father. They willed it to him. He and my mother moved to Colorado but kept the house as a summer retreat. My sisters and I loved visiting the lake."

Kitty cocked her head. "Sisters? I thought our grandmother was your only sister."

Aunt Polly looked away, quiet as we waited for an answer. "I had a younger sister, Margaret, but she's gone now. Your grandmother, Catherine, and I were very fond of her."

I burst in. "How did she die?"

Aunt Polly straightened in her chair. "I didn't say she died. I said she was gone." She stood up, still grasping the box, and turned to us. "Put the wall back the way it should be." She clumped out of the library back to her couch, taking the mystery box with her.

We pushed the wall back into place and scooted out the porch door to take a quick walk and conspire about what we'd heard. When we were far enough away from the house, I started. "Didn't die. Just gone. What the heck does that mean?"

"Did she run away? Was she kidnapped? Did she marry someone in Australia and never come back?"

"Was there some sort of family argument?"

Kitty nodded. "Maybe she left because Polly got the summer house."

"Or maybe she joined the circus and never came back."

Kitty stopped and raised her eyebrows. "OK, now you're just being silly. Have you ever heard Mom talk about a Margaret?"

I shook my head. "Nope. If we write to Grandma Catherine, maybe she'll tell us."

"That could take weeks! Maybe when Aunt Polly asks for her nightly brandy to relieve the pain in her ankle, we should bring a second glass. A few glasses could loosen her tongue."

"Wow Kitty, I didn't know you had it in you."

"The whole thing makes me so sad. Why does everything have to be a secret?"

"Speaking of secrets, I'm wondering if the blue key would fit the box you just found behind the bookshelf."

"I was wondering the same thing. Next time we get a chance, let's try it."

"Let's hope she doesn't hide this new box."

After dinner that night, Kitty started. "Ready for your brandy?"

Aunt Polly cocked her head to one side. "Sure. It's just for my pain, you know. The humidity is making my ankle throb."

Kitty scooted into the kitchen and came out with a small glass, along with the bottle, which she kept in full view. She handed the glass to our great-aunt, who downed the booze in two sips.

"My arthritis is really acting up. Hand me the bottle."

Kitty and I looked at each other with conspiratorial grins. This might work. She brought the bottle, and Aunt Polly poured herself a generous serving, again snarfed it down, and poured herself another.

I waited for half a heartbeat and dove in. "So, Aunt Polly, can you tell us anything more about your sister, Margaret?"

We watched her for a few moments. I thought I saw her good eye spinning in circles, so I hopped off the platform rocker and snatched the bottle. "I'll take this back to the kitchen."

When I got back, her head leaned against the back of the couch and her mouth hung open with a trail of brandy leaking to her chin. We snapped off her television and went upstairs, defeated.

Chapter 17

Sunday after church, the sun shone brightly as Kitty and I walked down the path along the lake side of the houses. We passed the O'Reillys and could hear a commotion coming from the back of their property. We quietly crept around the side of the house and watched Jimmy and Charlie skateboarding along their driveway. Beach Boys music blared from their portable radio, and they were barreling up a wooden ramp and then trying to stay on their boards as they landed on the cement. Charlie used one leg to gain speed and zoomed up the ramp, but his board shot out from under him, and he landed on the ground with a yelp.

"Ah-choo!!!" I had another sneezing fit from the bushes we were hiding behind.

Jimmy looked over and spotted us. He smiled and waved.

"Hey, there. What are you two up to today?"

I shrugged, tongue-tied. "Nothing much."

Kitty perked up. "Did you make that ramp?"

Charlie was still sitting on the ground rubbing his foot. "Yup. But I'm ready to trash it. I think it's uneven."

"It's fine," Jimmy said. "You just need to take the ramp faster and don't lean to the right. Stay balanced over the board."

Kitty turned to Charlie. "Are you OK? I mean, did you break your foot?"

Charlie groaned and hopped up. "I'm fine. Just a bruise. How's your great-aunt's foot?"

Kitty shrugged. "Seems to be doing pretty well. Hard to tell because she walks slowly even when she's not hurt."

Jimmy turned to me. "Want to give it a try?"

"Me? You mean the skateboard?"

"Sure, why not?"

"Oh, wow. I'm not very… well… OK. What do I have to do?"

Jimmy demonstrated how to get one foot on the skateboard and use the other to push off. "In a way, it's like ice skating. Use one foot to get momentum and then glide."

He handed me the board. I positioned myself at the end of the ramp.

I giggled nervously. "You make it look easy." I gingerly put one foot on the board and pushed off a little too fast. The board flew out from under me and sailed off, hitting Jimmy in the shin. "Oh. Sorry."

"I didn't see that coming," Jimmy said as he rubbed his shin. "Try to push off a little slower this time."

I couldn't believe he wanted to give me another chance. I

set the board down, positioned my right foot on it, and again took off with my left foot. I managed to stay on the board for 2.4 seconds, then it shot out from under me, and I landed on my bottom. "Ouch!"

Charlie smiled at me. "Must be the ramp. Now two of us are hurt."

I stood up and rubbed my backside. "I think this is beyond my coordination level."

Jimmy lowered his voice. "Say, would you two like to take a drive?"

I nodded. "Sure, yes. I mean, that would be great."

"Come on, Cindy. Let's run back and tell Aunt Polly," Kitty said, and we sprinted into her house.

We found Aunt Polly lounging on her favorite couch, popping Fig Newtons, and relaxing in front of Gunsmoke.

Kitty approached her quietly. "Um, Aunt Polly? Sorry to wake you."

"I wasn't sleeping."

"Uh-huh, OK. Cindy and I would like to go for a drive with Jimmy and Charlie."

"Why?"

"They asked us to, and we thought it'd be fun," Kitty said.

Aunt Polly stared at us for a moment and eventually said, "Get my purse," which we did. She took out ten dollars and said, "If you pass the Dairy Queen, we're out of Dilly Bars. Bring back the change."

Kitty pocketed the ten-spot, and we dashed out the door, excited for a taste of freedom.

Jimmy and Charlie held the doors of the Barracuda, and we slid inside, me in the front seat next to Jimmy, Kitty and Charlie in the back. "Where would you like to go?" Jimmy asked.

"Anywhere!" Kitty and I spoke in unison. We were desperate for adventure.

Jimmy started the engine. "I know just the place." He cranked up the music, and when "Help Me, Rhonda" came on the radio, even I sang along. We rolled down the windows and let the wind muss our hair. The music melted our teenage angst. For a few blessed moments, I shook off my anxiety and let a flood of happiness wash over me. Life was good. We laughed and sang as we sailed along in the Barracuda, feeling as if we were invincible. When Petula Clark came on the radio, we belted out the chorus of "Downtown" as we passed cars along the highway. Finally, Jimmy pulled into the parking lot of a city park, and we piled out, eager for a stretch in the warm, humid air. The sight of the shining sun was invigorating.

We walked along a sidewalk surrounding a fishy-smelling pond until we came to an isolated picnic bench far from the road. Jimmy's expression turned conspiratorial as we sat. "We asked our parents if they knew anything more about your great-aunt."

I sucked in a quick breath. "What did they say?"

Jimmy swatted a fly. "They said her father was wealthy and well known."

We nodded. Old news. "Anything else?" I asked.

Charlie steepled his fingertips. "They remember she had a younger sister, but they haven't seen her in years."

Kitty gasped. "We just learned about her!"

Kitty and I filled the boys in on what happened the day before.

Charlie laughed at my speculations. "Well, we know she wasn't working as a circus act."

I frowned at him. "That's not funny. They probably didn't have a circus during the war."

Charlie raised a hand. "OK, I'm sorry. I didn't mean to offend you. But can you imagine any sister of your Aunt Polly as a trapeze artist? I mean, if she was the same size as your great-aunt, imagine her doing handstands on top of an elephant? Or jumping through a flaming hoop of fire?"

I frowned as long as I could and then cracked up and laughed until my side hurt. Laughing was infectious, and for a few moments, the four of us were wrapped in waves of it.

Kitty stepped off the bench. "Let's play on the swings for a few minutes."

Dark clouds threatened to unload on us, but we thought we'd have a few minutes of fun before it rained. We ran to a set of swings and competed to see who could soar the highest as we pumped our legs faster and faster. But the clouds didn't wait, and a crack of thunder was followed in quick order by a pop-up shower overhead. The others jumped off their swings, but I was enjoying the sensation and sang out. "Swinging in the rain, I'm swinging in the rain…"

Kitty hollered as she jumped off her swing, "It's singing in the rain, not swinging." Charlie grabbed her hand, and they took off toward the car.

I leaped off. Jimmy reached for my hand, and we ran toward the safety of his car. We were soaked by the time we were safely inside. I turned to Kitty. "I thought swinging was correct."

She shook her head and smiled. "You're always mixing words."

Jimmy tossed a small towel at me, which I used to dry my arms and then passed to Kitty. "Since pop-up showers are common, I keep a little towel in the car. Let's find a malt shop."

This day was getting better and better. I couldn't think of anything to say on the way to the drive-in, and I was afraid if I started to chatter, I'd sound like an immature chimp, so I kept my trap shut. Kitty and Charlie cozied up in the backseat, so I didn't turn around again.

Jimmy pulled into the parking lot of a drive-in restaurant and pressed the knob on the tall metal post next to the car. He ordered four chocolate malts, and soon a girl on roller skates delivered them to the car window. We sipped and slurped like a pack of thirsty dogs. Kitty and I tried to tame our enthusiasm since girls were supposed to have tiny appetites, but a cold malt on a hot summer day was pretty close to heaven. And being with the boys of our dreams made them all the sweeter.

On the drive home, Kitty remembered our great-aunt's request, so we swung by the Dairy Queen and picked up two boxes of Dilly Bars. Before we reached their house, Charlie said, "Let's go sailing again tomorrow. It's supposed to be sunny."

Jimmy nodded enthusiastically. "Great idea! We can take a picnic to that little island in the middle of the lake," Jimmy said. "What do you think?"

Kitty giggled. "What's not to love? Another afternoon away from our great-aunt sounds like paradise, don't you think, Cindy?"

"Sure. Yes. Fun," I said. "I'll bake brownies." I was still worried about going sailing again, but I reminded myself that last week we had fun, and I didn't get thrown overboard.

We set a time to meet and headed back to Aunt Polly's right away so our ice cream bars wouldn't melt.

That night after dinner, Kitty and I said we were sleepy and headed to bed early so we could read the newspaper articles in the scrapbook we found. We still had a handful of letters to read but wanted to finish the scrapbook first.

We started at the beginning and found articles that announced the Schultz family would return to Minnetonka for the summer. Kitty read aloud from a 1903 paper: "Catherine and Alexander Schultz are returning to the area for their daughters' summer holiday from school. Daughters Catherine (12), Polly (10), and Margaret (7) will be attending the First Presbyterian Church of Minnetonka. Mrs. Schultz says she is planning to assist the Ladies Aid with a bake sale while Mr. Schultz works from his company's Minnetonka branch. A nanny will accompany the girls. The older two will take tennis and swimming lessons, along with conversational French. Mrs. Schultz says she will receive guests on Tuesday and Friday mornings from 10 a.m. to noon."

Kitty put the newspaper down and frowned. "How creepy to have your travels listed in the newspaper. What an invasion of privacy."

"Yes, but we know there was a younger sister now for certain."

We put our noses back in the scrapbook and kept looking for clues. We reread the articles about Aunt Polly's college graduation in 1915 and her worldwide cruise. Another piece stated that she was in Paris, studying French. "I suspect she was also studying French pastries," I said.

"You think she learned to make any?"

"No, silly. Eat them."

We continued browsing through the scrapbook and found an article that was not on the society page like the others. This was a front-page story about a boating accident dated September 3, 1912.

"Kitty! Listen to this. 'Sixteen-year-old Margaret Schultz, a summer resident of Minnetonka, was injured in a boating accident in Colorado. She dove off her motorboat and became entangled in the motor. She was taken to the local hospital, but her condition is unknown. The accident is under investigation.' How gruesome!"

I looked up at Kitty, whose hand was covering her mouth. Her eyes were watery. "Is that it?" she asked.

We scanned the rest of the articles, but none mentioned Margaret Schultz.

"There isn't an obituary, so maybe she's still alive?"

Chapter 18

We awoke eager for our sailing date. I peered out the window to ensure the weather wouldn't trick us and send another storm. But the puffy clouds looked like they were smiling at us. "It's going to be so much fun today," I said into the window.

Kitty stretched and yawned as she shook off dreamland and stood up. "I'm so glad Aunt Polly hurt her ankle. I don't mean because she's hurt, but because we've gotten to see the guys."

I turned and nodded. "I agree. At first, I was afraid we'd be stuck here alone with her, day and night. But this is turning out to be the best visit ever."

"I can't wait to see Charlie again. The picnic sounds perfect."

I sat back down on the bed and the springs creaked. "I'm surprised Aunt Polly is letting us spend so much time alone with the guys."

"Me too. Sometimes I feel like she's pushing us to hang out with them, and other times she seems angry that we are."

After breakfast, I called home to get a brownie recipe and immediately baked them so they'd cool in time for our outing. After rummaging through the cupboards, I found a clean container and put most of the brownies into it.

"I'm leaving a few brownies in the pan for you, Aunt Polly," I called from the kitchen.

"What? I wasn't invited to go sailing?" she answered in her highest voice.

Kitty and I froze as we looked at each other.

"Well, I mean, with your foot. It's a long walk. I didn't think you'd want to…" I stuttered.

She barked out a laugh. "I was kidding."

"Oh, thank goodness… I mean, good… I… I didn't think…"

"Just go," Aunt Polly said, and we took off before she could change her mind.

We wore swimsuits with shorts over the bottoms, sandals, and towels slung over our shoulders as usual. We exploded out the back porch door with an air of confidence. We shook our loose hair as if we were Minnetonka girls. But, of course, we weren't.

When we were out of earshot, I ranted to Kitty, "That was close. What would we have done if she really wanted to come along?"

"She'd never be able to walk to the lake, and she doesn't have the balance to get into the small boat, even without the walking cast. So we're safe. Now let's have fun."

"She'd likely tip the boat if she did try to get into it." I took a breath.

Wayne sneered a greeting when he answered the door. "Look who's here. Again." We stood outside waiting for friendlier faces.

Jimmy pushed past him. "Hi! Ready to go? Mom packed a lunch." He wore navy swim trunks and a light blue T-shirt that matched his eyes.

I brightened. "Yup. All set. I brought brownies."

"Any funny stuff in those brownies?" Wayne asked, poking his head out the door.

I wrinkled my nose. "Just regular brownies." I felt like sticking my tongue out at him, but held back.

"Too bad," he said and slunk back into the house.

Within minutes Charlie flew down the staircase from their second floor and jumped over the porch to land outside next to us. His eyes were bright, and his cheeks were glowing, perhaps a reflection of his red T-shirt. "Hi, there! Let's blow this pop stand!"

We giggled, and the four of us took off. Jimmy and Charlie carried the cooler, swinging along with their usual vigor. I was relieved Wayne wasn't joining us but uncomfortable with the way he openly disdained us. Was it because we weren't from Minnetonka? Or that we were from a large Catholic family? Or because we weren't sophisticated like all the lanky blonds we saw everywhere? I needed to shake off the negative feelings like a puppy shaking water after a dip in pond scum. I pushed Wayne—and my doubts about

Jimmy's attention—out of my mind and focused on not tripping.

We hiked over to the bay where the boat was tied. Kitty and I pitched in to get the boat ready, and when it was, Jimmy pushed off, and we set sail for a small island.

It was the kind of day my grandmother called a bottle day—one we wished we could bottle for the winter and uncork when it was 20 below and the winds howled.

I was determined not to end up "in the drink" again, so I paid attention to the "coming about" commands, even while watching seagulls dive for fish. Within thirty minutes, we reached the tiny island in the middle of the lake, and I realized we were literally the only visitors, other than the sparrows, chickadees, and robins who flitted back and forth in the birch and poplar trees. As we hopped out of the boat, I was surprised at the density of the trees. "There aren't any bears here, right?"

Jimmy laughed. "Bears? No. Not unless they're excellent swimmers. Not enough forest for them in the middle of the lake."

I felt my cheeks warm, but at least I knew we wouldn't get eaten by bears while we enjoyed lunch. Ever since I went camping as a child and a bear tried to get into our tent, I got nervous whenever I was surrounded by a forest.

"Let's eat," Charlie exclaimed as he snatched the picnic basket from the boat. We found a sandy spot and circled the basket as he handed out ham and cheese sandwiches, potato chips, and soda cans. But it wasn't soda.

I looked at the cans and wrinkled my nose. "Beer? Beer. I can't drink this."

Jimmy and Charlie looked at each other conspiratorially. "Sorry. We thought you might like a cold one since it's so hot today," Jimmy said.

Kitty grinned. "I'll take one."

I shot her a stink eye, but she ignored me and reached for the beer. It blasted open after being rocked in the boat, and foam poured onto the sand. "Oops," she giggled, again in full flirtation mode.

She tasted it and turned to offer me a sip. I didn't want to be a party-pooper, so I gingerly took the can and tasted the bitter beer before shaking my head and returning it to her. "No thanks. Any colas?"

Jimmy smiled and handed one to me. "Sure. Here you go, Cindy."

Our lunch was extra delicious, as food always is when eaten outside with people you enjoy. Despite my hesitation over the beer, I relished time spent in the sun so close to Jimmy. My heart still sped up whenever he looked at me, said my name, or came close to me.

As we munched, Kitty filled them in on our latest family discoveries. "We learned something about Aunt Polly's younger sister."

Charlie turned to her playfully and grabbed a lock of her long hair. "Oh yeah? Breaking into rooms again?"

Kitty flashed a quick smile. "No. We decided to read the rest of the newspaper articles from the scrapbook and found one about an accident." Kitty told them about Margaret and the boat.

"What year was the accident?" Jimmy asked.

"1912, while Aunt Polly was away at college," I said.

Charlie was philosophical. "Just shows how life can change in a moment." He took a deep breath, stood up, and yanked off his T-shirt. "Let's enjoy our youth! Carpe Diem," he shouted and ran into the water. "Come on, you guys. The water's perfect."

Jimmy followed in a moment, stripping off his shirt and diving in without hesitation while Kitty and I scooted out of our shorts and stepped cautiously into the lake.

When I was standing in water up to my knees, I shivered and turned to Kitty. "Perfect? It's freezing. I don't think I want to be emerged."

"Immersed, you mean. Let's just take it a step at a time."

Kitty and I gradually adjusted to the temperature while Jimmy and Charlie were already swimming in deeper waters twenty feet out. As Kitty and I inched our way, Jimmy and Charlie appeared and started playfully splashing us.

"Come on, you two!" Charlie said. We squealed and turned away from the cold-water sprays, but they kept splashing us until we were soaked.

Finally, we walked farther and plunged in up to our necks, to the cheers of Jimmy and Charlie. They swam toward us and grabbed our arms to swirl us around in circles. Being weightless in water was a magnificent feeling. We did backward flips to see who could come up the fastest. At one point,

Jimmy swam to me, put his arm around me, and pulled me to him. He planted a kiss on my forehead, and I brazenly put my arms around his shoulders, delighting in the strength of his muscles. When he leaned down and kissed my lips, I nearly fainted. Then suddenly, he pulled back and shouted, "Let's play keep-away!" He ran to the boat and brought back a red and white striped beach ball.

Charlie immediately agreed. He crouched in the water, Kitty climbed onto his shoulders, and Jimmy handed her the ball. I was supposed to do the same to Jimmy, but I wondered if the spell of weightlessness would be broken once my full weight was seated upon him.

"Come on, Cindy," he urged as he crouched down.

"I hope you're strong enough," I tittered.

He shot back, "You don't think I'm strong?"

Had I hurt his pride? "No. I mean, yes, I do. It's just that I'm... Never mind." I climbed onto his back.

Jimmy groaned. "Ugh. Oh my!"

I slid off his shoulders, embarrassed, and when I looked up, he was laughing. I splashed water in his face and turned away, hurt. Now he was making fun of my weight. Jimmy reached for my arm. "Cindy, I was kidding. You don't weigh anything at all. Hop back on."

Tears threatened to spill when I turned back to him. He pulled me into a hug. "I'm sorry. Really. I was teasing." He crouched down, and I climbed onto his shoulders. He let out a battle cry to let Charlie and Kitty know the game had begun.

I wasn't sure of the rules of keep-away but pretended I knew what to do. Somehow Kitty and I were supposed to grab the ball back and forth while also trying to topple the other. There were squeals and screams as we rallied and lunged at each other in good-natured fun. I was grateful no other swimmers were near as we battled to stay afloat, or they'd think a team of rabid monkeys had overtaken the island.

Finally, I reached too far backward for the ball and was thrown into the lake. We played another round and eventually decided to dry off in the warm sun. Jimmy lay his proper beach towel in the sand next to my faded bath towel, and Kitty and Charlie sunned themselves a short distance away from us. After a few moments, Jimmy flipped over onto his stomach and propped himself on his elbows. I opened my eyes and saw his face coming closer. His blue eyes seemed darker as he leaned in. He smiled and brushed my hair off my forehead.

"Having fun?" he asked.

"Yes. The best." I was nervous, wondering what would happen next, but I didn't have long to wait. He planted soft kisses on my mouth, and I responded in kind. But when he ran his tongue over my lips, I panicked.

Chapter 19

I SQUINTED FROM THE INTENSE SUN in my eyes. "Let's go for a walk, Jimmy," I said. This kissing business made me nervous, but I didn't want to tell him and risk looking like the dork I knew I was.

He frowned uncertainly. "Um, OK. Sure." He sprang to his feet in one easy movement, then reached down to help me. "Want to explore the island?"

"Yeah, let's see what's here," I said. "I've never been over here."

"Not much to see, but stretching our legs sounds good." He put an arm around my shoulder and directed me to a gravel path with heavy tree cover. "I'll let you know if I see signs of a bear."

I looked at him and gave him a little push with my free hand. "Very funny."

As we walked along, I removed his arm, bent down to pick up rocks, and set them in patterns along the way.

"What are you doing?"

"It's something we learned in Girl Scouts. The stones tell us to go straight or to turn in a specific direction, depending on how we stack them."

"Are you worried about getting lost?" he asked.

"No, but if we get kidnapped by pirates, Kitty will know what direction we went."

Jimmy burst out laughing. "You're kidding, right?"

I grinned up at him. "Well, we don't have any breadcrumbs to mark our path."

"OK, Gretel." He put his arm around my waist and pulled me closer to face him. "You're a funny one."

I looked up at him, enjoying the closeness and the smell of the lake on his skin. "Thanks, I think." The heavy tree cover was sheltering us from the blinding sunshine, and a cool breeze swatted the perspiration from my forehead. "I think I'm glowing."

"Is that another code for something?" Jimmy asked.

"My great-aunt says only horses sweat. Men perspire, and women glow."

He laughed. "So, are you glowing any specific color?"

"Hopefully not green. Just a rosy glow."

"I think I can make you glow brighter," he said, pulling me close and leaning in for another kiss. I kissed him back, this time enthusiastically, and we quickly found the passion escalating. When his tongue explored my mouth, I was unsure what to do at first, but soon responded with mine. He tasted salty, and his breath held a hint of beer. His hands initially surrounded my waist, but I pulled back when he dropped them down and squeezed my bottom.

"Whoa there," I said. I took a deep breath and stepped out of his arms. Mysterious heat was radiating in my lower region, and I was sure it was a sin to feel that good. "We'd better get back." His breathing had quickened, and I could see the disappointment in his eyes, but I was uncomfortable going any further.

Jimmy smiled. "You don't want to glow any brighter?"

I shook my head and grinned. "This is as rosy as I'd better be."

He turned serious for a moment. "Can I ask you something?"

"I guess so."

"Am I the first guy you've kissed?"

I looked at our bare feet and traced a circle in the sand next to the path. "Am I a bad kisser?" I asked.

"No. I was just curious. What's the circle? Another sign?"

"Yes. I'm letting the aliens know where to find me," I said, glad for the change of subject.

Jimmy shook his head and reached for my hand. "I think we can find our way back."

We walked back to the same beach where we ate our picnic lunch and found Kitty and Charlie locked in a passionate embrace. My cheeks turned red when I saw them. I wondered if I should alert them to our presence. But Jimmy took matters into his hands. He found a can of beer, shook it up, opened it, and aimed the spray of foam and beer at Kitty and Charlie.

"What the? Hey!" Charlie said as he sprang to his feet.

Kitty squealed and leaped up as the cold beer hit her warm skin. Charlie grabbed her hand, and they ran into the lake to wash off the beer and cool down as Jimmy and I laughed. Well, Jimmy did. I wondered if Kitty would be mad at me for interrupting them. We rarely argued, and I didn't want any tension with my sister.

Soon, the four of us picked up the remains of our picnic, jumped into the sailboat, and headed back. My mind was a jumble of emotions on the ride back. Did Jimmy really like me? Or did he think I was "easy"? The nuns in our girls' high school often warned us about horny teen boys and told us not to be easy. But how much kissing was "easy" and how much was affection? Kissing Jimmy was fun, but was too much fun a sin? My mind hurt trying to figure it out.

We splashed apple cider vinegar on our sunburned skin that afternoon to cool the heat. We were quiet at dinner while we pushed our SpaghettiOs and Smokies around our plates, which prompted questions from Aunt Polly.

"You girls are certainly spending a lot of time with those boys."

Kitty sighed. "I hope you don't mind. We're having so much fun swimming and sailing."

Aunt Polly scrutinized Kitty's face. "Don't let things... you know... get out of hand."

"We're just having fun," Kitty said. She looked to me for support.

"They're really nice guys." Did that sound believable? I mean, they were really nice, but also, they were, you know, boys. Horny teen boys. And we were budding teen girls. Before she could guess about kissing and stuff, I needed to change the subject, so I decided to pry for details about her past. We could search this house forever for clues, but the answers were hiding in front of us inside her memory.

She was already seventy-two, so who knew how long she'd live? Or how soon she'd lose her mind, if she hadn't already. Maybe it was too late, and all the answers had already fallen out of her brain.

"So, Aunt Polly, did you have any boyfriends when you were our age?" I asked.

"What kind of a question is that?" she snapped back.

Kitty cut in. "We were just wondering. You were young once, like us, so were there any boys you were sweet on?"

Aunt Polly straightened a bit and sniffed righteously. "First of all, we weren't allowed to date until we turned eighteen. The young man would have to come to the house and meet our parents. And we weren't allowed to be alone with a man. We did a lot of double dates."

We listened in awe at what sounded like a different planet. "Wow," I said, "things sure have changed."

She raised her eyebrows. "Little has changed. Men are still full of hormones, and they will always seek loose women to use. I'm letting you go out with the O'Reilly boys because they come from a good family, and you are staying together. Double dating."

Kitty nodded her head as she bit her bottom lip. "Right, we're double dating. We'll stay safe, won't we, Cindy?"

"Safe. Yes. Sure. We are. We're safe."

Aunt Polly stared at me as if she thought I was having a stroke. Was she reading my guilt? I could feel the color creeping from my cheeks to my neck, and now my ears were burning. Can you go to Hell for kissing too much before marriage?

I had to change the subject. "Dessert! Who wants a brownie?"

That night, Kitty and I were upstairs sitting on our beds, sifting through the handful of letters we'd retrieved from the rolltop desk. But I couldn't focus.

"Kitty, Sister Louis Marie from our religious studies class told us that kissing for more than seven seconds was a mortal sin. Do you think she's right?"

Kitty rolled her eyes. "How could something that feels so great be a sin?"

I looked down, trying to sort out my conflicting thoughts. "But aren't we supposed to wait until we're married?"

Kitty was aghast. "To kiss? Are you kidding?"

"Well, I mean to kiss the way you and Charlie were kissing."

"How do you know what we were doing?"

"When Jimmy and I returned from our walk, you were sprawled on the sand in front of God and everyone, and it was way longer than seven seconds."

Kitty stood up. Her raging face looked like shriveled

squash. "You were counting? Is that it? You got a stopwatch and counted?"

I stood up too, in case she was going to attack me. "No! But it seemed like a long time, and he was on top of you, for heaven's sake! Were you just counting slow? Like 'One Mississippi, two Mississippi, three Mississippi'?"

Hands on her hips, she shouted at me, "Cindy, stop! I mean, Sister said all kinds of crazy things, but what do nuns know?"

"But she said we shouldn't arouse a boy because we'd be responsible for what happened."

"I can't believe you listened to that nonsense. She also told us not to wear white because it'd remind guys of bed sheets." Kitty's hands were on her hips, and she shook her head in disbelief. "You're being ridiculous. You can't possibly believe all that."

I took a step back and looked down. "Well, no, but yes. Some of it. I ditched my patent leather shoes after she said they'd reflect our undies. Just in case."

Just then, we heard Aunt Polly's shrill call to action. "Girls, girls!" We burst out the bedroom door to the top of the staircase, glad for a distraction from the accelerating discussion. She was standing at the bottom of the stairs red-faced.

"Girls, what's all the kerfuffle about? I can hardly hear myself think!"

"Nothing!" I lied.

"We were playing a guessing game," Kitty added, breathing quickly from the argument. "Sorry we bothered you."

"Yes, we'll be quiet," I said.

Aunt Polly frowned. "I should hope so." Then she turned, muttering to herself, and clumped to her front living room, and we skulked back to our room. We flopped on our beds for a few moments to regroup, and then Kitty rolled on her side, rested her head on one elbow, and whispered, "So, what were you and Jimmy doing? I saw you going into the woods together, and you looked pretty cozy."

"We did kiss a little, but I stopped him before… you know… anything happened."

"Anything Sister would disapprove of, you mean?"

"Kitty, stop making fun of me and mind your own bumblebees. I don't want to go to Hell."

Kitty shook her head and then flopped onto her back. "Mind your own beeswax, not bumblebees. Sr. Louis Marie can just mind her own beeswax!"

I snatched a few letters and held them up to Kitty. "Like we're doing? We're reading Aunt Polly's private letters."

"Shh. Keep your voice down. We don't want her hollering again."

"I can't believe she could hear us. I thought her hearing was going, but she has a bat-like radar."

"Maybe she is part bat. She was staring at us at dinner as if we were guilty of something," Kitty said.

"Well, we are guilty of several things. Are we going to get into trouble if she finds out what we've been doing in her house?"

"Cindy, how will she find out? The only ones who know

are Jimmy and Charlie, and they're not going to run over and snitch on us."

I nodded. "That's true. And I swear, I'll never tell."

"And neither will I. Besides, it's ancient history."

"What if they get mad at us, Kitty? They might tell Aunt Polly out of spite."

Kitty smiled and winked. "Then we'll have to ensure we don't disappoint them."

I scrunched up my face. "Eew. I'm not sure I like what you're suggesting."

She sighed. "Nothing like that, silly. But I hope we get to see them again soon."

Chapter 20

AUNT POLLY LET US SLEEP the next morning, which was a relief. I tossed and turned from my blazing sunburn, dreams of fiery kisses, and the heated words between my sister and me. When Kitty awoke, I sidestepped difficult subjects and focused on safe ones. Like weather.

"Looks rainy today. And cool."

Kitty looked out the dirty window and sighed. "I guess we won't be swimming or sailing."

"Another long day here with Aunt Polly. Maybe we can play Parcheesi again."

"I'd rather swing from the chandeliers!"

I grinned. "After so much fun yesterday, it feels like a big letdown just hanging out all day."

We slid into our bell-bottom jeans, T-shirts, and Keds, braided our hair, and headed downstairs to gauge Aunt Polly's mood. We found her lounging on a wicker recliner on the front porch wearing a blue and yellow floral eye patch that matched her floral house dress. She looked like a giant parakeet, and I waited to see if she'd say, "Polly want a cracker?"

"Good morning, girls. I thought you'd never wake up."

"Morning," we grumbled back.

She pointed toward the lake. "There's a storm coming. I thought I'd watch it from the porch. Always fun to see the clouds roll in over the lake."

I was terrified of thunderstorms. "Another storm? Is it going to be a tornado?"

"No, just lightning and thunder. You girls can bring our breakfast onto the porch."

I hesitated. "Mmmkay, but aren't we going to get wet if we sit on the porch?"

Aunt Polly was out of patience. "You'll be fine. Just bring me some breakfast. I've been up for two hours already waiting for you girls."

We turned and headed to the kitchen to scout for breakfast fare, but the milk was sour again, and the cereal was almost gone. We made cheese on toast under the broiler, poured glasses of orange juice, then lugged it out to the porch and sat at a small table as far from the screened windows as possible. The sky was greenish-gray, devoid of songbirds who must have hunkered down in their nests. A few seagulls were frantically squawking, probably warning their friends, but otherwise, it was eerily silent. Even inside the screened-in porch, I could smell the musty, dusky scent of the air heavy with moisture.

For a few moments, it felt as if the earth was waiting for

a signal, like a race's starting gun. And then boom! There it was. A bolt of lightning flashed across the sky and skipped across the lake. I screamed involuntarily.

"Oh, for heaven's sake! What's the matter with you?" Aunt Polly said, glaring at me.

"Sorry. It just startled me."

When the deafening thunder and cracks of lightning intensified, I bolted down my breakfast, and Kitty and I cleared away the dishes.

"I'm going upstairs to read, Aunt Polly. I'll feel safer in my room."

"Your room, huh?"

"Well, I mean the room we're staying in," I stammered.

"Suit yourself," she said, calmly watching the sky turn dark and light up with barbed flashes like knives across the sky. The edgy atmosphere seemed to mirror her mood.

We marched upstairs. I was angry. I turned to Kitty when we were safely inside our bedroom with the door closed. "Why does she have to be so mean?"

Kitty shook her head. "Who knows? But now I want to read the rest of those letters even more. I don't feel bad about prying into her life and her sister's life."

"I'm with you. I told her I would read, but I didn't say it was a book. Let's start with the letters in the dresser drawer we haven't read yet. Then the next time she leaves, we can put those back and bring up another handful."

"There were others addressed to her parents and a few from some guy named Anthony."

"Right. And the letters from her sister Margaret. I wonder if there are any from Grandma Catherine."

"I don't remember seeing any. That's weird. Maybe they weren't close." Kitty looked at me hesitantly, and I felt rotten about the argument we had the night before.

I pulled my knees up to my chest. "I hope we stay close."

Kitty smiled at me. "Me too. Let's not let anything come between us."

I nodded in relief. "Agreed. Even boys."

"Yes, but stop calling them boys. They're nearly grown men, so let's call them guys."

I nodded. "OK, I'll remember. Now back to the letters. The ones we brought upstairs were the ones addressed to Aunt Polly. Let's get started before she interrupts us again."

We separated the letters according to their dates and spread them into piles on our beds. We began to open them one at a time. We found notes written to Aunt Polly while she was away in college and looked for one with a similar date to the newspaper article about her younger sister's accident.

"Kitty, I found it. From her mother. But inside the envelope is a telegram in addition to the letter. I'll read that first.

"It reads: 'Margaret hurt in boating accident. In hospital. Look for letter with details. Love, Mother'"

Kitty's hand flew to her mouth. "Can you imagine receiving a telegram like that? So abrupt."

"I can't. But a letter must have followed a week or so later to explain. Here it is." I read:

Dearest Polly,

I hope you are well. Please try to stay away from desserts. Your figure has no more room for additional poundage. Now, on another matter, I'm sorry to tell you that your dear little sister, Margaret, has been in a ghastly boating accident. I won't go into too many details, but I do assure you she's getting the best possible care in the hospital. The doctors aren't sure of her prognosis because she is still in a coma. I'll send another update as soon as I have more information. Please don't let this distract you from your studies. Your father is counting on you to make him proud.

Love, Mother.

"Her mother sounds more interested in Polly's weight than Margaret's condition. What an odd family. Imagine receiving a letter like that. She couldn't very well fly home to Colorado in 1912, so she had to worry all alone at college."

"Right. And no phone calls. And I suppose it took weeks to get a letter out." I shook my head, thinking about how I'd feel in a similar situation. "How could she focus on her classes? I couldn't if something happened to any of our sisters."

Kitty sighed. "Me neither. I don't know. It's horrible. Let's keep reading and see if there are other clues."

We searched for the letters that followed in chronological order.

Kitty was quiet as she read and then gasped, "I think I found our answer. Here's a letter dated October 24, 1912, from her mother:

Dear Polly,

I hope your studies are going well. I'm sorry to inform you that your sister's injuries have not healed. She has limited abilities because of the brain injury, and we've been forced to admit her to an institution. We had no other choice. I know you were fond of her, but try your best to forget her. Don't bother to write to her because she won't be able to read your letters. We plan to visit now and then, but she doesn't seem to know we're there when we do. It's as if she's died and left her body behind. I realize this is difficult news, but please don't let this upset you. Push it out of your mind and focus on your studies. I'll share more details when I see you at Christmas."

I snatched the letter from Kitty to read it myself. "So that was it? Just left her in an institution? What?"

Kitty was shaking. "What happened in that accident? What sort of injuries did she have?"

"Yes, and what sort of an institution? This is so creepy!"

Kitty's eyes were wide with concern. "Do you think Aunt Polly was able to forget her? Is that why she won't talk about her?"

"How could anyone forget a sibling? This doesn't make sense. What sort of a life did Margaret have?"

"She'd be sixty-nine if she was still alive. Do you think she ever got better?"

We sat thinking about our poor Great Aunt Margaret. We couldn't ask Aunt Polly any more questions without stirring her anger.

I sat up straighter. "I'm asking Mom about this. I don't

care if we get into trouble for finding the letters. We're family, and we deserve to know the truth."

Kitty nodded. "You're right. Let's ask Mom. But Cindy, our great-grandmother sounds like a cold piece of work."

"She certainly does. How can we be related to some of the folks we're related to?"

By now the storm was over, and we tramped down the stairs to find our great-aunt still on the front porch.

"You missed a good storm, girls." She struggled to her feet and started moving toward the front of the house. "I need to go to the podiatrist to take care of my corns. Do you girls want to come along?"

"No thanks," we said in unison.

Aunt Polly found her large brown faux-leather purse, put it over her elbow, and shuffled out of the house. "Don't entertain those boys while I'm gone."

"We won't," we said in unison.

When we heard her engine roar to life and saw a plume of black smoke, we knew the coast was clear.

CHAPTER 21

KITTY TURNED TO ME. "Should we call the guys over and make out?"

"Not funny. We promised not to entertain while she's gone."

"So now we're going to start obeying her?"

I sighed. "Let's call Mom."

She marched to the phone and dialed home. Colleen picked up.

"Hi, Colleen. Is Mom there?"

"Sure, but how long do you have to stay there?"

"Not sure."

"What do you do all day?"

"We cook, clean, fetch, and carry. We're like her personal servants."

"Sorry. But I'm glad I'm not there."

"Your turn will come. Now can you go get Mom?"

I put my ear next to the phone, and we heard Colleen yell for Mom. We could also hear squealing from our little sisters.

Finally, "Hello," Mom said in a melodic tone.

Kitty started. "Hi, Mom."

"How are you, girls? Ready to come home?"

Kitty looked at me and shook her head. "Not really. We're doing OK."

"That's a switch. So what's on your mind?"

"Well, Cindy and I found a telegram and some letters about Aunt Polly's sister Margaret and they were really upsetting."

"Where did you find the letters, dear?"

"That's not important. But we want to know what happened to her in the boating accident."

I grabbed the phone from Kitty. "Yes, and was she put in an institution for the rest of her life?"

Mom sighed. "I told you not to snoop around, and that's exactly what you're doing."

I was insistent. "We're bored, and there are lots of interesting things lying around. Now please, just tell us the truth. We're almost adults."

"Where is Aunt Polly? Why don't you ask her?"

"She's at some doctor doing something about vegetables."

Kitty shook her head and grabbed the phone from me. "Mom, she's at the podiatrist having the corns shaved off her feet, which sounds gross. But we can't ask her things because she gets furious. We don't know how long she'll be gone, so please tell us."

"It sounds like you know most of the story already."

"But we still have questions," I said.

She let out a sigh of resignation. "OK. Let me shoo the girls into the other room. They don't all need to know about this."

We heard Mom over the phone as she herded our youngest sisters outside to play on the backyard swings and glider. Finally, her footsteps got louder as she reached for the kitchen phone.

"Still there?"

Kitty and I huddled around either side of the phone as I held the receiver. "Yup. Still here."

"Hard to know where to start."

"We read a newspaper article about a boating accident," Kitty said.

"Yes, Margaret was with friends in a motorboat when she decided to dive off the boat to swim. Somehow the boat swerved near her, and her hair was caught in the motor. It sucked her in, and she had a severe head injury. It was pretty gruesome. Her friends dragged her into the boat and raced to the shore to find help. I believe they wrapped her head in a towel and drove to the nearest hospital since phones were rarely available in 1912."

I cringed and looked at Kitty, hoping she wouldn't be sick. One hand was over her mouth and the other was holding her stomach.

I made a face. "That's horrible. Her head! I can't believe she didn't die."

"Yes, it was horrific. You're sure you want me to go on?" Mom asked.

Kitty and I looked at each other and nodded. "Go on, Mom."

"It was somewhat of a miracle that she didn't die on the way to the hospital, but it almost would have been better if she had. The doctors did surgery to patch her up the best they could. Margaret was in a coma for several weeks with swelling in her brain, if I recall. My mother said she couldn't walk or talk when she finally opened her eyes. Someone had to physically feed her, and she just stared straight ahead."

"Was our grandma able to visit her?"

"Yes, my mom, your Grandma Catherine, lived close by since she attended college in Colorado. She told me she went with her parents to visit Margaret, but there was never a change in her condition."

"Why didn't they let Polly go and see her?" Kitty asked.

"Polly was in college in Minnesota, and the only way to reach her quickly was through a telegram. They were expensive and only allowed something like fourteen words. Obviously, they wanted her to know about her sister but didn't want to alarm her. Travel was slow and difficult. It would have taken weeks away from Polly's studies to travel to Colorado, so her parents insisted she stay at school."

"Did Margaret ever recover?" Kitty asked.

"Not that I know of. She was sent to an institution that dealt with people who had brain injuries."

I was appalled at the lack of information about her. "It's

like she was erased from the family history. How long did she live like that?"

We could hear our younger sisters in the background. "Mom, Maureen hurt herself on the glider."

Mom was distracted. "Uh girls, I've got to go."

The screams of a hurt child got louder and louder as the gaggle of little girls rushed into the house.

"She ran in front of our swings," Joanne explained to Mom.

"She pushed me," sobbed Maureen.

"Is Maureen OK?" I asked.

"She'll be fine. Head wound. We'll talk soon." And she hung up.

Kitty put the phone down. "That head injury sounded gruesome."

"Maureen's? Or Aunt Margaret's?"

Kitty looked pale. "Both. But let's hope Maureen's is just a minor cut. You know how those head wounds bleed."

"Let's think about something else. Maybe some of the letters still in the desk have happier stories. We should check them out while Aunt Polly's gone."

"I wish our grandma lived closer so we could ask her about some of this."

"Me too, but I wonder if she's as closed about the past as Aunt Polly. Maybe it's too painful to remember."

We ran upstairs, gathered the letters we previously read, and retrieved the key to the desk. Downstairs in the formal living room, we crept to the desk at the far end, opened it, and pulled out the rest of the letters. We thought we had them all, but as I was replacing the others, I noticed a small door inside the desk. The previous letters were stuffed into pigeonholes, but I found another packet of letters tied with a ribbon when I opened the partially hidden door.

"Kitty, look at this!"

"Who are they from?"

I whispered. "Anthony Walker. I'll bet they're love letters."

Kitty squealed. "Cool! I can't wait to read them."

"Do you think she really had a boyfriend? Seems so unlikely given the way… she is."

"Well, she was young once, hard as it is to imagine that."

As we tiptoed across the worn, faded rug, I tried not to look at the oil portraits hanging on the walls. "I feel like they're going to tell on us."

"Don't be silly. But we should ask Aunt Polly who they are. I mean, she can't get mad about that."

I kept my voice low. "I can't talk about it in front of them. I know they're supposed to be dead, but the way their eyes follow me, I feel like someone is lurking behind the paintings."

"Maybe there's another secret room behind the paintings where people sit and spy on us."

I hesitated for a millisecond and considered the possibility as I looked at the wall they were hanging on. Then I shook my head. "Not possible."

Kitty laughed. "Let's get out of here."

Once upstairs, we again sorted the letters into piles

according to who they were addressed to. And then we found one letter addressed to Anthony Walker.

"Why would she have a letter addressed to someone other than her parents?" I asked.

"Cindy, look at the stamps. It says return to sender. She must have had the wrong address."

"Maybe he moved. Let's organize the letters from him by date so we can read them in order."

Kitty shook her head. "You do love order."

"I'm just trying to be logical," I said. "I'll take the first one, and you take the next."

I slid the letter out of the delicate envelope. "Here's the first: 'October 1916: My dearest Polly,' Ooh, so it is a sweetheart!"

"Just keep reading."

"Sorry. 'I'm so happy to hear you are finally coming home after all your travels. It will be wonderful to see you again. When will you next visit Minnetonka? Yours truly, Anthony.' So definitely a boyfriend. Or gentleman caller, as they said back then."

Kitty frowned. "There's quite a gap in the dates. This one is from July 1917 from Anthony: 'My dear one, we reached the port of Saint-Nazaire, France, without incident. In fact, the locals cheered us upon arrival. I can say no more about our mission other than the food is terrible, and the conditions are grim. I sincerely hope you are well and that you'll await my return. Yours, Anthony.' Wow, it must have been serious."

"I'll bet Aunt Polly didn't have many boyfriends, so he must have been special."

We put those two letters in the "read" pile and chose the next two. "And just as we suspected, he went to war. But why would our great-aunt be there? Women didn't usually serve in wars, did they?"

Kitty shrugged. "I don't know."

The subsequent two letters had similar sentiments. But Kitty frowned as she read the next one. "My dearest Polly, I understand you want to be with me, but it is far too dangerous for you here in France. And it would be nearly impossible to find me as we are moved from camp to camp to stay ahead of the enemy. Please reconsider and stay where you are safe. Yours, Anthony."

I looked at our little pile. "That was the last one. But now we have the letter she sent to him that was returned." I took it out of the envelope and read it aloud. "My dearest Anthony, I must see you in person. There is something I need to tell you. Because I speak fluent French, the American Red Cross can use me to assist in the war effort. Please don't worry. I'll search for you as soon as I arrive in France. Yours always, Polly."

"She must have been desperate to sign onto a war effort just to find him and talk to him in person. Let's find the letters to her parents from the same months."

We searched through the piles, found letters from the summer of 1917, and started looking for clues.

Kitty read one and shouted. "Bingo. This is from Polly

to her parents in August 1917: 'Dear Father and Mother, as you know, I'm in France helping with the Red Cross. Please don't worry. Since I don't have medical training, I assist with sorting mail, serving meals, and translating when needed. Simple tasks. I've tried to locate my dear Anthony but haven't had any success, so I plan to stay another month. I'm visiting hospitals in the hopes of helping soldiers write letters to their families and sweethearts. Love, Polly.'"

"Here's a letter from September 1917: 'Dear Father and Mother, I'll be leaving France by the end of this month and heading back to Colorado to see you. I am well, but disappointed that I haven't located Anthony. My work here is simple, but I have a sense of fulfillment. Of being needed. The soldiers are grateful whenever I bring them mail or serve them meals. And I enjoy using my French. After all those courses, it's wonderful to be able to speak it. However I visited a war hospital, and it was gruesome. I'm looking forward to seeing you in a matter of weeks. Love, Polly.'"

Kitty shook her head. "To look at her, you'd think she'd been on her couch most of her life popping peppermint candies and munching cookies. It's hard to imagine her helping in France. She could barely help herself even before she hurt her foot. I wish I could have seen her in action, buzzing around, helping soldiers, and speaking French."

"You speak a little French. Why don't you try a few phrases on her and see if you can loosen her tongue at dinner?"

"We can play dumb and act as if we didn't know she spoke French, and maybe she'll tell us why she was there." I didn't want to admit to Kitty or anyone that my French accent was appalling. Would you?

"I think I heard her car backfire. What should we tell her about what we've been doing while she was gone?"

"Just reading. That's not a lie. If she asks us what book, just name one you brought."

"Right. Nancy Drew and *Pride and Prejudice*. What about you?"

"*Wuthering Heights* by Emily Brontë. She can't argue with that."

We tucked the letters into safe dresser drawers and headed downstairs carrying our books, but I hoped we'd find something exciting to do for the afternoon. Maybe involving two guys from next door. A girl can dream.

Chapter 22

The next day the air was heavy with humidity. Kitty and I went for a walk after lunch.

"This air is making me feel as if I'm trying to race underwater with weights around my ankles," I said, and Kitty agreed. We walked down the lake side of the homes and cast a few pennies in the Ericksons' wishing well.

"Penny for your thoughts," I asked Kitty.

"I wish I could see Charlie again. What about you?"

"I like Jimmy, and it'd be fun to hang out with them again. But I'm getting homesick. I miss our little sisters and sleeping in a room without mosquitoes buzzing around my head."

Kitty grinned. "And not worrying about mice in the cupboards…"

I continued, "…or squirrels running through the house…"

"…or Aunt Polly shrieking for us to fetch and carry…"

"…and not jumping over cracks in the house…"

"…and being able to cross my arms…"

"…or put my hands on my hips…"

Our voices ramped up in volume with each complaint.

I took a deep breath. "I feel like a prisoner in Pollywood."

Kitty kicked a stone as we continued along the path. "I hoped to make some money working as a carhop this summer."

"Right. And here we are, working for nothing."

"Well, she's paying for our food."

"Oh yes, all the cornflakes and Dilly Bars a girl can eat."

Kitty giggled. "Don't forget the moldy strawberries and curdled milk."

"And moldy bread and moldy cheese."

"Mom's not a great cook, but at least she does cook. We do everything here while she lays on her couch reading those racy novels, watching TV, and ordering us around."

I stopped and purposely put my hands on my hips. "And don't forget her temper. We never know when it's going to blow like a torpedo."

"Do you mean volcano?"

"OK, fine. Volcano."

"I know. You want to go home. I think she still has another few weeks before her ankle's healed."

I lowered my voice. "We're getting close to the house, so we'd better whisper. Remember she has bat-like hearing."

"She's batty, all right. Let's keep walking and pass the O'Reillys'. Maybe the guys are outside. That'll cheer us up."

I agreed, although I also wondered if we were too forward. They lived next to us, so if the guys wanted to see us, wouldn't they just pop over? As we passed their backyard, I took a moment to sniff the air. "I love the smell of these Mongolian bushes."

"Say what? Do you mean magnolias?" Kitty said, laughing.

"What's the difference?"

"Mongolia is a country. Magnolia is the name of a tree, not a bush."

I shook my head. "Fine. You win." Geography was not my strong suit.

We walked around their front yard but saw no sign of them, so we dawdled back to Aunt Polly's. Just as we reached the back porch, Charlie came running up.

"Hey there!"

Kitty's face lit up. "Hey yourself. What's up?"

"Our friends are having a party tonight, and we wondered if you two would like to join us."

Kitty and I spoke as one voice. "Sure!"

"Great. It's at that park where we went a few days ago. Some of the guys are entertaining with their band."

"Live music. Cool," I said.

"Come over about eight, and we can drive to the park."

Kitty was grinning like she'd been saved from starvation. "Eight! Perfect. See you then."

We were silent for about ten seconds as we entered the porch, and then we looked at each other and mouthed, "Yay! Finally." In truth, it had only been a few days since we'd seen the guys, but in the land of Pollywood, it was an eternity.

We found Aunt Polly lounging in the front living room watching her "stories." She nearly sat up when she saw us.

"Did I hear one of the boys?"

Kitty put on her sweetest voice. "Why, yes, Aunt Polly. Charlie came by and invited us to a gathering tonight. We're going over at eight, if it's all right with you."

"Groups are safer, you said," I reminded her.

Aunt Polly was less than impressed. "Eight o'clock? That's a little late to start a party. What sort of gathering is this?"

Kitty shrugged. "Just kids hanging out, talking, and listening to music, I guess."

Aunt Polly's face screwed up as she thought about this. "Dancing?"

"No," I said. "Probably just talking."

"Yes, lots of talking," Kitty echoed.

Aunt Polly was quiet for so long we thought she was in a coma, but finally she spoke up. "Fine. You may attend the party, but you must be home by ten p.m."

Kitty protested. "Ten? But Aunt Polly, you know we're on summer break. Why do we have to be home so early?"

"Because I said so. I need to go to bed by ten, and I want to be sure you're home safe by then. Either agree to my curfew or don't go. Your choice."

I wasn't sure which eye to focus on since she wasn't wearing one of her patches. "Fine," I said, glancing back and forth at both of her eyes just to make sure. "We'll be home by ten."

The afternoon dragged on as we looked forward to the party. Kitty and I made hamburgers and corn on the cob for dinner and served it on the front porch, which pleased our great-aunt. She sat in a sturdy chair looking out over the lake and didn't seem to notice the humidity rolling over us in waves.

"You'll have to make more of that Parcheesi cake, Cindy," she said.

"Sure. Maybe tomorrow. I don't think we have all the ingredients."

Now that her belly was full, she seemed more amiable. "Looking forward to the party?"

We both nodded.

"Yes, but it's so hot. I'm going to take a bath to cool off," I said.

"Me too," Kitty said, and we eagerly climbed the stairs to get ready for our date.

We bathed and washed our hair, applied nail polish to our fingers and toes, then dressed in skirts, clean cotton T-shirts, and sandals. We rolled waistbands to make our skirts shorter, something the nuns at school forbid. We left our hair long, parted down the middle with no braids or ribbons, then turned to makeup. We liberally applied blue eye shadow and a dusting of blush to our cheeks before we drew eyeliner that swept up at the outside of our eyes like cats, followed by a heavy hand of mascara.

"Mom always says my eyelashes are straight, but this mascara seems to help them curve upward," I said as I swept the magic wand up and over my eyelashes again and again.

"Mom's not exactly a makeup expert. One day I found lipstick and mascara in her drawer, and I asked her about them since she never wears makeup. She told me those were from her wedding. Twenty-one years ago!"

"It must have been all dried out."

"The mascara was. I told her to throw it away, but Mom said, 'Waste not, want not.' She's so cheap."

"Mom calls it thrifty. Gets it from the Scotch side of her family."

"You mean Scottish. Scotch is booze."

I rolled my eyes at her. "Mom says Scotch."

"Mom is wrong."

"Whatever." I applied another round of mascara as if it would save me from a life alone in a cave surrounded by bats. And then I sneezed three times.

I looked in the mirror, hoping to see someone else's face looking back. I wanted to look like the models on the cover of Seventeen magazine—big eyes with eyelashes that winged out, swollen, pouty lips, flat stomachs, and long legs. Instead, I saw a short, pudgy girl with a flat nose, clumped eyelashes, smudged eyeliner, and muddy mascara smeared below my eyes from my violent sneezes. I turned to Kitty, my nose twitching and pools forming in my eyes. "Why am I so plain?"

Kitty turned and saw my dilemma. "Don't cry. It'll only make things worse. Let me help you."

"I'm so fat."

"Don't be silly. You're just curvy. At least you don't have to wear a padded bra." She licked the end of a Q-tip and smoothed out the eyeliner, then removed the puddles of mascara below my eyes. Finally, she found a safety pin to get the clumps out of my eyelashes. As she approached my eyes, I put my hand out to stop her.

"Wait! What if you poke me in the eye?"

"It's fine as long as you don't move. Or sneeze. I'll just pull your eyelashes apart."

I closed my eyes and winced.

"Open your eyes, Cindy. This will only take a moment."

The things we do for beauty. I stood stock-still staring ahead, eyes as wide as they would go. She separated clumps of eyelashes one at a time. I held my breath, afraid that even breathing would render me blind from a pinprick.

"There. Now look in the mirror," she said.

The smudges were gone, and my eyelashes were long and thick without clumps. "Much better. Thank you."

We both finished with some goopy pink lipstick and a spray of Chantilly perfume and headed downstairs, ready for a night of fun.

Aunt Polly came from her kitchen armed with a new package of chocolate-covered graham crackers. When she saw us, she frowned as her eyes took in our short skirts and heavy makeup. "Is this a costume party?"

Kitty answered sweetly. "No, just a fun night of music in the park."

"Where did you get those short skirts?"

"Well, all the girls wear them like this. We don't have miniskirts, so we rolled ours up at the waist," Kitty giggled.

"Roll them back down. You look like hussies. Didn't you say you were just going to listen to music and talk with the boys?"

We rolled the waistbands of our skirts down and tried to laugh off her insults. "Yes, just a fun night in the park," Kitty said as I stood silent, afraid she'd put the kibosh on the whole evening.

Aunt Polly shook her head. "Humph. Be back by ten."

We dashed out of the house before she could change her mind, and as soon as she was out of sight, we rolled our skirts back up.

Jimmy and Charlie were wearing tie-dyed shirts and jean shorts with sandals. They smelled of English Leather and Brut, but at first, I couldn't tell who was wearing which one. The car was ablaze with aromas, with all four of us freshly spritzed.

Jimmy drove with me next to him again which made me somehow feel more mature. Kitty cuddled up to Charlie and sniffed his cheeks. "You smell heavenly. What are you wearing?"

"Brut," Charlie proclaimed as if it were a character trait.

"So, where is this party?" I asked.

Jimmy responded. "Down by the docks in that park we were in before. Some guys we know have a small band named Grassy Marsh, and they're setting up in the pavilion. Should be a groovy night."

Charlie piped up from the backseat. "Get ready. They plan to rock on all night."

I peeked at Kitty in the backseat. "All night?"

Kitty took over. "That sounds like a gas. But we might have a tiny problem."

Jimmy turned away from his driving to look at me. "Oh yeah, what's that?"

I chewed on my lips. "Um. Our great-aunt said we had to be home by ten tonight, not tomorrow morning."

"Whoa, bummer," Charlie said.

"Sorry," Kitty replied.

"I guess we can bring them home and then come back out," Jimmy replied, looking at his brother in the rearview mirror.

I turned in time to see Charlie pull Kitty into an embrace. "Let's make hay while the sun shines."

Kitty snuggled into him. "Sounds nice."

Jimmy soon turned into a tree-lined driveway that rambled through a park lush with evergreens and oak trees. He found a place to park, and we drifted toward the pavilion.

The four of us followed the music and found a crowd of teens enjoying the band. We stayed by the stage, listened to the music, and enjoyed the warm evening and the freedom from adults. Others walked by and greeted Jimmy or Charlie or both.

"School friends," they told us. Occasionally, they'd introduce us to their friends, but it was a casual scene. Several girls lingered closer, and Jimmy turned to chat with them. They were rail-thin, with flowing blond hair and perfect makeup, and were wearing hot pants and bright, form-fitting tank tops.

If Aunt Polly thought we looked like hussies, she should get a load of these floozies, I thought. Secretly I wanted to look just like them. You would have too. Such confidence.

I stood awkwardly, wondering what to do. Charlie had his arm around Kitty's shoulders as they stood nearly attached to each other, listening to the band. They drifted off into the crowd. I felt stupid standing alone, so I pretended to listen to the music of the Grassy Marsh, but after several minutes I tried to become more than wallpaper.

"Hi," I said, turning back to Jimmy and the floozies, interrupting their flirtations.

"Oh yeah," Jimmy said. "This is a family friend who's visiting. Cindy, this is Robin and Marci."

I gave a little wave. "Nice to meet you."

Robin looked me up and down. "Where did you come from?"

"Minneapolis. South Minneapolis by Lake Harriet."

Marci nodded as if that made sense. "Visiting someone locally?"

"My aunt. Well, great-aunt. She hurt her foot, so we're staying here to help her for a few weeks."

"So which high school do you go to?" Marci asked.

"Regina."

"Ray what?"

"Regina High School in Minneapolis."

"Oh, you mean Ra-jeye-na High School! Like vagina! ." Robin and Marci started to laugh.

"It's pronounced Ray-geena."

Jimmy followed the conversation like a ping-pong match and seemed bewildered, unsure which team he was rooting for.

Marci snickered and turned to Jimmy. "Have we played Regina's football team?"

Jimmy opened his mouth to answer, but I barged in, "No. We don't have a football team." This was getting more uncomfortable by the minute.

Robin wrinkled her nose. "No football team? So Raj-eye-na is a school for slow students?" She raised her eyebrows and shot a look toward Jimmy.

"Ray-geena is a girls-only high school," I corrected her. "Not for slow students. In fact, 80 percent of Regina graduates head for college."

"So no football, then."

"No football."

"I suppose no basketball either?" Marci asked.

"No sports teams. At all." Could I make it any clearer to her fuzzy brain? I didn't want to be rude because we Regina girls were taught to be polite in the face of stupidity, hostility, or absurdity, but I had my limits. And if she reached my limits, I might pull her hair or scratch her arms. Because we were ladies, we didn't punch, but pinching and pulling hair were prominent in our playbook for scuffles.

"Is this one of those Catholic girls' schools?" Robin asked.

I took a deep breath and let it out slowly. Very slowly. "Yes." I felt like a cornered animal and wished Kitty was nearby to take the heat with me. Or at least to keep me from lunging at Marci's throat. Robin giggled and flipped her hair over her shoulder. "I suppose you have like fifteen kids in your family?"

"Yup, something like that." I glared back at her, hoping my eyes would become lasers and punish her with boils or cause her hair and teeth to fall out.

Robin and Marci turned their attention back to Jimmy, talking about people I didn't know and events I wasn't invited to. I stood like a statue for as long as I could.

About eleven seconds.

"I'm going for a walk," I said to the wind and stormed off, not sure where to go but sick of the inquisition and rudeness. I tried to crane my neck to look for Kitty, but short necks don't extend much more than the width of a dragonfly's wing. I was only five feet, two inches tall, and my chances of finding anyone in a crowd were less than my chances of finding bigfoot. Kitty and Charlie must have wandered deep into the dense crowd, so I gave up and walked toward the water and out onto a dock. The sky was turning sherbet colors, preparing for sunset. I tried to slow my breathing to keep from crying. I sat down at the end of the dock and dangled my feet inches above the water. Water always calmed me—unless a storm was rolling over it. We lived in the middle of a chain of lakes and a short distance from Minnehaha Creek, so water was always within reach. I relaxed back on my elbows and thought about the last time friends and I rode our bikes to Minnehaha Falls and the fun we had exploring caves. OK, so we didn't have a football team, a basketball team, a rugby team, or even a bowling league, but my friends didn't make me feel like a freak.

Within minutes, I heard my name and ignored the calls, but as they got louder, I realized Jimmy must have spotted me. I mentally rearranged my face as he sat down next to me.

"Hi, kiddo! What's going on?"

"Just needed some air."

He put his arm around my shoulders. "Sorry about all the questions." He handed me his glass of beer. "I brought you this."

"No, thanks."

"They were just curious about your school."

I lifted my chin and looked up at him. "I'm really proud of my school."

"Sure. I think everyone feels that way about their school."

"She made it sound like we're freaks, oddballs, just because it's a girls' school."

"I guess we don't know much about Regina. I'm sure I'd love it. If they'd let me in."

A smile tugged at my face. "I'm sure you would love it. All those girls. You're quite a flirt."

"Me? I'm just friendly."

"It was pretty funny when she thought we had a football team. I can just see us playing in our two-toned saddle shoes and brown knee socks."

Jimmy took a swig of his beer. "That's what you wear?"

"On our feet, yes. We have a gray plaid skirt with a brown wool blazer. Imagine that on the football field."

Jimmy laughed. "You'd need new football digs."

"That's the only flaw you see in this scenario?"

He emptied his glass, then squeezed my shoulders. "You're a nut! Let's take a walk."

We hopped up and walked around the park hand in hand, which felt comforting. He left those floozies to find me, so he must like me. The heaviness from the humid air lifted, along with my spirits. The scene was like something in a movie set, with a gentle breeze dancing off the water cooling the night air, lively music, and happy faces. Jimmy passed a few more classmates, waved, and kept going, not stopping to chat.

As we got closer to the band area, they started to play "The House of the Rising Sun."

Jimmy swung me around and said, "Let's dance." We danced and howled along with the words. The Grassy Marsh was so loud no one could hear us anyway. Later they played a collection of peppier songs, and there on the grass, we shimmied, twisted, and danced the Watusi. I'd never felt so free, except for the times I stepped on his toes. But he laughed it off. I felt almost grown-up.

Kitty and I loved playing loud music on our house's third floor and practicing the latest dance moves, so I knew most of the steps. Dancing to a live band with Jimmy was better than anything I could have imagined. When the band played a slow song, he wrapped me in his arms, and I could feel his muscles. I put my head on his chest and heard his heartbeat. His actual heart! I couldn't believe I was dancing on a cloud of grass with… Jimmy. The guy I'd had a crush on for over a year.

I looked up at him as we danced the Teddy Bear, and he bent down and kissed me. And again. And again. And then I heard Kitty calling me.

"Cindy, we've got to go. It's 9:45, and we turn into pumpkins at 10."

Jimmy didn't let go. "What'll she do to you if you're late?"

"Turn me into a frog? Carve me up and hide my body? I don't know."

Jimmy bent and whispered in my ear, "Stay a little longer. This party's just getting started."

I nearly melted.

Chapter 23

KITTY WAS THERE AT OUR SIDE. "Come on. We've got to get out of here."

Jimmy let me go, and it was like dragging two magnets apart. We followed Kitty and Charlie to the car and slipped inside it.

On the drive back to Aunt Polly's, Kitty tapped the back of my seat. "I have an idea. Aunt Polly usually goes to bed at ten, so if you want to wait a bit, we could pretend we're going upstairs to sleep, and then we could escape down the ladder."

"What? Are you crazy?" I asked.

Jimmy nodded. "I wondered why your dad left the ladder up. Maybe he's trying to help us out here."

The thought of climbing down a rickety ladder terrified me. "I'm sure he didn't think about us using it. It's probably not even safe."

Charlie's enthusiasm was palpable. "If the ladder's safe

enough for your dad, it'll be fine for you. I mean, he must weigh lots more than you girls."

"I sure hope so," I mumbled under my breath.

When we approached the house, Kitty finalized the plans. "OK. You two drop us off, and we'll go inside and convince her we're going to bed. We'll wait a few minutes and then turn the lights on and off in the upstairs sun porch. Then, hopefully, we'll be able to get a window open, and we'll climb down."

I still wasn't convinced of the plan. "What if she hears us?"

"Her room is on the other side of the house."

"What if we can't get the window open by the ladder?"

Charlie answered. "We'll watch to see what window you open and make sure the ladder is beneath it."

"OK, but what if I fall off the ladder?"

Jimmy answered. "What if, what if, what if… Come on, Cindy. What if you live your whole life afraid and never do anything daring?"

I took a shaky breath. "OK, let's do this." My brain was working overtime, wrestling with the angel and devil both breathing in my ear.

"What's the worst that can happen?" my evil self asked.

"I could fall and break my neck and die," my angel replied.

"Yes, but at least I would have been kissed by a gorgeous guy," my evil self replied.

"True, that," my angel replied and settled the matter.

The guys walked us to the house and pretended to say good night with chaste kisses. Kitty and I made a big show of saying good night and walked past the ladder and into the back porch. We let the screen door slam to alert Aunt Polly that we were home and startle her awake. She abruptly awoke on her lounger in the front living room where Peyton Place was just ending on her black-and-white television.

She shook the cobwebs from her sleepy brain. "Oh, girls. You're back."

I emphasized our punctuality. "Yes, right on time, just like you asked us."

Aunt Polly stretched her arms a little bit. Not over her head like most people do, but her arms stiffened a bit and flexed. "Did you have fun?"

Kitty's cheeks were still flaming. "Yes. There was a band and music, and… we talked a lot." Sure we did!

"Well, I certainly hope the fellas behaved"," Aunt Polly said. "If you want some cocoa, fix it yourselves."

I faked a yawn. "Not for me. 'I'm worn out. I think 'I'll head up to bed"."

Kitty followed. "Me too. Tired out. Good night, Aunt Polly"."

Aunt Polly slowly got up from her lounger, turned off her television, and headed to her first-floor bedroom, while we tramped upstairs, nearly tripping over each other as we pretended to go to bed.

Kitty and I whispered as we waited until we thought our great-aunt was asleep. We reapplied lipstick and a spray of perfume. Then we crept down the back hallway, hopped over the hole in the floor, and quietly stepped into the upstairs porch.

We brought towels to swing around our heads to collect cobwebs so they wouldn't be plastered to our hair. I mean, what guy wants to kiss a gal with a wad of cobwebs clinging to her locks?

The porch was often used as a sleeping porch on hot nights, lined with cots and walls of windows. Each cot held an old wool-green army blanket, which held a snoot full of dust. The summer screens 'hadn't been installed in probably twenty or fifty years, so we were stuck trying to loosen the storm windows. With no tools. We knew that even if our great-aunt heard us going into the porch, we could always say we were sleeping on one of the cots. It would be believable since she had no idea of the room's condition, as she likely hadn't climbed the stairs to the second floor since World War II.

I walked to the window closest to the ladder. I yanked and pulled with no luck. Kitty pushed me aside and put her back into the attempt. Nothing.

She looked panicked. "What now"?"

I hugged my stomach. "Um, let's try the other windows."

"But they aren't near the ladder."

"The guys can move it. Or we can forget this plan and go to bed."

"Never! What's the matter with you, Cindy? This is our chance to have some fun for once."

I was rocking back and forth on my heels. "I'm afraid of getting caught or falling off the ladder."

"Shush. No more of that. We need to find a window that will open. Cindy, focus!"

We took turns moving from window to window on the porch, banging our shoulders against each to see if one would loosen.

"We're making too much noise. She'll hear us," I said. "Maybe you can slip through that hole in the floor."

Kitty glared at me. "Not funny! Even if I could slip through it, you'd have to follow. So think about that. And didn't Dad just fix that hole?"

"Yeah, but he said he needs more shingles or something."

Kitty stage whispered, "Let's go down the hall to the next bedroom on this side of the house and try those windows."

Again, we tiptoed down the hall and approached the windows with hope. The first two were painted shut, but the third window budged a bit. Just a sliver. Kitty and I looked at each other and nearly squealed. We took turns pushing, pulling, and cajoling the stiff window until finally, miraculously, it opened enough to allow our escape. But of course, it was a long way from the ladder.

"Now what?" Kitty whispered.

"Maybe I could run down the stairs and move the ladder, then we can climb down," I suggested.

She spoke through gritted teeth. "Cindy! We don't need the ladder if we can run down the stairs. But we can't take the stairs because we'll wake Aunt Polly."

"No need to get in a snit. I see your point."

Kitty shook her head and took a few deep breaths. "Let's blink the lights in this window and see if we can get Jimmy and Charlie's attention."

I clutched my stomach again, unable to control the shivers of nerves pulsing through me. "Sure, and their parents. The whole neighborhood's going to think something's up."

Kitty put her hand on her hip and pushed her face close to mine. "What's your big idea, then?"

I backed away. "Let's just turn on the light in this room and hang out and whisper their names."

"And wait for the bats and the bugs."

"We have to find a way to talk to them, Kitty."

"We'll take turns at the window. You first."

I shook my head and muttered. "This whole thing was your idea. You should go first." I turned on the overhead light.

"Fine. But it'll be your fault if I eat a bug or get bitten by a bat." Kitty hung out the window and shouted as quietly as one can shout while whispering, "Charlie! Jimmy!" Then she popped her head back into the room, and we waited. Nothing. "Your turn. I think I swallowed a bug."

I stepped over to the window, bent down, and thrust my head and shoulders out the opening into the dark night. "Jimmy! Charlie!" In a few moments, the guys appeared outside of the window.

Jimmy shook his head. "What are you doing over there?"

"We couldn't get the stupid window open. This is the only one that'll budge," I said. "Please move the ladder."

Charlie and Jimmy pulled the aluminum ladder toward them, and each took an end. The metal complained at the movements, and we hushed them from upstairs. When they set it against the wall just below our window, I heard a small scrape and held my breath for a moment to make sure the coast was clear.

Kitty turned to me. "You go first."

I was shaking all over. "Why me?"

She arched an eyebrow. "Because you'll chicken out after I've gone down, and then I'll have to climb back up and throw you out the window."

I started to hyperventilate. "I see your point. I wish I wasn't wearing a skirt. I didn't think about them standing on the lawn waiting for us. Maybe I should go change."

She grabbed my arm and pushed me toward the window. "Don't think about it. Just get going. We've got to get out of here before she hears us."

I bent in half and thrust my right foot out the window into the nothingness while I clung to the windowsill filled with dead bugs and paint slivers. I wiggled my foot around and heard Jimmy doing his best whisper-shout, "More to the left." I was never great with directions, as I told you before. Soon I heard Jimmy again. "The other left!" Was he making fun of me?

My foot connected with the ladder's top rung, and my knees started shaking. Have you ever been terrified of heights? Really, really terrified? I thought I'd throw up, but then I remembered that I rarely throw up. That was Kitty's mode. "I don't think I can do this."

Kitty held my shoulders. "Yes, you can. Don't look down."

"What if I fall?"

"Jimmy will catch you. Won't that be romantic?"

"Sure. I'd probably crush him. Then I'd be charged with his murder."

Kitty gritted her teeth. "Cindy, stop it. Now look at me and stick your left leg out and onto the ladder. The party will be over by the time you get down the way things are going."

She helped steady the top half of me while I cautiously backed my right foot out the window and onto the ladder. Jimmy held it steady.

"I wish I was wearing prettier panties," I said as both feet struck metal and my upper half was still inside the porch. As if I had prettier panties. Who was I kidding? Mom only let us wear white cotton high-waist granny-panties without lace or even the days of the week written on the fanny.

Kitty shook her head. "Too late. Now walk down a few rungs."

Carefully, I stretched one foot and then the other down one rung and then two before I stopped. "Kitty, remember to leave the window open a crack so we can get back in later on."

She nodded impatiently. "Right. Will do. Now focus."

My legs shook violently as I climbed down at the speed of an inchworm.

I missed the last few rungs of the ladder and fell gracelessly onto the ground, popped up, pulled the hem of my skirt down, and tried to make light of it. Jimmy shook his head and laughed, then gave me a hug. "You did it!"

Charlie held the ladder for Kitty, who seemed to glide effortlessly down as if she performed this task regularly. When Kitty was nearly on the ground, Charlie grabbed her by the waist, swung her around, and hugged her. We silently screamed a victory chant, ran like our clothes were on fire, and hopped into the Barracuda.

Jimmy held up his hand instead of turning on the engine. "Wait. Everyone out," he ordered. "We can't start the engine without causing suspicion. Kitty, sit in the driver's seat and steer. Everyone else, push." He put the car in neutral, and she slid into the driver's seat. The three of us pushed the Barracuda down the lane until it was nearly onto the main road, and it was safe to start the engine without waking the neighborhood. Kitty got out and Jimmy, Charlie, and I climbed back in. Jimmy started the car, and we were off.

Once again, I felt the thrill of freedom and the fear of consequences. But for a few glorious hours, I pushed the fear to the back of my mind. I was alive. I climbed down a rickety ladder and lived.

"Let's grab some grub before the drive-in's closed," Jimmy said.

I nodded. "Sounds good." I liked the way this guy was always hungry.

We headed to the same drive-in restaurant as before.

As we sat in the parking lot slurping chocolate malts and munching crisp, salty fries, Kitty cut through the silence. "Aunt Polly had a boyfriend."

"Seriously?" Jimmy said. "I don't mean to be rude, but I can't imagine it."

I giggled. "We can't either, but she wasn't always old and, you know, huge. There's still so much we can't figure out. Just when we think we've found an answer, we find more questions. But it has helped pass the time."

Jimmy looked at me with something like hurt in his eyes. "I hope you think we've helped you two pass the time."

"Yes, of course. I didn't mean it that way. You and Charlie have been lifesavers," I said.

Charlie thumped Jimmy on the back. "Literally lifesavers at least once, right?"

Jimmy nodded. "Oh yes, the time you got knocked off the boat." He looked at me and smiled.

My face turned red, and I was glad it was dark in the car. "Yes, thank you for that."

We finished eating, drove to the park, and were greeted by music, swelling crowds, and unfamiliar smells. The party was in full swing, with people everywhere.

Jimmy opened his door. "Let's party!" He reached for my hand.

"Wow, this has gotten huge," I said, sniffing the air and trying to figure out the bitter smell.

"Far out!" Charlie said.

We melted into the masses, with Kitty and Charlie behind us.

Chapter 24

I'D NEVER SEEN SUCH A CROWD. But in truth, I'd only been to a few parties that included guys. Before high school, we weren't allowed to go to boy-girl parties or even to speak to boys on the playgrounds in elementary school. And now... well, we didn't get many invitations. Maybe if we had brothers who brought their friends home, it would be different, but going to an all-girl school, as wonderful as it was, had its limitations.

Jimmy and I surged into the crowd, hand in hand. We soon lost track of Kitty and Charlie as we pushed toward the stage area where kids were dancing. The night turned cool, which was a relief from the day's humidity, but the air had an odd scent. As we roamed through the crowds, I hoped we didn't see Marci and Robin from my earlier encounter. New friends greeted him, and occasionally they held out a cigarette. They weren't a brand I recognized.

"I didn't know you smoked," I shouted over the noise.

"Different kind of smoke. Want a puff?"

"What is it?"

"A reefer."

"A what?"

"Don't tell me you haven't tried weed!"

I wrinkled my nose. "You're smoking a weed? Like dandelion?"

Jimmy threw his head back and laughed. "Mary Jane."

I shook my head. "A weed named Mary Jane. Must be something you grow in Minnetonka."

Jimmy sucked on the reefer and held in the smoke until it spurted out of his nose. He barked out a cough. He put his face close to mine and grinned. "You must be the most sheltered person on the planet. Come on! Give it a try."

I didn't want to, but I didn't want him to think I was living in a convent. He held it close to my lips, and I sucked in a small puff. And then hacked an unladylike bark of my own. "That's horrible."

He smiled. "It's an acquired taste."

"Why would you want to acquire it?"

"Because of the way it makes you feel. Try again and hold it in a little longer."

I can be fun, I told myself. He held it to my lips. I gave it a try, this time taking a bigger puff and attempting to suck it into my lungs, but instead I erupted like a car backfiring. I felt my brain twitch. Was that it? Was that what I was supposed to be feeling? I swayed slightly. "Whoa."

"Groovy, right?" Jimmy said, looking into my eyes and grabbing my arm. "Let's dance."

We kicked off our sandals and danced on the dew-covered grass. My head was spinning as if I were standing in the middle of a merry-go-round.

Jimmy pulled me to him, and our dancing turned wilder. Soon one of his friends approached with a large glass of beer. "Jimmy, there's another keg over by the dock. Here's one to get you started."

"Thanks, man," Jimmy said. He took a gulp of the beer, then offered me some. I was thirsty, so I swallowed the bitter ale and made a face.

"What? No beer either?" Jimmy frowned.

I shrugged my shoulders. "More of a chocolate malt gal, I guess."

He laughed and swatted me on the butt. "That explains this."

"Hey now. What do you mean by that?"

"You're well padded."

I couldn't believe he said that. "You mean fat!"

"No, just a little plump. I like girls with a bit of flesh on their bones."

I put a hand on one hip. "Unlike most of your classmates?" Most of the Minnetonka girls rivaled the models in magazines, with no shortage of confidence or cleavage.

Jimmy shook his head to indicate the subject was closed. He finished his beer, grabbed my hand, and twirled me around. "Don't be mad." I tried to shake off what felt like an insult. Probably was an insult. But he seemed to like me as I was. Didn't he? I twirled the question in my mind as we danced the Swim, the Shimmy, and the Twist.

When the Grassy Marsh took a break from playing, Jimmy went for another glass of beer while I stayed behind by a tree. I looked around to find Kitty but couldn't see her in the crowd, which seemed to grow by the minute. Even without the band playing, it was difficult to hear anyone. When Jimmy came back, he offered me a sip of his beer.

I wrinkled my nose after swallowing. "Still tastes the same," I shouted.

Jimmy shook his head. "Can't believe you don't like it. Woo hoo! I love summer." He threw his head back and howled like a coyote.

His sudden enthusiasm startled me, but I wanted to show him I was no stick-in-the-mud, so I copied his howl. He chuckled his approval and pulled me closer for a kiss, holding me with one arm around my waist and the beer in his other hand. We kissed again and again.

The band soon returned from break, and I was relieved to be dancing again since I couldn't hear Jimmy well over the crowd and couldn't think of anything to say. Kissing him was amazing, but I didn't want it to go any further.

Another couple dancing nearby waved to Jimmy and passed him a reefer, which he inhaled and again put to my lips. Despite my nagging conscience, I took another hit. Jimmy finished the reefer and pulled me closer to dance next to him, even during the fast dances.

So this was what summer was like for Minnetonka kids. Parties, sailing, beer, and reefers. It was a different universe from our world of babysitting, reading, and rules. Rules at school, more at home. In eighth grade, a group of us girls went to a movie together, and the boys from our class found out and came and sat in a row behind us and planted M&M'S candies in our ratted hair. We giggled at them and flirted, but went our separate ways when the movie ended. Someone in our class spotted us and reported it to the nuns at school on Monday. The nuns called our parents and warned them that we were headed for a life of ruin, babies out of wedlock, flunking out of school, the lot. All because we flirted with boys at a movie. Maybe the nuns were right. My head was exploding with guilt.

After his third beer, Jimmy kissed my neck and then held my arms over my head with one hand while he kissed my lips repeatedly. I responded to his kisses, but when he let go of my arms, and his hands wandered over my breasts, I pulled back. My head was fuzzy, and the sensations pulsing through me were thrilling and terrifying.

"I can't do this," I said and backed away from him.

"Sorry," he said. "Want to go for a walk?" We strolled away from the crowds into a part of the park umbrellaed with oaks. As we approached a secluded area, Jimmy stopped and again pulled me close to him. I felt his sultry breath in my ear as he kissed my neck. He backed me up against a large tree and pinned me with his body until I could feel the scratchy bark against my legs as he reached under my skirt.

"Jimmy, stop," I said, trying to wiggle away from him.

"Come on, Cindy, loosen up," Jimmy slurred, still holding me against the tree.

"I just wanted to dance. This is too much for me."

He tilted his neck back. "I thought you Catholic girls wanted more action."

I shoved him and untangled myself from his grip. I wanted to slap him but didn't. "Is that what you think of me?"

He stared at me, then shook his head like he was resetting his brain. "I didn't mean it. I thought you were enjoying it."

"I was, but things are going too fast. I'd better go home," I said and turned toward the crowd of dancers.

Jimmy caught my hand. "Cindy, Cindy, why don't you chill out? Let's just stay and groove with the crowd."

"I can't. This doesn't feel right to me."

"Right to you? I thought you liked it. Now what? You planning on becoming a nun? Or you want to end up alone like your aunt?"

"Great-aunt! And just because I don't want to be with you doesn't mean I'll end up alone."

"Oh, so it's me. Thanks a lot."

"Jimmy, you're stoned and drunk. It's a turn-off."

"Turn-off. You've done nothing but cozy up to me all summer. Just when I think I'm giving you what you want, you clam up."

"Sorry if I've misled you, but I've had enough. I want to go."

I pulled away from him and walked into the crowd looking everywhere for Kitty. I had no idea where I was going, but I was tired of fending off Jimmy's advances, as enticing as they were. I finally found Kitty and Charlie dancing and kissing in a dark corner of the park.

"Kitty, hi. I'm ready to go."

"What?" she yelled above the music.

"I want to go!" I said louder.

Charlie looked at me and shouted back, "Where's Jimmy?"

I shrugged. "I thought he was following me."

Kitty looked concerned. "What's wrong?"

Tears threatened to spill. "I don't want to talk about it. I just want to leave."

She could see the concern in my eyes and turned to Charlie and mouthed, "Sorry. We'd better go."

We looked for Jimmy and finally found him slumped under a tree.

Charlie grabbed him under the arms. "Come on, Jimmy. Get up." He staggered to his feet.

Kitty looked at me. "What happened?"

I just shook my head.

Kitty said, "I have my driver's license, so I can drive home if you don't have yours yet, Charlie."

Charlie dug into Jimmy's pocket, pulled out the keys, and handed them to Kitty. "Be my guest."

Jimmy leaned against me in the backseat as we drove back to their home in silence. When we arrived, Kitty and I said we could find our way back into the house, but Charlie and Jimmy insisted on helping us. Jimmy seemed to have regained some of his senses.

Aunt Polly rarely locked the doors, so we decided to see if

we could sneak in without waking her. The back porch door was unlocked, so we crept through the porch, but the door into the house was locked. We tiptoed back out of the porch.

"We're going to try the front door," I whispered. "If we get in, we'll blink a light."

Kitty and I crept around to the front of the house, but that door was also locked.

"Shoot! Now we'll have to go up the ladder," I said.

Charlie and Jimmy were waiting in the yard, but Jimmy was still out of sorts.

"Still locked?" Jimmy shouted.

"Shush," we all said to him, and Kitty and I nodded that yes, the doors were locked.

Kitty turned and kissed Charlie passionately and said she'd go up the ladder first. Jimmy and I stood several feet apart, trying not to watch them. Finally, Kitty started up the ladder. She was halfway up when a light came on and a giant marshmallow carrying a gun appeared. It was Aunt Polly in a long white nightgown with a hunting rifle.

Chapter 25

"Who's there?" our great-aunt hollered.

Kitty climbed down the ladder.

Aunt Polly opened the door to the porch, pointed the rifle into the darkness, and thundered onto the porch. "What's going on?"

In unison, the four of us shouted, "Don't shoot."

She stepped outside and swung around to face us, pointing the rifle in our direction as her eye tried to adjust to the darkness. "Who's there?"

"Aunt Polly, it's us. Kitty and I."

"And Jimmy and Charlie," Kitty added. "We couldn't get in because the doors were locked."

Aunt Polly looked at the four of us and then at the ladder. She walked closer to us, still pointing the gun, and I realized her glass eye must still be sitting in a dish by her bedside. I could hardly look at her.

"You girls thought you were going to climb up the ladder?" She was incredulous.

Kitty was eager to smooth things over. "Yes, we didn't want to bother you."

Aunt Polly sniffed the air. "Bother me? You were out drinking and carousing?"

Charlie stepped out. "Miss Schultz, they weren't drinking. We were just dancing and having fun. Now, maybe you could put down the rifle."

"Well, the fun's over." She gestured with the gun. "Get in the house, girls, and go to bed. Boys, remove that ladder. We'll discuss this in the morning." She waited to make sure the guys placed the ladder on the ground.

Kitty and I walked in the house like chickens about to be slaughtered. We quickly climbed the stairs into the safety of our room. Since Aunt Polly rarely if ever climbed stairs, we wouldn't have to face her until breakfast.

Kitty whispered to me, "I didn't know she had a gun."

"Does she know how to use it?"

"I doubt it."

"How creepy was that seeing her without her glass eye?" I shuddered.

"Eewee. I know. I didn't know it came out."

"I guess there aren't veins and ligaments or thingies to hold it in. Gives me the shivers."

Kitty looked worried. "Do you think she'll send us home?"

I shrugged. "I don't know. I'm ready to go home."

"Why? What was going on with you and Jimmy?"

"I don't want to talk about it. I'm exhausted, and I just want to go to bed."

"Are you sure?"

"Yes, Kitty, I'm sure. Just tired. It's been an insane day, and I'm ready for it to be over. I think my legs are still shaking from going down that ladder."

We changed and climbed into bed. For once, I was happy to pull the sheet over my head to keep the bugs away so Kitty couldn't see my tears. I tossed and turned, asking myself what I was doing with a guy like Jimmy.

He was using me. I thought back to our conversations and the mild insults that ran through them like a thread of chocolate in fudge ripple ice cream. Not that I was thinking about ice cream, because I wasn't. He basically said I was naive, chubby, and odd. And he felt because of all that, I'd be… easy. But my reputation wasn't up for grabs, and I was done with Jimmy. Not a great night for sleeping, with my mind like jumping beans, but finally the voices quieted and I slipped into dreamland.

When I awoke the following day, my head was still foggy. My world seemed unsteady.

Kitty was getting dressed and turned to me when she saw I was awake. "Wow, did I sleep well after all that dancing. But I'm dreading talking to Aunt Polly."

I nodded. "What do you think she'll do to us?"

"Make us drink curdled cocoa? Eat moldy strawberries? Moldy cheese? No, wait! She's already insisted we do all of that."

"Let's just call Mom and go home."

"Dad will kill us if he finds out we used the ladder to escape."

"Yes, but Aunt Polly is bound to tell him, so we'll have to face him sometime."

Kitty plopped back onto her bed and faced me. "But go home? We're having so much fun."

I looked out the window toward the lake and thought about last night. I sighed. "Are we?"

"Cindy, don't you want to see Jimmy again? It looked like you two were having a blast."

I shrugged. "I'm not sure."

"If we go home, all we'll do all summer is babysit our sisters. Is that what you want?"

"I thought you wanted to get a job as a carhop and earn some money."

"Yes, I did, but if we leave now, I won't get to see Charlie until when? Next summer?"

I picked at my bedspread. "You never know. Maybe he could come to Minneapolis to see you."

She searched my face. "Don't you like Jimmy anymore?"

"I don't want to talk about it. Let's go down and face the music."

We slowly descended the hardwood stairs and skulked into the front room like prisoners waiting for their sentence. Aunt Polly was up and already watching game shows on television.

"I thought you girls were never going to get up. I suppose with all your carousing, you were tired," she charged as we marched in front of her. I was relieved to see her glass eye was back in place.

We nodded. Then Kitty put on her sweetest voice and forced a smile while I lurked behind her. "Good morning, Aunt Polly. How are you today?"

She blasted back like a shrill whistle, "Well, someone, or rather some folks, disturbed my sleep last night and gave me quite a fright. How do you think I am?"

Kitty's voice lost a bit of its pep. "Tired, I suppose. We're sorry we gave you a fright."

I nodded. "Yes, sorry, Aunt Polly."

"I told you girls to be home by ten so I'd know you were safe. Never in a million years did I think you'd pull a stunt like this and climb out a window."

Kitty seemed up for the fight. "We just wanted to stay at the party. They had a live band, and things were just getting started when we had to leave. And besides, we have to babysit our little sisters all the time at home, and we aren't allowed to go out like other kids our age."

"It's true. We rarely go to parties or even out for pizza."

Aunt Polly wasn't buying what we were selling. "Enough excuses. What you did was wrong and dangerous. I have half a mind to call your father."

Kitty and I exchanged quick glances. Calling our father would mean we'd be grounded for months. Maybe years.

"Please don't call Dad. He'll make us go home. Don't you want us to stay and help you while your ankle heals?" Kitty asked.

Aunt Polly gave that some thought. "I enjoy having you girls here, but if I have to worry about you sneaking out every night, it's not worth it."

"We won't sneak out again. We promise. Right, Cindy?"

"Sure. I doubt there'll be any more parties."

"It's not just the parties I'm worried about. You two are spending a lot of time alone with those boys. This could put you in a life-altering situation."

Kitty wasn't giving up. "No. They're great guys, aren't they, Cindy?"

"Yeah, sure," I shrugged with little enthusiasm.

Aunt Polly gave me the evil eye. I shrank from her piercing one-eyed glare and looked down at the floor for a moment. "Cindy? What's going on with you and Jimmy?"

I snapped back. "Nothing. Just having fun." Nothing that I wanted to talk about, anyway. And certainly not with my elderly great-aunt. Aunt Polly continued to stare at me, and I looked away in case mind reading was another of her superpowers. "Things can get out of control with boys, and then it'll ruin your life. Not just your reputation. And if one of you gets pregnant on my watch, your parents will never forgive me."

"Pregnant! No! Nothing like that is happening," I spit back. When would this conversation end?

"I need to think about this. If you girls stay, I don't want you going out at night alone with those boys. You'll need to regain my trust."

We nodded. That was our punishment. Supervised visits

like they have in prisons. Or chaperones like they had in the 19th century. It was either that or going home to face Dad.

Aunt Polly sat a little taller. "Now, I'm starving. Let's get on with breakfast."

That was our cue to start serving her, and we'd better make it snappy. She had the home-court advantage and used it every chance she got.

Fortunately for us, Aunt Polly had a hair appointment after breakfast, so once again, we looked forward to a few hours alone. She came out of her room wearing a purple floral dress and matching purple eye patch, grabbed her oversized black purse, and slowly made her way to her car. She was too mad to ask us to help her, which was fine by me. We waited until we heard the usual backfire from her engine and knew she was gone and couldn't hear our conversations. Unless her superpower hearing extended for miles, which I hoped it didn't.

"It looks like she's going to let us stay," Kitty started. "And hopefully she won't call Dad."

"True. Dad would blow his stack. He'd probably send you to join a convent."

"As if it's mandatory that each family sacrifice one girl. Well, it's not going to be me."

I let out a sigh. "Actually, a cloistered convent doesn't look so bad right now. We either go home and face Dad's wrath and Mom's scorn, or we stay here as our great-aunt's personal house servants."

Kitty snapped back at me. "You can't be serious about

the convent. I mean, they aren't allowed to talk all day. How would you survive?"

"You mean how would YOU survive, Kitty. Besides, they only take virgins, and the way you're going, you won't qualify for long."

She huffed her indignation, hands on her hips. "That's not funny."

"OK, well, maybe you should think about where you and Charlie are headed."

"What about you and Jimmy? I saw you dancing like two gyrating lizards."

I shook my head. "Nothing's going to happen. And I don't think lizards gyrate."

"Well, I'm not willing to give up. Going home's not an option. Let's hope this thing blows over in a few days, and we can go back to sailing, swimming, and movies."

I picked at my fingernails. "I guess so."

"Cindy, you don't sound very excited. What's going on?"

"Let's finish reading those letters while we have the chance. She should be gone at least another hour."

"OK, but I know something happened between you two. When you're ready to talk about it, I'm here."

"Thanks, Sis."

"Let's get back to our detective work. It'll get our minds off our troubles."

Chapter 26

WE TOOK THE LETTERS from our dresser drawer and searched for ones we hadn't read yet. There were a few from Aunt Polly's parents, which we arranged by date. Then we plopped down on our beds to begin reading.

I did a quick review. "Let's look for the ones around 1917 and start there. We know before this she was either at college, on a cruise, or hanging out in France. But she came home for a while and joined the Red Cross when America got into the war."

Kitty gestured with an unopened envelope. "And her sweetheart was called to France. Don't forget that. How romantic to go searching all over France for her lover. Wait. Lover? Do you think he was?" Kitty said.

I scrunched up my face, disgusted. "I have no idea. Nothing about Aunt Polly seems romantic." I rifled through the pile and held up a letter. "Here. I found one dated October 21, 1917: 'Dear Polly, we're relieved you're back safely in the U.S.

Why not come back to Colorado? Surely the summer home is drafty, and winter will be here soon. Please consider traveling west. Love, Mother.'"

"Any more from 1917?"

I handed one to her and then read a different letter aloud. "This one is from November 15, 1917: 'Dear Polly, we hope you are well. Your father and I would love you to join us for Thanksgiving. We're sending money for train fare, so please don't disappoint us. Love, Mother.'"

"This must be the next one. December 12, 1917: 'Dear Polly, we're so happy you visited us for Thanksgiving. It's wise that you stay in the summer home away from others. I'm working with a doctor who will help our situation. Please stay well. Love, Mother.' So was she sick?"

I frowned. "Sounds like it. But whatever it was, she survived. If she was sick, why would they want her to stay in the drafty summer home which was never winterized? Wouldn't that make her sicker?"

Kitty gazed out the dirty window for a moment. "Why didn't she return to her parents when she came back from France?"

I rubbed my cheek. "Maybe she wanted to be alone."

"But why? And didn't she need a job?"

"Good point. She went to college and was trained to teach school, so what was she doing? I wonder if we could ask her about her career. Maybe she'd explain a few things without realizing we were poking around in her past."

Kitty became more animated. "Right. Maybe if we act

interested in her career, she'll reveal more about her life. We are interested, so she should be flattered, wouldn't you think?"

I felt lighter. "You're right. She should be happy to share her history. Our other grandpa is always going on about things that happened when he was a kid."

"How many times have we heard Grandpa say, 'When I was your age…'?"

I sat up taller. "True. This isn't spying. We're on a noble pursuit of the past."

The burning inquisition into Aunt Polly's past kept our minds off the festering plague of trouble we were in. There were no more letters from her mother, so we were forced to confront the present.

"We need a plan. She'll be home soon," I said.

Kitty stood and stretched. "Let's surprise her with lunch and act as if nothing's happened. Maybe you can make a cake again."

"Good idea. Let's ply her with sugar and hope she forgets."

"Start baking." We hid the letters and tore down the stairs.

I found a spice cake mix and put the cake in the oven to bake, knowing its power over Aunt Polly. Well, over me too, if I was honest. You feel the same, don't you?

We prepared a lunch of tuna fish sandwiches, carrots, and potato chips, Aunt Polly's favorite, served with cola, also her favorite.

When we heard her car backfire, we arranged our faces into angelic expressions and enthusiastically greeted her.

Kitty opened the door and helped her into the house. "Doesn't your hair look nice, Aunt Polly."

Aunt Polly seemed a bit skeptical but played along. "Thank you, Kitty. What were you girls up to while I was gone?"

"Up to? We were reading again, and we made a delicious lunch."

"Lunch sounds great." She sniffed the air. "Do I smell cake?"

"Yes. Cindy made a spice cake."

"With Parcheesi frosting?" She was falling under the magic cake spell.

"I'll make the frosting after lunch. Shall we eat on the front porch? Such a lovely day."

Kitty was a bit over eager. "Yes, just have a seat, and we'll bring the lunch right out."

Aunt Polly shuffled out to the porch, and I whispered to Kitty in the kitchen as we did final preparations, "Don't be too obvious."

"I'm not sure that's possible, but I'll try."

We carried the plates to the porch, set them on the wobbly table, and Aunt Polly dove into her sandwich and chips with gusto. When she finished, we were still eating. I was afraid she might reach for my plate, so I moved my chair back and kept hold of my plate.

Kitty started probing. "Aunt Polly, do you enjoy teaching?"

"Yes, why do you ask?"

"I'm still trying to decide what to major in. I've only got

two more years of high school. Did you start teaching in New Mexico right after you graduated?"

Aunt Polly slurped her cola. "No. My parents treated me to a cruise around the world. I was gone for three months."

"Wow! That must have cost a fortune," I said.

"Don't be vulgar, Cindy. It's not polite to discuss money. Yes, my father was a man of means and prominent in the state. He was proud that his two daughters graduated from college before women even got the right to vote."

Kitty continued. "What about your mother? How did she feel?"

"Actually, my mother was also a college graduate and considered herself a suffragette, working for women to get the right to vote."

My mouth was hanging open. "Far out! That's so cool. But were you alone on the cruise? I mean, did your sister or a friend go with you?"

"There were many other passengers on the cruise, and I was friendly with several since we were on the ship together for so long."

Kitty brightened. "Did you meet anyone special?"

I nearly ducked when she lobbed this question, but Aunt Polly was in a nostalgic mood.

"I met several wonderful friends. In fact, I later went to France to spend time with one."

"Ooh la la. A Frenchman?" Kitty asked.

Aunt Polly's eyes narrowed at Kitty. "I didn't say it was a man. It was an American who was doing some work for a company in France. I minored in French in college, and my cruise only stopped for a week in Paris, so I thought it'd be fun to spend more time there."

Kitty was dreamy. "I'd love to travel like that. How long did you stay in Paris?"

Aunt Polly sat back in her chair. "Let's see. I think for about four months, and then I returned to this lake home."

I scrunched up my face. "But your parents were living in Colorado, weren't they?"

"Yes. You girls are certainly inquisitive today. What's gotten into you?"

Kitty took a sip of her cola. "I guess we started thinking about our futures and then realized we don't know much about what you were doing when you were our ages."

Aunt Polly looked dubious but not angry. "Well, that's enough for today. It's time for my stories." She got up, ambled to the front living room, and turned on her television to watch soap operas. Kitty and I collected the dishes and followed behind her on our way to the kitchen. When we finished washing the dishes and cleaning the kitchen, we decided to take a walk.

The sun was bright as we walked along the lake side of the houses and pondered our situation. Leaves on the oaks overhead had turned from a light spring green into deep emerald hues. A fishy smell tickled my nose, wafting up from the lake just down the hill and across the road. Ever-present seagulls laughed at each other and splashed in the water hunting for prey. I envied their simple existence. My life suddenly seemed as complicated as the mystery surrounding hot air balloons. At least, it was a mystery to me.

I threw a penny into the Ericksons' wishing well. "Aunt Polly seems to be in a good mood. At least she didn't threaten to call Dad," I said.

"I think we threw her off by asking about her travels. I'll bet that's where she met Anthony Walker. How can we drop his name without revealing that we found the letters?"

"Oh, Kitty, I think we're on thin ice here. We'd better not press our luck."

"Still so many unanswered questions. Like what happened to Margaret? Is she still alive?"

"True. And why did she have to go to France to tell Anthony she was sick?"

"If she was sick. We don't know that for sure. What if she was pregnant?"

"Don't be daft! She was way too proper for that," I said.

We looked down into the wishing well and reflected on our great-aunt's curious life. Thinking about her past helped us forget the hot water we were in from sneaking out the night before, but my heart was still hurting from the way Jimmy treated me. I felt cheap and dirty. Even though I stopped his advances, I was insulted that he thought he could manhandle me when we'd only been out on a few dates. Kitty leaned against the well. "Do you think she'll call Dad?"

"I think if she was going to do that, she would have already called him. Maybe she's giving us a pass."

"That'll be our punishment. Keeping us in the dark about

what she intends to do. Honestly, she has it easy as long as we're here taking care of her."

"But do you want to keep taking care of her instead of going home to our family? I don't. I'm ready to risk Dad's wrath just to be home again." I sighed and looked away.

"I hate it when you keep secrets from me," Kitty said.

"Secrets! That's the theme of this summer at the lake house. Keys that don't unlock anything. Boxes, desks, and rooms that are locked. People that should be part of our lives but aren't. All we have are more secrets."

We walked back down the lane, and as we got closer to Aunt Polly's house, we saw Jimmy and Charlie skateboarding on their sidewalk. They looked up and waved, then left their skateboards and met us partway down the lane. As usual, they looked like cover models, wearing tight T-shirts and cut-off jeans. When they got within earshot, Charlie was the first to speak.

"Hey, there. How are you two doing?"

I shrugged, but Kitty jumped into the conversation. "So far, so good. No one has cut off our hands or called our dad."

"Is your great-aunt still hopping mad?" Charlie asked as he moved closer to Kitty.

Kitty smiled at him. "We placated her with food and our good manners. I think she's cooled off."

Charlie seemed relieved. "So you're staying?"

"I think so. Don't you, Cindy?"

"I guess. For now."

Jimmy and I stood further apart. I couldn't look him in

the eye, even though I knew I hadn't done anything wrong. Well, other than a few puffs of a reefer and a few sips of beer. But I felt guilty for enjoying his advances.

Charlie snickered. "She was a sight last night in her white nightgown, carrying the gun, and without her glass eye. I'll have nightmares about that forever."

"She did look spooky. I didn't know she had a rifle," Kitty said.

We stood for a moment, no doubt each of us remembering the vision of Aunt Polly from the night before.

Kitty broke the silence. "Well, back to Pollywood. We don't want to keep her waiting."

I was happy to step away from Jimmy and my conflicted thoughts.

Chapter 27

After our brief walk, I went into the kitchen and took out the ingredients for the Parcheesi frosting, as Aunt Polly now called it. She would consider cake the most essential dinner element, so I didn't want to disappoint. Just as the butter and brown sugar were melting, there was a knock on the back porch door. I turned off the burner and was stunned to see the petite Mrs. Erickson from down the lane. She was wearing another long caftan and casual shoes. I opened the door and greeted her.

"Hello, Mrs. Erickson. Would you like to come in?"

She looked at the state of the house and shook her head. She seemed breathless from the walk up the lane.

"Are you here to see my great-aunt?"

"No, actually, I wanted to talk to you." She stayed on the broken concrete path.

She lowered her voice to assure me this would be an

uncomfortable conversation. "What happened some days ago when the fire department showed up?"

"Aunt Polly had a little trouble, but she's fine."

She squinted at me over her glasses. "What kind of trouble?"

"In the bath."

"Do you mean she had a stroke?"

I lowered my voice so my great-aunt wouldn't hear me. "She couldn't get out of the tub."

Mrs. Erickson gasped. Then smiled. Then chuckled. "That's a good one!"

I didn't appreciate her attitude. "She turned her ankle."

"Oh my! Will the fire department have to come out every time she needs a bath?"

"We had a plumber come out and put in a shower, so she's safer now."

She glanced at my soft middle. "Well, let that be a lesson to you. Don't let her fatten you up."

"Was that what you wanted to talk to me about?" I mean, seriously!

"No, no. I'm wondering if you're going to be around this weekend."

"Yes. Kitty and I are staying a few more days. Why?"

"Mr. Erickson and I are going away for the weekend, and we need someone to look after Anastasia."

"Oh, yes, your cat. Is Marjorie going with you?"

"Yes, just a weekend trip with Marjorie."

I shrugged. "Sure, you can bring Anastasia by."

"Oh, no. She can't stay here. She'd be frightened to death having squirrels and animals running through the house."

"You want me to stay at your house?"

"No, dear, that's not necessary. I just need you to come by and feed her and keep her company three or four times a day."

I was a bit taken aback. "Three or four times a day for how many days?"

"Just three. And I'll pay you five dollars."

"Five dollars a day?"

"No, no. Five dollars for three days. I mean, it's not too much trouble. Easy money for a girl like you."

What did she mean by that? "OK, sure. I'll do it." I guess a girl like me can't be too picky.

We worked out the arrangements, and she went on her way without stopping to see Aunt Polly.

I went back into the house just as Kitty came downstairs. I explained the arrangement with Mrs. Erickson.

"Why didn't you invite her in?"

"I did, Aunt Polly, but she said she couldn't stay."

Aunt Polly bit her bottom lip and her shoulders drooped as a slight sigh escaped.

Before the Ericksons left town, I popped over, and she showed me where the cat food, bed, and litter box were kept, along with a suggested schedule. Then she gave me a key to their home and instructed me to come and go by the back door.

The first time I visited Anastasia, I found a note addressed to me sitting on the kitchen counter. "Cindy, please don't forget to give Anastasia her medication each evening. It will relax her and help her sleep without me. See you Monday."

I put the pill box on the note and left it as a reminder. Each day I went back and forth down the lane to take care of Anastasia. Once she got used to me, she was easy to find and seemed to enjoy my presence. I spent time petting her and tossing a ball of yarn around to entertain her. Occasionally Kitty came with me, but I went alone on most of the visits.

Sunday after church, as I was about to visit the cat, I asked Kitty if she wanted to come with me.

"No. I'm enjoying my book. Maybe next time."

I walked down the lane and marveled at how quickly the weekend had gone. Even though I'm allergic to cats, Anastasia was a non-allergenic breed which kept sneezing to a minimum. But on this visit, I found the back door ajar. I must have forgotten to shut it all the way. "Anastasia," I called as I cautiously entered. I couldn't find the cat. I went into the kitchen to get a can of Fancy Pants Cat food, but I heard something odd.

"Anastasia," I called again louder. When the cat didn't come, I started walking through the house calling her name. But then I stopped. I heard something that sounded like breathing. I took a few steps toward the second floor and stopped and listened. There it was again. Almost like… snoring. The hairs on my neck stood on end. I dashed out of the house and back to Aunt Polly's.

Aunt Polly and Kitty were in the front living room reading when I barged in, breathless.

Kitty looked up, alarmed. "What's going on?"

"I couldn't find the cat, but I could hear breathing. Heavy breathing!"

Aunt Polly laughed. "Don't be silly. You can't imagine a cat breathing so loud you could hear it from another room."

"I'm not kidding. Something was creepy. I could hear heavy breathing."

Kitty stood. "I'll go with you. I'm sure it's nothing."

Aunt Polly just shook her head. "You have such a vivid imagination."

I told Kitty about the back door on the way to the Ericksons' house.

"You must have forgotten to pull it closed last time. Don't worry. It's probably nothing. Everything was fine yesterday, right?"

"Yes, but I'm sure I closed the door. What if the cat escaped?"

"We'll figure it out."

We walked in the back door and into the kitchen and called for the cat. We went from room to room on the first floor but couldn't find her. Then Kitty and I started up the steps to the second floor, and the breathing got louder with each step. She looked at me, alarmed. We stopped yelling for the cat and carefully walked up the rest of the carpeted steps. At the top of the stairs, Kitty quietly pushed open the door to the first bedroom. A middle-aged man with a scruffy beard and filthy, torn jeans was lying on the bed snoring. The scent of alcohol hit us from ten feet away. He looked and smelled as if he hadn't bathed in over a month.

Kitty and I backed up, and she whispered, "Run. Just run and don't stop until you reach Aunt Polly's."

Chapter 28

WE DASHED DOWN THE STAIRS and out the back door, carefully closing it tightly without locking it. We ran as fast as we could without looking back, terrified that he'd follow us. We burst into Aunt Polly's house and told her what we saw while panting to catch our breath.

"What?" As we relayed the scary episode, Aunt Polly's cheeks flushed, her eyes opened wide, and her hand flew to her throat. She snatched the telephone and dialed the operator. I'd never seen her so alarmed.

My insides were shaking, I was so afraid. I reached for Kitty's hands for reassurance.

"I'm sorry I doubted you," Kitty said between breaths as we clutched each other to stop shaking.

"I've always felt so safe here," Aunt Polly said. "This is most unusual."

Within minutes, we heard a police siren and walked to the edge of Aunt Polly's property so we could watch from a safe distance. On the phone, Aunt Polly told them exactly where the guy was sleeping and which door was unlocked, so we saw police go around to the back of the property. I held my breath as we waited for what seemed an eternity. Then another squad car showed up, along with a man in plainclothes with a large camera. Finally, two cops escorted the man out of the house, put him in the squad car, and left. We dashed back inside.

Now what? My adrenaline was racing, and I felt the need to go for a walk, but I was too frightened to go outside for long, even though I knew they had the dude in custody.

I peppered Aunt Polly with questions.

"How long before we know something definite?"

"I'm sorry, I have no idea."

"What's the police protocol? Will they share what they learned? Will we have to wait until a newspaper report's printed?"

She answered patiently, "Cindy, nothing like this has ever happened, that I know of. I don't have any answers for you."

Kitty and I walked outside together and peered down the lane, watching for additional signs. Was the camera guy a reporter? We watched for what felt like an eternity but finally gave up and went back inside. I played the piano to soothe my nerves, and when that didn't work, we played a game of Parcheesi with Aunt Polly and ate the last of the cake. But after that, I got up and walked in circles around the living rooms and dining room.

Aunt Polly watched me pace.

"Cindy, would a warm cup of cocoa help? Or perhaps you

should lie down or read a novel. Anything to get your mind off this."

I stopped pacing, glad she didn't dismiss my feelings. "Thank you, Aunt Polly. I'll go get my book, but I want to stay downstairs in case an officer comes by."

Finally, a car pulled up to the driveway.

A uniformed officer knocked on the porch door. I don't know why, but my insides started to shake when I saw him. Was I afraid of him or what he would tell me? Either way, I swallowed my fear and invited him in, and he followed me into the front living room where Aunt Polly and Kitty were waiting. Aunt Polly sat up straighter on her couch.

"Hi. I'm Officer Harold Kline. Have you got a few minutes?" He removed his black, flat-top hat with the badge prominently displayed.

"Yes, please sit down," Aunt Polly said and gestured to one of the platform rockers.

His tall frame sank into one of the narrow, uncomfortable chairs, but he quickly stood up. "I'll just stand. This won't take long."

He took a small pad of paper and a pen out of his light blue shirt pocket and wrote down our names. Then he asked Kitty and me to recount every tiny detail of our encounter with danger. He listened intently and probed for more information until he was satisfied he understood what happened.

"First of all, thank you, girls, for helping us catch that guy. We suspect he assaulted other women in this area in the past few weeks."

Aunt Polly was shocked. "He wasn't a burglar?"

"No, he's a, well, he preys on women and girls." Then he turned toward Kitty and me. "Sorry to be so blunt."

I turned to Kitty, who looked as if she might faint, and was glad she sat down. Our eyes locked, and the thought of what could have happened went through us like shock waves. As horrifying as it was, I wanted to hear everything Officer Harold was willing to share.

"He's a drifter, a homeless guy who's been terrorizing this area recently. He looked for open windows or doors, apparently found a window unlocked, and crept into the house that way. He likely was leaving the door ajar so he could come and go, waiting for Cindy."

I gasped. "Why me?"

He turned to me and spoke carefully. "The perp must have guessed that the Erickson's weren't home. He likely saw a note addressed to a Cindy, so he guessed a female would be coming over soon to feed the cat. He may have been coming and going for a few days, figuring it was a great hiding place because we were looking for him."

"So he might have been there yesterday?" My knees were shaking.

"We don't know when he first got into the house, but it was likely late at night. Today, while he waited, he got into their liquor cabinet and drank himself into a stupor."

He turned to me with great sympathy in his voice, but his words were like piercing swords. "Lucky for you, he passed out, because he intended to harm you. I'm sorry to tell you this."

I nearly fainted, realizing how close I had come to being attacked, and sank into a chair, shaking and nauseous. My head felt fuzzy, and I had trouble concentrating on the officer's words. Kitty went into the kitchen to bring me a glass of water, which I sipped.

Officer Harold tried to reassure me. "Don't worry. He's off the streets now."

"But, but, what about their house? Is it safe to go back?"

"Yes. We did a thorough search of the house. A few detectives took pictures and searched for other evidence. We found a frightened cat, but otherwise, everything was fine. The cat's still in the house, by the way."

"Aunt Polly, can I bring Anastasia here until the Ericksons get home?"

"Certainly."

"I'll go with you if you like, and we can bring the cat back and ensure the house is secure. Then we'll contact the Ericksons," the officer said. "The note listed a number where they can be reached."

"Yes, thank you."

Kitty piped up. "I'll go too."

She must have been scared to go back into the house, and it meant a lot to me to have her volunteer to come with me. I wasn't sure I could face that house again, but I had to find Anastasia. That poor kitty must have been terrified.

Jimmy and Charlie were in their yard silently watching as we followed the officer down the lane. I couldn't think of anything to say and half-heartedly waved as we went by.

By the time we got to the house, my insides were shaking, and I was breathing hard. Officer Harold entered through the back door into the kitchen. My shoes squeaked on the tile floor as I gathered the kitty's food, dishes, and litter box while calling her name. But her pill box was missing.

Officer Harold stayed close by our sides as we looked in the vast living rooms, dining room, library, and other first-floor spaces for the cat. We searched under furniture and inside closets. Finally, the officer said, "She must be upstairs. I'll come with you. It'll be good for you to face your fear and see that bedroom again."

Kitty and I looked at each other and held hands while we slowly climbed the stairs, remembering what we saw and heard earlier. When we reached the bedroom where the intruder was caught sleeping, Officer Harold went ahead of us and pushed the door open confidently. We stepped closer and peeked in to confirm that he wasn't there. But I couldn't bring myself to go into the room.

"I doubt Anastasia's in here with the smell of that man lingering in the air," he said. Something caught his eye, and he walked to the nightstand next to the bed and picked up a bottle. He read the label. "These are for the cat. Did you leave them here?"

He brought them to me. The bottle was nearly empty. "No. I left them on the kitchen counter by the note. Where are the rest of her pills? It was nearly full. They're to help the kitty sleep while Mrs. Erickson is gone."

He threw back his head and laughed. "So, the perp had

himself a great nap using kitty tranquilizers and booze." Then he turned to me.

"Sorry. That wasn't very professional of me. But you don't see many people taking cat pills."

I didn't smile. "Those pills helped save me." Kitty squeezed my hand. "Save us."

He turned serious. "Yes, pills, booze, and your quick thinking. I hope you're proud of yourself for listening to your instincts."

"I felt the hair on the back of my neck stand up. Is that what you mean by instincts?"

He smiled at me. "That's one way. Sometimes folks get goosebumps, their stomach tightens, their heart races, or they get a shiver down their spine. You must learn to trust those signs. Trust your gut."

I thought about that. "I think I had all those feelings at once." But I didn't tell him that trusting my gut was difficult because it usually just wanted cookies.

Officer Harold smiled reassuringly. "We'd better find that cat."

We went into the next bedroom and coaxed Anastasia from under the bed. Relief. Kitty and I flew down the stairs, with me holding the cat close to my heart. I could feel her heart pumping next to mine. I wrapped her in a small blanket and headed for the door. We gathered the rest of her supplies as Officer Harold made a last check of the first-floor windows to be sure they were all locked and then pulled the door shut with a satisfying click. We headed back to Aunt Polly's, and he got into his squad car and left after handing us a card with his phone number on it.

"Let's hope we never need this," I said, and Kitty agreed.

Inside, I set out Anastasia's food, water, and litter box and then reached down to hold her on my lap. Her motor started, and the vibrations were a soothing balm. "I'm so glad you weren't hurt," I whispered.

Aunt Polly seemed genuinely concerned. "What a fright you girls had!"

Kitty nodded. "Thank you for saying that."

"Of course. I was worried about you."

My mouth dropped open. "Really?"

Aunt Polly looked at me quizzically. "Why wouldn't I be worried? You came very close to being attacked."

I nodded, and tears formed in my eyes. "Yes, we did. It's just that my parents always seem to dismiss our fears."

"Certainly, they wouldn't dismiss a near attack," she said.

I took a deep breath. "Last year, I was walking home alone from school after play practice, wearing my Regina school uniform. A man in a Cadillac pulled up and said he knew my dad and asked if I wanted a ride home. I said no. He asked several times in different ways, getting louder each time. Finally, he got angry and shouted, 'get in the car' over and over. I turned and ran and then kept crossing the street back and forth so he couldn't pull up next to me and drag me into his car. I finally ran down our alley and into our house. My heart was beating fast and I was breathing hard. I went to the front window to keep an eye out to see if he figured out where I lived. Kitty, you remember, don't you?"

"I do. You told me, and we both were looking out the front window when Dad asked what we were doing."

"Right. I told him, but he completely dismissed me. He glanced out and said, 'There's no one there.' That was it. He acted as if I made it up. It was terrifying, and I couldn't understand why he was so unconcerned."

Aunt Polly looked away thoughtfully. Her lips twitched back and forth as if she was trying to think of the right thing to say. "Perhaps he dismissed your concern so that you wouldn't dwell on it. I don't know what it's like to be a parent, but he has a lot to juggle with eight daughters."

"There's no way I'd forget something as scary as that."

Aunt Polly's good eye seemed softer, somehow. "For generations, people have been taught to forget, rather than talk about difficult subjects. He probably thought he was helping you move on. Sometimes parents make mistakes." She looked away and was quiet for several minutes.

I licked my lips and nodded while keeping Anastasia on my lap. I wasn't sure which of us was comforting the other, but I was happy to sink my hands into her silky fur and let my racing heart quiet.

Maybe if I kept my mind on other things, terror would evaporate. Just move on, like they say.

Chapter 29

As long as Aunt Polly acted sympathetic, I decided to ask again about her sister. Keeping my eyes focused on Anastasia, I searched for a way to begin.

"Aunt Polly, I don't mean to cause you pain, but will you please tell us where your sister Margaret is?" Kitty shot me a look of alarm, but I gave her a quick nod to tell her I knew to tread gently.

Aunt Polly sighed and looked at her lap. For a while we thought she was angry, but when she finally looked up, her good eye seemed far away. "Margaret was in a terrible boating accident where her head got caught in a motor."

Kitty and I gasped at the gruesome thought. Even though we read about it in a newspaper, hearing our great-aunt describe it graphically was shocking. And we had to convince Aunt Polly that this was the first time we heard about it. We listened intently as she continued.

"The injury affected her brain. She never recovered. She

was in the hospital in a coma for weeks, and my parents had to put her into an institution where she stayed until her death a few years later."

Kitty spoke up. "You said she wasn't dead, just gone."

"That's the way I've always felt. I was gone at the time at the university, but it was as if she was swept away. I was very fond of her, and it was a painful blow in my life. People didn't travel much then, and I couldn't come back right after the accident."

"Did you ever see her again?" I asked.

"Once. While I was on a summer break, I went to the institution. She was there physically, but there was no way to communicate with her. She couldn't eat or breathe on her own, and it felt like she was dead."

Kitty proceeded carefully. "Why doesn't anyone ever talk about her?"

Aunt Polly snapped back. "Because it's too painful. Even now. She was only sixteen when she was hurt. Your age, Kitty. Imagine having your life snatched from you now. That's why you have to stay safe."

We were silent, not sure what to say or do. Aunt Polly broke the silence.

"When an old person dies, you know they've had the chance to live their life, but when a young person dies, it's a tragedy because they weren't able to experience life. To travel and become educated and meet people."

"Like you did. Travel and graduate from college," I said.

"Yes. And meet people."

"Anyone special from your past?" I dared to ask.

Aunt Polly reared up and sent piercing arrows my way with her eye. "What kind of a question is that?"

"I was just curious."

"Well, don't be." We sat silently for what felt like an eternity until she spoke again.

"Kitty, please make more popcorn with butter and salt."

"Sure." Kitty went into the kitchen, and we heard the clang of the large kettle on the top of the gas stove. My mouth watered at the thought of this savory treat. Soon enough, we heard the popping inside the kettle as the kernels exploded and hit the metal lid, and then the air was filled with the heavenly scent of popped corn. Kitty melted butter and salted the warm corn before she brought out three large bowls.

I set Anastasia on the floor so I wouldn't get butter on her fur, and she went off to explore the house. We munched in blissful silence for a time. I was grateful to learn more about our Great Aunt Margaret but wondered if I could push Aunt Polly a bit more. I debated internally as I chewed. Should I ask her about her visit to France in 1917? But I couldn't reveal that I knew about that without admitting that we had gotten into the forbidden room. I decided on a safer topic.

"Aunt Polly, remember that box we found behind the wall in the library?"

"Yes. Why?"

"Do you have any idea what's inside of it?"

"Probably some old jewelry or a few papers."

"Do you think we could try to find a key for it and see what's inside?"

"You're certainly in a nosey mood! I have no idea where the key is."

Kitty brightened. "We could look for it. Like a scavenger hunt. I think it'd be fun."

Aunt Polly looked dubious. "Fun, huh. Fine. If you girls want to look around, go ahead."

Kitty and I finished our snack, washed our hands, and set to work looking through drawers, desks, and closets on the first floor where Aunt Polly could see us. I was pretty sure one of the keys we already found might fit. We ransacked our way through both living rooms, both dining rooms, and the library but found nothing new.

I made a bold suggestion. "Aunt Polly, what about the room off the kitchen? Maybe there's a key in there."

She reared up and barked back. "Stay out of that room. I've told you that before. It's off-limits."

My bold wave shrank into a meek puddle. "We'll look upstairs then." We headed upstairs to retrieve the keys we found weeks ago. We pretended to look through dressers and made more noise than necessary to punctuate our progress.

Kitty whispered. "Which keys are left?"

"The blue one and the large skeleton key. Let's bring down the blue key and hope it fits."

"Unless we find another one up here. We might as well look in a few more places now that we have permission."

We headed to bedrooms further down the main hallway

that we'd scarcely searched on previous hunts. We looked inside drawers, outside of old dressers, along the legs of fainting couches and settees in dressing rooms. And bingo.

"Kitty, look!" A small gold key was taped to the back of the leg of a fainting couch. I was giddy with our success.

"Which one should we bring down to her?" she whispered.

"Let's bring them both." Before we took them downstairs, we quickly searched for Anastasia and found her asleep on my bed. I sat beside her on the chenille bedspread and petted her until her motor started up again, and she burrowed into my hand. Although I had washed off the butter, she picked up the scent and licked my fingers with her sandpaper tongue. But I didn't dally for long. Anastasia looked comfortable, so we left her alone and pounded down the stairs.

"You two are like thundering elephants," Aunt Polly said. "What's your hurry?"

Kitty held up the keys. "We found two keys upstairs. One behind a dresser and the other taped to the leg of the fainting couch."

Aunt Polly shook her head. "I'm uncomfortable with you girls digging around in those bedrooms."

"But you told us we could search," I protested.

She shook her head. "Well, I wasn't expecting you to go to such extremes. But very well. Go into my bedroom and retrieve the box."

We nearly tripped over each other in our excitement. Her bedroom was likely built as a maid's room when the home was first built. A single window covered with a faded, blue chintz curtain shed light into the small space containing a twin-sized bed, small bedside table, and a dresser. There was a closet at the far end. The space was neat, with two extra pairs of sturdy shoes sitting against a wall.

We found the box on top of her dresser, brought it out, and handed it to our great-aunt. She tried the small gold key first, and it went in but didn't open it. When she put the blue key in the lock, we heard a click, and the lid popped up.

We waited to see if she'd let us see the contents. She lifted out an odd box with a small contraption inside it and an old handwritten letter.

She gasped. "The sugar tongs! I thought my sister hid these."

"What are they?" Kitty asked.

"History, that's what. Family history. They disappeared years ago, and your grandmother, Catherine, accused me of taking them. Everyone knew she was the one who would inherit them, and she thought I was jealous."

I looked at her. "And were you jealous?"

"Not enough to hide them. They disappeared before I left for college, so I wonder if Margaret hid them as a prank. She loved to play games."

"Do you think she knew about the hidden wall in the library?" Kitty asked.

"I'm not sure. But if she didn't, then perhaps Mother hid them to protect them until it was time for Catherine to inherit them."

I wondered what the big deal was about an odd-shaped thing called sugar tongs encased in a plastic box.

Aunt Polly took the letter and began to read it silently until I protested, "Please read it aloud."

"Fine, but sit down. I don't like having you breathing down my neck."

We sat as we were told, and she began to read.

Chapter 30

Aunt Polly cleared her throat and held the faded handwritten note close to her eyes.

"The sugar tongs are of Dutch design and ancestry and were supposed to have been brought to America by one Cornelis Melyn, Patroon of Staten Island, from Antwerp in 1639 as a part of his household silver."

"1639! Far out," I sputtered.

"Yes, far out indeed. Now, if I may continue. 'The first of the Catherines who owned them was Cornelis Melyn's great-granddaughter, Catherine, born in New York in 1695. Then the sugar tongs passed from one Catherine to another over several hundred years.' These rightfully belong to your mother, the seventh Catherine, and then you, Kitty, will inherit them someday." She handed the document to Kitty.

"Me? But I'm Kathleen, not a Catherine."

"Your mother didn't want to name one of her girls Catherine because she was sick of all the confusion over the names.

But she named you Kathleen, which your mother said was close enough to inherit them."

"Wow. What did someone do if they didn't have a girl?" I asked.

"Wait for a granddaughter," Aunt Polly said.

"But what if…?" I started to ask.

"It's never happened, Cindy. Girls run in our family lines."

Kitty examined the letter. "Look at this! It says the third Catherine in the line was married to Captain Jesse Leavenworth of New Haven. During the Revolution, when the Hessians were plundering, she buried her silver, including the sugar tongs. Her daughter died young, so the next in line was her granddaughter and she asked that they be handed down through the Catherines in the family."

"What did she mean by the Hessians plundering? Who were they?" I asked.

Aunt Polly assumed a teacherly bearing and sat a little taller. "During the Revolutionary War in the United States, some 30,000 German soldiers called Hessians came and helped the English soldiers. While on a rampage, they ransacked homes and farms looking for valuables and food. That's why our ancestor buried the silver."

"Is this the reason we can't go in the room off the kitchen? Because you thought family valuables were there?" I asked.

"No, it is not. I had given up on finding these. The room off the kitchen contains personal items from my life, and it's still off-limits to you two snoops."

"Sorry I asked."

Aunt Polly shook her head. "I don't know why you're so interested anyway. Now, Kitty, let's put everything back in this box and tape the key to the top. Then I'll give it to your mother when she comes to fetch you Monday."

"Monday? Tomorrow?" we said in unison.

"Yes. I think you've been away from your family long enough. The Ericksons will be back tomorrow morning, so your cat sitting will be done. After the scare with the intruder, I thought you might want to see your mother and sisters, so I called your family while you were retrieving the cat. Your family will come up for the afternoon to swim and have dinner. It gives you time to say goodbye to the boys and to pack your things."

"That'll be fun, won't it, Kitty? Or should I call you Catherine?"

"Very funny. Mom is the next Catherine in line."

There was a knock on the porch door, and Kitty hopped up eagerly to answer it. Charlie stood, looking confused.

"Hi. Just wondering why the cops were here. Are you all right?"

Kitty was animated. "We are now, but we had quite a scare."

Aunt Polly called from the living room, "Who is it Kitty?" When she explained, Aunt Polly suggested we pop over to the O'Reillys' and tell them in person so they wouldn't have to read about it in the newspaper.

Kitty and I walked over, and Charlie called for Jimmy, Wayne, and his mother to hear about our encounter with danger. He invited us in, and we stood awkwardly in their foyer while they assembled. They peppered us with questions simultaneously.

"What was going on earlier? Why were the police here? Is there any danger? Was anyone hurt? Did they catch the perp?"

Kitty and I filled them in on the drifter and relayed what Officer Harold told us.

Mrs. O'Reilly's hand flew to her heart. "Girls! I'm so glad you weren't hurt. What a terrible ordeal."

Jimmy and Charlie seemed uncomfortable with the topic but expressed appropriate concern. Wayne smirked and shook his head. "What a loser he was."

Mrs. O'Reilly glared at him. "Yes, but also a violent, troubled criminal." Wayne smirked and walked into another room.

"I'm glad you're OK," Jimmy said, and Charlie nodded.

"How'd he get in?" Charlie asked.

"Apparently the Ericksons forgot to lock one of the windows. He was coming and going for two days," I said.

"Creepy," Charlie commented.

"And their house wasn't the only one. He assaulted several women in this area in the past two weeks," Kitty said.

"You boys need to check all the locks on the windows," Mrs. O'Reilly said.

"Because of all this, our family's coming tomorrow. We're going home with them after dinner," I said.

"We certainly have enjoyed having you girls around this

summer," Mrs. O'Reilly said. "I'll let you and the boys talk." We thanked her, and Jimmy and Charlie ushered us outside for a walk.

Charlie sounded hopeful. "It's a warm afternoon. Want to go swimming?"

"Swimming? Like now?" Kitty asked.

"Sure. Let's walk down the hill and swim from the dock. Such a hot afternoon."

Kitty lit up. "That sounds great. We'll have to ask our great-aunt, but it should be OK."

As we walked back into Aunt Polly's house, I wasn't so sure. "You really think she'll let us after the party?"

"It's just an afternoon swim to cool off," Kitty said, and we trudged inside to ask her.

Chapter 31

After Aunt Polly agreed, Kitty dashed back outside and told the guys we'd be ready in ten minutes.

We were quiet as we changed into our swimsuits and sandals, put our hair in braids, and grabbed bath towels. My mind was trying to figure out what to say to Jimmy. Kitty noticed my mood didn't match hers, and before we went back downstairs, she questioned me again.

"Cindy, what is wrong? We're going to have fun. FUN! Why are you acting like you're on the way to a funeral? Don't you love swimming?"

"Of course, I want to go swimming. It's a hot afternoon, and it'll be nice to cool down. Let's just go."

She shook her head. "Try to be more enthused."

"Why? It's just swimming. If I don't feel like doing cartwheels, I'm not going to," I snapped. "And after the morning I've had, I'm still upset."

She cocked her head to one side and a braid flipped over

her shoulder. "Yes, but the guys will think you're a drag if you keep acting this way."

I flipped my braids back. "I'm not worried about what they think of me. I'm not trying to impress them."

"So you think I am?"

"No, I think you're flirting like you usually do," I said.

"Fine. Let's just go. I don't want to fight about this."

"Good."

We walked toward the O'Reilly house and saw Wayne lounging outside.

I cautioned Kitty, "Don't be too loud. Wayne's outside in the hassock."

Kitty frowned and then spotted Wayne. "You mean the hammock. Hassocks are those things you rest your feet on. Hammocks are tied between two trees."

"Here we go again."

She sighed. "I'm just trying to help."

Jimmy and Charlie were already waiting in front of their home. We walked together down the hill, across the road, and over to a small sandy beach sporting a dock and small diving board. One by one, we discarded our towels and sandals and dove into the water. Despite the warm air, the water temperature was still cold enough to take my breath away. Lakes were like slow cookers that warmed slowly, but as soon as August hit, the air could turn chilly, so July was usually a prime swimming month. Such was life in Minnesota.

We swam together, doing somersaults and taking turns diving off the board. The water was refreshing once I got used to it. I felt my tense muscles loosen as I swam, but I kept my distance from Jimmy. Several times he swam toward me as if he had something to say, but I just turned and swam in the opposite direction. Meanwhile, Kitty and Charlie were flirting and kissing as she wrapped her legs around him and held onto his neck underwater. Soon I decided I'd had enough.

"I'm heading in, Kitty. See you inside." I gathered my sandals, dried off with my towel, and walked off the dock, but as I was crossing the road, Jimmy caught up with me and grabbed my hand to stop me.

"You don't have to leave because of me."

I shook his hand away. "I'm done swimming, that's all."

"Are you sure that's all?" he asked.

"I had a terrible scare this morning on top of everything from last night."

He took a breath and looked into the sky. "Look Cindy, I know I was a jerk last night. I had too much to drink, and I'm sorry."

"It wasn't just your behavior. You and your friends insulted me, my family, and my school."

He drew his hand through his thick blond mop. "I'm sorry. I thought they were just messing with you."

I looked down, not wanting to meet his eyes. "And you made me feel cheap."

"I'm sorry. I am. It was the booze. But I like you, and I hope we can be friends."

"Just friends."

"OK. I understand. We can still enjoy hanging out, right?"

"Right. Well, maybe next time we visit. We had a lot of fun together. And I'm grateful for that."

Jimmy smiled. "Let's walk down the lane. You can fill me in on your latest detective work."

"Great." I breathed a sigh of relief. My stomach was always in knots if there were arguments and tensions in relationships. I didn't know how to push through the conflict without breaking ties. Was it possible I didn't have to ignore Jimmy forever just because of his behavior last night? He was smart and funny, and I enjoyed being with him. And did I mention that he was a hunk? Oh yes, I'm trying to forget that part.

We crossed the road and climbed up the hill, and instead of going to Aunt Polly's, we walked down the lane with our towels draped around us. We found a park bench and sat down to dry off in the sun.

"Have you discovered anything new?" Jimmy asked.

I nodded. "We did learn a few juicy details about Aunt Polly."

Jimmy was facing me, squinting a bit from the afternoon sun. "That she murdered three people over a plate of spaghetti?"

I giggled. "Nothing like that. We found letters showing Aunt Polly was in Paris looking for her sweetheart during the war, and she had something she needed to tell him. We think she may have been sick."

"She traveled all the way to Paris to tell a guy she was sick? Sounds more like she was, you know, expecting."

"She told us today that she met someone while she was on a three-month cruise after she graduated from the university."

"Her dad must have been loaded."

"I don't know much about him, but we think he was president of some grain company. The two older sisters graduated from the university and then were treated to cruises around the world."

"Far out! Imagine getting to see so many countries and cultures."

"Yeah, the farthest I've gone is to see Hershey, Pennsylvania, in a station wagon with nine of us and a tent strapped on top of the car."

Jimmy laughed. "I thought there were ten of you."

"There are now, but this was three years ago before Ann Marie was born."

"So your family knows how to travel in style."

I playfully swatted him. "Hey, don't knock it until you've tried it. Three people to each seat, riding all day for three days, eating bologna sandwiches out of a cooler. Then when it was finally dark, my dad would look for a campground, and we girls would have to pitch the tent while my parents slept in the back of the station wagon."

"Sounds like a laugh a minute. Where was your luggage?"

"No luggage. We each got a sleeping bag, and our clothes and toiletries were rolled up in our bag. They were all strapped on top of the station wagon along with the tent."

"What if it rained?"

"Dad threw a makeshift tarp over the whole works and loosely tied it down."

"How did you manage not to kill each other?"

"Mom's a Girl Scout leader, so she made us sing songs, and we played license plate games, that sort of thing. We each had a book, and when we finished them, we'd swap books. But by the time we got close to Hershey, we were ready to get out of that car."

"Your folks must be really patient."

"Mom's usually patient or passed out from exhaustion. Not Dad. He's quite stern, but he has a wacky sense of humor. When we were still far from Hershey, he shouted, 'Girls, smell the chocolate. We're here.' We all stuck our noses out the nearest window and inhaled deeply, but instead of chocolate, the stench of a dead skunk greeted us." I laughed. "He's a funny guy, my dad. One minute he's really strict, and the next he's playing jokes."

Jimmy was thoughtful. "You sound a bit homesick."

"I am. We've been here for weeks, and I miss my family and my own bed."

He nodded. "I get that."

"I think it's different when you have much younger siblings. We older girls have helped to raise the younger ones, so we're pretty close."

"Sounds like a lot of work when you're just kids yourselves."

"Mom and Dad both work really hard. He's had to change

careers, and we all learned to pitch in while he built his new business. But it isn't all work."

"No? Sounds like it."

"Now and then they come up with wacky ideas. One time they told us company was coming over after dinner. We cleaned and prepared snacks and got ready. After dinner, Mom and Dad told us they were going to their bedroom to change and told us to answer the door when the company arrived. Within minutes they were at the front door and shouted, 'Surprise.' The party was for us."

"So they tricked you into cleaning?"

"Well, yes, but then we had a party."

"They went up to their room? So how did they get to the front door?"

I put my hand over my mouth as I remembered. "They climbed down a ladder from the second floor and ran around to the front of the house."

"This ladder business is genetic?" Jimmy laughed.

"I forgot all about that. Dad can't get too mad at us. We'll tell him he gave us the idea."

"Pretty funny coincidence. Maybe he'll put a ladder up to your room at home so you can practice coming and going the ladder way."

"I hope not. My room's on the third floor. I was terrified just going down from the second floor here. I can't imagine climbing down from the third floor."

"Practice makes perfect. I'm going to come into town someday and insist you climb down."

I stood up. "Very funny. Thanks for the chat, friend. I should probably go in, get changed, and think of something to make for dinner."

We walked back to Aunt Polly's. We stood awkwardly at the back porch door, as Jimmy kicked the ground with his toes. He looked up and I thought for a moment he was going to kiss me.

I moved toward the door. "Thanks again for… everything."

"Sure. I'll see you again before you go."

I smiled and moved toward the door. "OK."

Inside, Aunt Polly was lounging.

"Where have you girls been?"

"We were swimming, Aunt Polly. You remember."

"Oh yes. Where's Kitty?"

"She and Charlie wanted more time in the water. I'll start dinner. I'm sure she'll be back soon. " At least, I hoped she would.

I fixed pigs in a blanket and carrots for an easy dinner.

Chapter 32

After we finished the dinner dishes, I looked at Kitty and moved my eyes upward so she'd catch my drift. "I think I'll go upstairs and start packing." Kitty followed me.

We shook out our braids to help our thick hair dry. My mind swam with a few other things we needed to do before we left for home.

I stood by the dresser trying to make a mental list. "We need to put the letters back in the rolltop desk, put the scrapbook inside the trunk, and set the picture album on the desk in the forbidden room. How are we going to get this done without her catching us?"

"We'll think of something. I'm excited to see our family but sad to go home."

"Because of Charlie?"

"We were getting really close."

I turned back to the dresser and started removing items. "Too close, if you ask me," I mumbled.

"What's that supposed to mean?" Kitty shot back.

I swung around to meet her. "Every time you and Charlie are together, you're practically wrapped around each other. I'm worried that you'll get into trouble."

"You worry too much. Is that why you broke things off with Jimmy?"

"Why do you keep asking me about it?"

"Because we're sisters, and we shouldn't have secrets. If something happened between you and Jimmy, I think you should tell me."

I sat down on my bed and reached for the sleeping cat and put her in my lap. "Fine. Jimmy was getting aggressive, you know… physically. And he was smoking a weed and drinking beer. He scared me. And besides, he and his school friends made fun of our family and school. They made me feel like some kind of freak, and I felt Jimmy was using me."

She sat back down on the bed. "Why didn't you tell me?"

"You seemed so happy with Charlie. I thought maybe I was being silly and oversensitive."

"Does Jimmy know you're mad at him?"

"Yes. When I left him at the park, he got the idea. But it's the girls who pay when things get out of hand. If one of us gets pregnant, we'd have to quit school and go to one of those homes for unwed mothers while the guy just carries on with his life. Scotch free!" I said.

"You mean scot-free. I know what you mean." She was quiet for a moment. "If Aunt Polly got pregnant, what happened to her kid?"

"I have no idea, but I'll ask Mom when we get home. Now how are we going to put everything back?"

Kitty thought for a moment. "Start with the letters. We can sneak those downstairs, and then I'll play the piano while Aunt Polly's in the other living room watching TV. You can put them back in the desk and lock it."

"Where should I hide the key?"

"Where did we find it?"

I mentally ran through the list of keys. "Inside the jewelry box in the forbidden room. We have to get back into that room one way or another. Too many things have to be returned there."

"I think our only chance will be to sneak in there tonight after she goes to bed."

"Let's hope she doesn't blow us away with her rifle if she catches us."

Kitty shrugged. "It should only take a few minutes. We can loosen the window when she's not looking after dinner."

I held the cat tighter and listened to her purr. "I don't know. What's the harm if we just leave everything upstairs in a desk drawer?"

"Once her ankle heals, she may come up here and check on things."

"I doubt she comes up here more than once a decade. But if some of our sisters come to visit later this summer, they'll find the items and may ask her about them. So back to plan A—you play piano, and I'll put the letters back in the desk.

Once Aunt Polly goes to bed, you slip in through the window, and we put the rest of the items back."

Kitty nodded. "And then we'll go to confession."

"Right. As soon as we get home alive."

We carried out the first part of our plan while Aunt Polly ate Twinkies and watched TV. Kitty pounded away on the piano, and I carefully opened the rolltop desk and replaced all the letters. I tied the love letters with the original ribbon and replaced them behind the secret door. When the coast was clear, I gave Kitty the signal, and we pretended to do more packing upstairs while we scanned the items for more bits of information before they had to be replaced in the forbidden room.

Once we were satisfied, Kitty turned to me. "Let's go down and watch Perry Mason."

"Good idea. Mom and Dad never let us watch that one."

Aunt Polly seemed glad to see us when we settled in the platform rockers just as Perry Mason was starting. We knew we weren't supposed to say anything during the program, so we sat in silence.

At ten p.m., as the credits rolled, it looked like Aunt Polly was nodding off. Candid Camera was about to begin. I feared she'd become interested in it, so I jumped up and turned the knob to "off." The sudden movements woke our great-aunt. She looked at us and blinked.

"Our last evening together. Let's watch Candid Camera and have some ice cream."

My nerves were on edge thinking about how to replace all

the smuggled items. Still, ice cream sounded good to me, so I turned the TV back on and went into the kitchen to dish up bowls of maple nut, her favorite flavor. We watched the show in silence as we relished the cool texture of the ice cream mixed with the flavored walnuts. Bedtime treats were frowned upon at home, as was watching television after 9:30 p.m. My palms were sweaty, and I kept going through the plan in my head.

Finally, the credits rolled, and our great-aunt followed suit and rolled off the couch and onto her feet. She took her time getting up and pulling her green muumuu away where it stuck to her sweaty body. Her rubber-soled shoes squeaked as she shuffled toward her room.

"Goodnight, girls. I'm heading to bed."

Kitty and I pretended to stretch.

I yawned loudly. "That was fun. Thanks, Aunt Polly."

"Yes, goodnight, Aunt Polly," Kitty said as she stood and walked into the hallway. As soon as we were out of her sight, we looked at each other, wide-eyed. This must be how burglars feel.

We dillydallied our way upstairs so that Aunt Polly wouldn't suspect anything. While waiting, we got ready for bed, finished packing, and fretted.

"Kitty, sit still. She's going to hear you bouncing on those metal springs."

"I'm so nervous. I thought we'd have more time to put things back."

"It'll only take a few minutes. Then we'll be home free."

"Says you! She nearly shot us the last time we tried to sneak back in."

"Don't remind me. But what alternative do we have? If we leave these upstairs, somehow we'll get caught, and she'll find out that we've read them. If we can put the scrapbook and picture album away, she won't be the wiser," I said while petting Anastasia to calm myself.

"Let's get it over with before I hurl that ice cream."

We cradled the confiscated items in our arms and crept down the stairs. By now, we knew which creaking steps to avoid. At the bottom of the stairs, we stopped and listened for any sound of activity coming from Aunt Polly's bedroom.

"I think we're clear," I whispered.

I held my breath while we crept barefoot through both darkened living rooms and squeezed open the door to the back porch, causing the rusted hinges to squeak. We listened. Nothing. Exhaled. A summer breeze coming through the screens tickled the hairs on my arms. We approached the porch window, still open a crack, thanks to our forethought. The moon cast a soft glow through the screens as my eyes adjusted to the near darkness.

We set the items on the floor and carefully pushed and shoved the stubborn window seal. Peeling paint flew into my mouth, and I spit it out.

"Shhhhh!" Kitty said.

"Can't help it. Paint in my mouth. Why isn't this window budging?"

"Humidity. Keep pushing."

Finally it budged. We worked our fingers into the gap and used our shoulders for momentum until we had an opening large enough for Kitty to crawl through.

"It was gross enough crawling in here in the daylight," she complained.

"Sorry. It's the only way. Climb in, and I'll hand you the stuff."

Kitty went in headfirst and landed on the travel trunk we left under the window weeks before. She stood and reached through the window.

"Hand me the photo album."

I passed it through the window but cautioned, "This goes in the dresser's top drawer, not the trunk."

"Right." She carefully made her way to the other side of the room and opened the top drawer. It complained with a loud screech. She stopped, and we waited, but nothing happened.

One down. I was starting to feel hopeful that we might pull this off. I suddenly had a flash of our future as jewelry thieves and then added that thought to the long list of things I needed to confess. Back to the present, we had to get the scrapbook into the travel trunk and shove it against the wall. Well, Kitty had to do this while I coached her from the porch. Kitty tripped over the bed frame on her way back to the window, and I shushed her.

"It's not like I tripped on purpose," she snapped back.

"Sorry. It's my nerves."

"Ready," Kitty said as I handed her the hefty scrapbook.

She set it on the floor as she opened the weighty lid, but when she reached for the scrapbook, the lid slammed shut with a thwack. We froze.

"Kitty, hurry. Just put it back and lock the lid."

She lifted the lid again but wasn't fast enough. We heard a rustle coming from Aunt Polly's bedroom.

Kitty dumped the scrapbook into the trunk, reached in her pocket, found the key, and locked it.

The light in the kitchen came on. I froze, as once again, our great-aunt appeared in a flowing white nightgown, pointing her rifle our way.

She made a beeline for the back porch as Kitty struggled to move the trunk inside the forbidden room. "What's going on? I expressly told you girls to stay out of that room!"

"Please don't shoot," I gasped, not knowing what else to say.

"I suppose Kitty's in there," Aunt Polly said, gesturing toward the open window with her gun.

I nodded. "Y... ye... yes. Kitty, you can turn the light on now."

Kitty turned the switch, and the single light bulb gave witness to our sleuthing.

Chapter 33

"WHAT'S THE MEANING OF THIS? And why is my travel trunk under the window?" Her good eye drilled into me until I had to look down at my feet.

I hoped Aunt Polly would put the gun down soon. "We were just curious." I tried to sound innocent.

"Curious about what?"

"Well, you know. About you and our other great-aunt and our grandmother."

"If you wanted to know more, you should have asked me. You didn't have to go slinking around like common criminals. Haven't we had enough of this?"

"No one wants to talk to us about the past."

"And suddenly, you two are interested in family history, is that it?" Aunt Polly pointed the gun at the floor and put her head through the window. "Kitty, come out through the door after you put the trunk back where it belongs. And lock that door."

Kitty turned out the light, then walked around to the porch, biting her bottom lip.

"Now hand me the key," Aunt Polly demanded, holding out her free hand.

"The key?" Kitty said.

"Don't play dumb with me. I heard the trunk slam shut, so you must have found the key."

Kitty reached behind her, retrieved the long gold key, and handed it over..

"Where did you find this key?"

Kitty and I looked at each other, trying to decide whether to make up a story or tell her the truth.

"Well?" Aunt Polly demanded.

"It was in a mink coat in one of the back bedrooms," I admitted. Finding the key was certainly a minor offense compared to all the rules we'd broken in the last few weeks. I could feel my heart pounding in my chest as I wondered what the next issue would be. Would she call the police? Our parents? I wasn't sure which was worse.

Finally, Aunt Polly found words to express her rage. "I'm very disappointed in you girls. It's a good thing you're going home tomorrow because I've had enough of your shenanigans. Sneaking out with boys, climbing down the ladder, and doing God-knows-what. Then breaking into rooms you were forbidden to enter and searching through clothing that isn't yours."

Kitty and I stood silently. I looked only at the glass eye, which seemed less menacing. At least she had it in the eye socket tonight.

"Now, shut the window and go to bed. And leave the past where it belongs." She clutched the gold key in one hand and gestured with her rifle in the other, demanding we exit the porch in front of her, which we did, like prisoners heading to a firing squad.

As soon as we realized she wasn't following us anymore, we dashed upstairs as quickly as humanly possible and fell onto our beds. Anastasia bounced onto the floor from the impact.

"I think I'm going to be sick."

"Put your head between your knees, Kitty, and take deep breaths." When my pulse settled down, I tried to think rationally about the past few weeks. "Kitty, look. It's not like we stole anything. We read some letters and newspaper articles. Aren't those public anyway? What's the big deal."

"The articles are public, not the letters. Luckily, she doesn't know about the letters. Yet."

I rolled onto my side, and Anastasia jumped back on the bed and curled around me. "Let's hope she never finds out."

"We have the key to the desk, and she rarely goes into that living room, so I think we're safe."

"Are you feeling better, Kitty?"

Her breath was shaky. "I think so. But what do you think she'll say to Mom and Dad?"

"She's a wild card, for sure. But how can she complain about a little investigating when we've been unpaid slaves for her for weeks? What were we supposed to do all this time?"

"She makes such a big deal out of everything."

"I could have made a lot of money babysitting this

summer. And even that newscaster's brats or the judge's grandchildren wouldn't have been as bad as putting up with Aunt Polly."

"I was going to get a job as a carhop," Kitty sighed. "I guess I still can."

We were lost in thought for a moment, listening to the cat's purring. Then Kitty broke in. "We did have some fun, though. Swimming, sailing, going on dates with the guys. That was the best part."

"Most of the time. Someday we'll laugh about climbing down that ladder."

Kitty snickered. "Why wait for someday? It was pretty funny."

"It was cool getting to know that she had a life. Her education, travels, and even a lover."

"We don't know that they were actually lovers."

"And I'm not asking her any more questions now."

"Me neither," I said. "Let's get to sleep. I'm exhausted." I pulled the sheet over my head.

It was an overwhelming day. As much as we dreaded seeing our great-aunt in the morning, we knew it was the last time we'd have to face curdled milk or moldy strawberries for breakfast. I fell asleep with disturbing images tumbling through my dreams. I dreamt that I was in a dark confessional in the back of a Gothic church, and suddenly the little door slid open between the priest and the confessor. Only instead of a priest, it was a one-eyed Aunt Polly. Her irate face filled the entire window, and she was foaming at the mouth.

Then suddenly her face morphed into the face of the vagrant man who nearly attacked me. I awoke with a little scream and sat up, my heart racing faster than a three-toed frog on a freeway.

Kitty sat up. "What's the matter?"

I whispered. "I think I'm going to Hell."

"Don't be silly. We haven't broken any laws. Mom always says things look better in the morning, so get some sleep."

"Mom. Ugh. And Dad. We have to face them tomorrow."

"Cindy, don't think about it. We'll face it tomorrow."

"Right. I'll try to forget about this entire day." I pulled the cat under the sheet with me, covered my head, and passed out.

My first nightmare was only the start of my night of horrors. My head hurt from the series of terrifying dreams when I opened my eyes the next morning.

The words of Officer Harold pounded in my ears. "He was leaving the door ajar so he could come and go, waiting for Cindy… Lucky for you, he passed out."

Before we went to bed, we were so worried about what Aunt Polly would do to us for breaking into her secret room that I pushed the episode out of my mind. But now, it echoed in my thoughts. I could have been attacked.

"Cindy, are you awake?"

I pulled the sheet back. "Yes."

"Did you get any sleep?"

"Not really. I had terrible nightmares."

"About Aunt Polly?"

"Yes, and the predator. I keep trying to forget about it, but my mind keeps playing it over and over. It was horrible."

Kitty was sympathetic. "Going home will help you forget, I hope. Let's get up and try to shake it off. Think about saying goodbye to the guys and then seeing our family."

"I'm so ready to go home."

We took our time getting dressed in jean shorts, T-shirts, and sandals and finished packing. Then we carried our small suitcases down the stairs.

Aunt Polly was sitting on the front porch. "It's going to be a beautiful day, girls."

Kitty and I exchanged hopeful glances. Had her anger disappeared like the clouds? Her glass eye was in, and she wasn't foaming at the mouth, so that was positive. Right?

I blinked toward the heavens and realized the sun was already high in a cloudless sky. "Yes, it looks like it's going to be warm," I said, clinging to weather as a safe topic.

We brought breakfast to the porch and made quick work of it while sticking to trivial topics. Aunt Polly's rage must have dissipated with the sunrise because she never brought up the escapades of the night before. We wondered if she was still angry but thought the best way to handle the situation was to quickly leave the house.

After we cleared the dishes, I fed the cat, and then Kitty and I decided to say a quick goodbye to Jimmy and Charlie. As we walked over to their house, I was still unsure what to say.

Jimmy and Charlie answered the door quickly. Jimmy and

I walked back toward Aunt Polly's house, and Charlie and Kitty walked in the opposite direction.

"Think you'll have time to go sailing?" Jimmy asked me.

I focused on the sidewalk as we walked along the lake side of the lane. "No, sorry. But it was fun. Sailing and… everything."

"Maybe we'll see you next summer."

"Maybe."

Jimmy and I finished our walk, and he gave me a chaste kiss as we said our goodbyes.

Chapter 34

I DECIDED TO READ IN THE BEDROOM while waiting for Kitty to return from her walk. The less time I spent around Aunt Polly, the less chance of her exploding at me. I sat on the bed and held Anastasia in my lap, enjoying the hum of her motor. When Kitty joined me upstairs, her cheeks were flushed with excitement.

"Charlie said he'll come to Minneapolis and take me out this winter. He promised to call every week and said we can keep going together."

"Wow. Like boyfriend and girlfriend. You're going steady?"

She turned and flopped on the bed. "I guess so. Isn't that exciting?"

"Does that mean you want to come back here next summer?"

"To see Charlie, yes. Don't you want to see Jimmy?"

"Maybe. But I don't want to spend weeks on end here again."

As we chatted, we heard the shrill voice of Aunt Polly calling us and went downstairs to see what she wanted.

"Girls, we need to go into town to get more groceries for tonight's dinner with your family."

We helped her to the car and held onto our seats as she backed up and lurched forward before puttering along to the grocery store. Once at the store, she honked the horn several times until Kitty stopped her.

"Do you have a list?" Kitty asked. Aunt Polly held it up with a twenty-dollar bill.

Kitty snatched the list and money. "Come on, Cindy. Let's take care of this." We opened the car door before our great-aunt could complain and went inside to do the shopping.

"Look at this list!" Kitty said. "Oreos, Lorna Doones, Fig Newtons. Nothing is for dinner tonight."

"Let's pick up hamburgers, hot dogs, buns, and coleslaw. She can restock her cookie supply another time."

"Right. Mom and Dad will be here, so she can't blow her top."

A sense of relief spread over me like warm milk running through my veins at the thought of returning home. Our home was chaotic and unpredictable, but nothing like the craziness we experienced with our great-aunt. We brought the groceries and put them in the backseat without an explanation.

Once home, I asked Kitty to walk down the lane with me to see if the Ericksons were back from their trip. We used the brass lion door knocker and waited. When it swung open,

I was happy to see Marjorie's concerned face. "Girls! I'm so relieved to see you."

Just then, Mrs. Erickson pushed her way to the door. "My goodness, you girls had quite a fright. The officer called and explained what happened. I'm so happy nothing was stolen, and Anastasia wasn't hurt."

"And, of course, the girls weren't hurt either," Marjorie added.

"I suppose you want your pay now," Mrs. Erickson said. "I'll have Marjorie bring that to you once we know Anastasia is safe."

Marjorie brightened. "I'll go with you to collect the cat and her things." She took off with us on the short walk back to Aunt Polly's.

"Are you visiting for the summer?" I asked Marjorie.

"No, just for a few weeks and my school reunion. I graduated from high school here thirty years ago."

Kitty piped up. "Wow! You don't look that old."

"Thank you. I'm actually forty-seven. I graduated when I was seventeen."

"I don't mean to be rude, but I don't see any family resemblance with your aunt," I said.

"Cindy! Don't be so nosey," Kitty said.

Marjorie laughed. "It's fine. I was adopted as a baby." She seemed so easy to talk to, I decided to keep asking questions. "I've never met anyone who was adopted. What's it like?"

Marjorie smiled. "I've never known anything else, so it's normal for me."

When we reached the house, we invited her in and introduced her to Aunt Polly. They stood shoulder to shoulder, apple cheeks to apple cheeks, and green eyes to green eyes. I blinked.

We collected the cat and her paraphernalia, but before we handed her over to Marjorie, she asked, "How much did my aunt say she was going to pay you?"

"Five dollars."

She reached in her pocket and handed me a twenty-dollar bill. "Split this. After all the trouble, you certainly deserve it."

Our family blasted in minutes later. I was happy to see my little sisters again. I hugged and kissed them and twirled Ann Marie around.

After dinner, Dad put the ladder back on top of the station wagon. Before we left, Aunt Polly brought out the box we found behind the wall in the library and handed it to our mom.

"Katie, I think this belongs to you."

Mom opened it and gasped, "The sugar tongs! I thought they were lost forever. My mother told me about them, but she didn't know where they were."

Our sisters gathered around and looked at the odd objects. Mom explained some of the history and how they were passed from Catherine to Catherine through the generations. "These will be yours someday, Kitty."

"But I'm Kathleen, not Catherine."

"Close enough. I always intended for you to inherit the sugar tongs, Kitty. And I'm thrilled they were found."

Aunt Polly turned to Mom. "I'm afraid your mother thought I hid them years ago. She held that against me, but it must have been Margaret who hid them."

"Who's Margaret?" Maureen asked.

"I'll explain more at home," Mom said. "It's getting late."

Kitty and I turned to say goodbye to Aunt Polly. She looked sad to see us go.

One by one, we piled into the station wagon, with Kitty and I holding our suitcases on our laps.

When we left, I felt an odd mixture of sadness and elation. But I couldn't wait to sleep in my own bed again, without mosquitoes, flies, and moths swarming around my head.

After a few days at home, Kitty and I still had questions about Aunt Polly. We cornered Mom one afternoon.

Mom was hesitant at first but then let down her guard.

"So, what do you know about her past," she asked us.

Kitty put her finger to her mouth as she recalled the details. "We know she graduated from college and then went on a three-month cruise. At some point, she met a fella named Anthony Walker, her boyfriend, I guess."

I chimed in. "We also know Anthony was sent to France in 1917 during World War I, and Aunt Polly went to France with the Red Cross."

Kitty interjected. "And that she was trying to find him, but we don't know why."

"It looks like Aunt Polly stayed in Minnetonka for a while instead of going back to Colorado with her parents. We found a letter from her mother saying a doctor was going to help her, so we thought maybe she was sick...."

Kitty's voice was quiet. "Or she was pregnant, we don't know."

Mom licked her lips. "Wow, you know most of it. You girls have been busy. I don't condone what you've done, but I'll answer your questions."

We nodded and waited as she calmly explained the rest of the secrets.

"My mother told me that Aunt Polly was pregnant with Anthony Walker's baby. She tried to find him to tell him in person but wasn't able to locate him. He died in the war a month before the baby was born and never knew he had fathered a child."

Kitty sighed. "So sad."

"It was also socially unacceptable for a woman to have a child out of wedlock, but Aunt Polly believed it was a loving relationship."

"What happened to the child?" I asked.

"She had a daughter in January of 1918. A local family doctor helped her find an organization that placed the child in a home with a couple who couldn't have their own children. That's all we know. Records are generally sealed after adoptions."

"Do we know if she's still alive?" Kitty asked.

Mom did a little math on her fingers. "We have no idea, but it's very possible. She'd be about 47 now."

"Did it cause a big scandal for her?" I asked.

"I believe she kept it very quiet and stayed in the family lake home until she delivered. But there may be some neighbors who found out and still hold a grudge against her."

"Her neighbors aren't very friendly. You think they know?"

"It's possible. Especially in a small community."

"Thanks for telling us, Mom," I said.

Later, Kitty and I were up on the third floor in our lilac bedroom, discussing the details Mom shared with us. Kitty sat at the makeshift makeup bench we made out of wooden orange crates and brushed her long hair. She put her hairbrush down and looked serious. "Did you notice how Aunt Polly looked like Marjorie?"

"I did. And her age is right. But there must be thousands of girls who were adopted that year."

"I still can't imagine Aunt Polly getting that close to a guy."

"You mean 'doing it.'"

Kitty turned to look at me and rolled her eyes. "Yes, it. Sex. Can't imagine it."

"And I don't want to. But she was young once."

"Like us—young."

"And she must have been in love."

Kitty snorted. "Or at least in lust."

"Don't laugh. That could have happened to one of us."

"I think Charlie respects me. He never pushed me too far. Sorry about Jimmy."

"He's too old for me anyway. And he was smoking weed and drinking at that party in the park. I never felt he saw me.

Me. Who I was. Not just a chubby girl from a big Catholic family. I realized I didn't want to be his girlfriend."

"You aren't chubby. I wish you'd stop saying that."

"Compared to all the models in Seventeen, I'm chubby."

"Let's cancel our subscription."

"Agreed," I said.

We thought for a few moments, and then Kitty broke in. "Do you think she'll forgive us for all the rules we broke?"

"I think she will since she has so few relatives other than us. But I doubt she'll ever trust us again."

Epilogue

June 1966, the following year

I played hide-and-seek with Ann Marie while Mom burned dinner in the kitchen. She looked up and shushed us. "Girls, listen." We heard the honking. Not a goose. Aunt Polly was back from New Mexico.

"Cindy, quickly pull the captain's chair around the table, and Kitty, please set another place," Mom said.

Kitty and I exchanged glances. Kitty pulled me aside as I put the chair at the end of our dining room table. "Either she's had the year to become angrier, or she's forgotten all about it, right?"

"I doubt she's forgotten. Let's hope she's not going to take some action against us," I whispered.

Kitty pulled back and frowned. "Action? Like what?"

I flapped my hands around uselessly. "File charges? Shave our heads? Brand our thighs with the word 'thief.'"

"Branding? Did you read The Scarlet Letter this spring?"

"Yes, why?"

Kitty momentarily closed her eyes and sighed. "Don't let your imagination get carried away. We waited on her hand and foot as she barked orders and made us eat rotten food. We could claim child abuse."

"Good. Yes. That's good." But then I thought about it. "Our parents would never stand by us."

Kitty put a hand out to stop me. "Let's pretend nothing happened and carry on as usual."

"There's nothing usual about her, though."

Mom came into the dining room and interrupted our fretting. "Kitty and Cindy, please go outside and help your great-aunt into the house."

"Can't Mary or Colleen help her?"

"Honestly! You girls. Go on."

As soon as we emerged from our front door, we saw neighbors peeking out windows, wondering what the honking was about. When she realized help was on the way, Aunt Polly stopped honking.

I faked a smile and a half-hearted wave. "Hi, Aunt Polly."

She shook her head, and her earrings twinkled. A bright yellow patch covered her glass eye, which matched her goldfinch-colored dress. "Hello, girls."

We helped her out of the car, up the stairs, and into the house, and the ritual hugs and greetings were accomplished. Next, I helped her into the captain's chair with the sturdy armrests.

Our family gathered around the table for dinner, said grace, and started eating.

Mom asked Aunt Polly about her year and her journey home. But when our great-aunt said that her house needed a bit of work to get it ready for the summer, Kitty and I focused on our plates.

"Kitty, Cindy, would you like to go back to the lake this summer?" Mom asked us.

But before we could answer, Aunt Polly skewered the idea. "I thought Colleen and Joanne would like to visit this summer."

She raised her eyebrows and gave Kitty and me a meaningful glance. I exhaled. Relief.

Mom nodded. "Colleen, you're fourteen now, so you can keep Joanne out of trouble."

Joanne frowned. "For pity's sake, I'm eleven. I don't need babysitting."

I piped up. "Speaking of that, I can take your babysitting jobs for you while you're gone, Colleen."

Colleen was less than thrilled with the idea of going to the lake. She shrugged. "OK, I guess. I'll give you the list. We'll have fun swimming, won't we, Joanne?"

Joanne nodded and the two of them went upstairs to pack.

Aunt Polly turned to me. "Be sure to give Colleen the recipe for Parcheesi frosting."

"Right. Yes. I will."

Mom piped up. "Parcheesi frosting?"

"It's Aunt Polly's pet name for the caramel frosting I made last summer," I said as I stood to clear the table.

Aunt Polly looked at me pointedly. "Yes, we have some great memories from last summer."

I froze. Was she going to spill the beans? I quickly bussed the rest of the dinner dishes.

"Time to start washing dishes, right, Kitty?" We dashed into the kitchen.

"Have fun," we said to Colleen and Joanne as they lugged their small suitcases out to Aunt Polly's beater of a car. When they returned to the house to help Aunt Polly to the car, I whispered in Colleen's ear. "Sniff the milk before you pour it."

And they were off.

Later, we finished washing the dishes.

I handed Kitty a plate to dry. "That was close. I was sure she was going to tell Mom about our transmissions."

Kitty laughed. "Transgressions, you knucklehead!"

"Whatever. But I thought you'd want to see Charlie again."

"Nah. He said he'd call every week and come into town so we could see each other, but he never called even once. Who needs that?"

*Q*UESTIONS TO *P*ONDER

1. Do you think current attitudes have changed about people who are very large or significantly overweight?

2. In the 1960s, magazines had tremendous influence over our culture. What has changed since then, and is this for the better or worse?

3. Have you ever been in a situation where you felt pressure to try something that makes you uncomfortable? How did you handle the situation?

4. Large families are becoming rare. Do you have many siblings? Do you consider yourself lucky to come from the size of family you have? Why or why not?

5. What family traditions are there in your family?

6. Do you know much about your ancestors and their lives?

7. If you want to know more about your ancestors, do you know where to research them?

8. There are many foods listed in Stay Out of That Room. Were there foods that were unfamiliar to you? If so, which ones?

9. Do you associate foods with favorite activities as Aunt Polly did with Parcheesi frosting?

10. Did your attitude toward Aunt Polly change by the end of the book? If so, explain.

11. Would you enjoy spending time with someone like Aunt Polly?

Facts about Stay Out of That Room

Aunt Polly was indeed a real person who lived in a vast Victorian summer home on Lake Minnetonka. It was in terrible repair and was eventually condemned, causing her to move to a senior apartment building. The creepy portraits of relatives and many antiques were lost to a realtor who swooped in and snapped them up before any family members knew it happened.

Aunt Polly loved to swim and was found dead years later in the pool of her apartment building from an apparent heart attack. She was likely happy that her passing from this life to the next was quick and painless while doing what she loved.

Regina High School was a Catholic Girl's School in south Minneapolis where five of us graduated. Regina closed its doors in 1987 after declining enrollment.

My father pressured me to join the Poor Clare Nuns, but

my allergies – and talkativeness - prevented me from being a good candidate.

The story of Princess and the eleven puppies was indeed true.

Yes, I have seven sisters, but their names were changed to protect the innocent.

Parcheesi frosting is still a family favorite today, paired with spice cake.

The story about the sugar tongs is true; one of the "Catherines" has custody of them and a record of their history.

My sister and I did indeed break into the mystery room, and what we found was…well, this is a work of fiction.

Parcheesi Frosting Recipe

Also called Easy Penuche Frosting – from Betty Crocker's New Boys and Girls Cookbook from the 1960s, with a few additions.

Ingredients:

- ½ cup butter
- 1 cup brown sugar, packed
- ½ tsp salt
- ¼ cup milk
- 1 tsp vanilla extract
- 2 cups powdered sugar

Directions:

1. Melt the butter and brown sugar in a saucepan over low heat for about two minutes

2. Add the milk and salt and bring it to a full rolling boil, stirring constantly.

3. Remove it from the heat and add the vanilla extract. Set the pan in cold water. When you can hold your hand on the bottom of the pan, it's cool enough.

4. Now add the powdered sugar and beat with an electric mixer to ensure there are no lumps. Keep the pan in the cold water and beat until it's thick enough to spread.

5. If it's too thick, add a few drops of milk. If it's too runny, add more powdered sugar.

ABOUT THE AUTHOR

I AM A WIFE TO ONE. Ken and I have been married for over 45 years.

Mother of three.

Nana to seven.

Great grandmother to one.

Sister to seven women. Yes, no brothers. My father said he felt like he was living in a convent at times as we ate in two long rows at the dinner table.

I earned an MS in journalism and mass communications when our three children were young. My career evolved from radio announcer to public relations and instructor at Iowa State University. I have been published dozens of times as a freelance writer and have now completed three novels.

Want to Hear the Latest Updates about the House of Girls Series?

Join my newsletter list. Just send your name and email address to: clarebills@live.com. I promise I won't flood your inbox or sell your name to terrorists. But I will happily answer every email.

Follow my Facebook page: Nearly Normal Writer
Instagram: clarebills2711
Website: clarebills.com

PLEASE WRITE A REVIEW

Dear Reader,

At Midwestern Books we have worked hard to make this excellent book available for you. We truly hope you have enjoyed it. It is our mission to tell stories from a Midwestern perspective that honors its culture. Thank you for including us in your reading selections.

Please, would you consider going to the Amazon website and write a review for this book. Reviews are crucial for helping others to know about this book and encouraging Amazon to promote it. We very much need help from readers like you to get the word out about our books and the enjoyable stories they share. Thank you for helping us.

Midwestern Books

OTHER TITLES FROM MIDWESTERN BOOKS

See Jane Run! Book 1 of the West River Mysteries. Amidst the scenic wonder of a quirky corner of western South Dakota, Jane Newell starts her career in a country school. She soon discovers that someone close to her is a killer, and she is determined to find out who it is.

See Jane Sing! Book 2 of the West River Mysteries. Just back from Thanksgiving break, Jane Newell stumbles over the body of a teenage boy while hunting for a Christmas tree. Jane ignores Sheriff Sternquist's warning not to investigate when she discovers a tangle of clues.

Cosmic Background Radiation. Grieving his brother, Josh confronts rural life to save his family. Strange dreams take him back 2,700 years to a parallel life with his brother alive and a girl he just met as part of the household.

Made in the USA
Monee, IL
24 January 2025

e979b6db-f912-4804-b761-8259b88304d8R01